SEP 2019

A PRISONER OF PRIVILEGE

A PRISONER
OF PRIVILEGE

Rosemary Rowe

This first world edition published 2019
in Great Britain and the USA by
SEVERN HOUSE PUBLISHERS LTD of
Eardley House, 4 Uxbridge Street, London W8 7SY.
Trade paperback edition first published
in Great Britain and the USA 2020 by
SEVERN HOUSE PUBLISHERS LTD.

British Library Cataloguing in Publication Data
A CIP catalogue record for this title is available from the British Library.

ISBN-13: 978-0-7278-8890-7 (cased)
ISBN-13: 978-1-78029-613-5 (trade paper)
ISBN-13: 978-1-4483-0230-7 (e-book)

All Severn House titles are printed on acid-free paper.

Severn House Publishers support the Forest Stewardship Council™ [FSC™],
the leading international forest certification organisation.
All our titles that are printed on FSC certified paper carry the FSC logo.

Typeset by Palimpsest Book Production Ltd.,
Falkirk, Stirlingshire, Scotland.
Printed and bound in Great Britain by
TJ International, Padstow, Cornwall.

To Andrea, with love

FOREWORD

The story is set in Glevum (modern Gloucester) in early 194 AD, when Britannia was the most far-flung province of a Roman Empire still reeling from the events of the preceding year. Following the murder of the Emperor Pertinax – a previous governor of Britannia and the supposed friend of the fictional Marcus in this story – by his own Praetorian Guard, for failing to pay them the bonus they felt that they deserved, the Empire had been virtually auctioned off to the highest bidder. The successful bidder, Didius Julianus, having been installed, found to his dismay that (as Pertinax had claimed) there really was not sufficient money in the Imperial Purse. He did not long survive.

From the outset there were counter-claimants to the purple, leading to a period of armed unrest – effectively civil war – with three other pretenders each being acclaimed as 'true successors' by their supporters, and each backed by several legions loyal to himself. Matters were resolved in early June when the geographically closest of the three, Septimius Severus, shockingly marched his forces to the very gates of Rome. Didius, abandoned by the Senate and the guard, attempted to negotiate, but he was executed and Severus duly proclaimed as Emperor.

The two other claimants did not capitulate at once. Clodius Albinus, the Governor of Britannia, was bought off with the courtesy title, 'Caesar and Co-Emperor of the West', and a (worthless) promise that he would be next in line. Pescennius Niger, who would probably have been the choice of the majority, refused such compromise. He continued to call himself 'Emperor' (indeed, is described as such in many texts), issued coinage in his own name and renewed his armed struggle against the 'upstart' Severus. Pescennius was not finally defeated for another year, and at the time of this story, might easily have won and been generally acknowledged as the Roman Emperor that he claimed to be.

It is against this background that the tale is set.

The whole Empire was buzzing with division and distrust. The legions in Britannia had declared for Clodius, of course, and – doubtful of his current compromise – were regarded with considerable suspicion by the new regime. Meanwhile, public figures around the Empire were being denounced for anti-Severan sympathies (often anonymously) and – accused of treason – were stripped of goods and office, and either exiled or killed.

This is the assumed fate of the old Commandant of the Glevum garrison, in this narrative, though there is no evidence of any such event occurring here. (Indeed, as has been acknowledged previously elsewhere, it is unlikely the fort at Glevum was by now much more than a guard and posting station for Isca to the west – though a late-second-century rebuilding of the fortified wall seems to counter the suggestion that it was no longer manned at all.) However, whatever the size and function of the garrison, it was ultimately under the command of Clodius. It can be imagined how the arrival of an alleged Imperial Spy would have inspired considerable alarm.

The Laurentius of this story is an ex-Praetorian – a member of that military elite and Imperial bodyguard which had engineered the fall of three previous Emperors, and whose loyalty had been so publicly for sale. Now retired, he would have served an earlier Emperor, in this case the capricious Commodus. Severus had feared the power of the Guard so much that almost his first act was to dismiss them all – with a parting bonus, he was not an idiot – and replace them with trusted members of the legions under his command.

Praetorians were in any case not popular. Generally of patrician birth, they were contracted for a shorter term, which – coupled with higher pay, better conditions, greater pension and retirement bonuses, splendid quarters and a tendency to be protected from actual combat in favour of guarding the Emperor in Rome – made them generally resented by the regulars. Meanwhile, their reputation for corruption and brutality made them feared and hated by the civilian populace. Laurentius, making no secret of his past, can hardly have expected a warm welcome in the town, although the garrison and council would be obliged politely to accommodate and entertain any traveller with an Imperial warrant for his stay.

The council – or curia – includes Libertus in this tale. He has unwillingly become a councillor. He holds the rank of local duumvir – one of 'two men', as the title indicates, sharing a single magisterial post. (This was a very senior rank in Rome but in the provinces it would appear that such shared roles, even for humbler posts, were not unusual – perhaps because there were fewer candidates qualified to serve, outside the capital.)

Libertus, having spent some years in servitude, not being of Roman patrician birth, and lacking the property qualification, should not strictly have been a candidate himself, but patronage could render such objections technical – and this is taken to have been the case, though Libertus is naturally anxious lest he be accused of holding a public post improperly.

The property qualification, in particular, is of some import-ance in the narrative – and here I fear history has caught up with me. When this series of novels was begun there were few examples known in Glevum of town houses dating from the second century (and those are mostly 'accounted for' in other narratives). It was assumed, therefore – since we know that, outside Rome (where apartment blocks were mostly frequented by the poor) members of the knightly class were by now moving into flats – that this was the case in Glevum, for these narratives. (The whole colonia was relatively new, but private development was moving in, so recently-built apart-ments might have been much larger and more luxurious than the crumbling, crowded tenements of the capital.) However, the recent discovery of more fine pavements (under the bus station) suggests that there may have been another whole area of expensive private homes – and it is likely that a man like Marcus would have lived in one.

But the series is fiction and must remain consistent with itself. Marcus continues to possess a flat in town, and property requirements are calculated from area, and not from the number of roof tiles as was the case in Rome. Thus Libertus meets the prerequisite for election by acquiring a sizeable apartment – albeit, only technically. His new role entitles him to a curial toga, with a stripe, for ceremonial use, but surrounds him with irksome prescriptions and taboos.

Another civic role was that of aedile, such as the class-conscious Rufus who figures in this tale. Becoming an aedile in Rome was a traditional first step on the ladder of civil and political advancement, for those of undistinguished patrician birth. Provincial aediles were members of the local curia, entitled to special dress and privilege, and acting effectively as market police, which gave them oversight of people like the argentarius – the official money changer for the town.

Argentarii were not members of the curia, indeed they were not often Roman citizens at all, though – since the position ensured acquaintance with the rich and powerful – they might hope to be nominated to that rank for 'service to the state'. Members of an exclusive guild, which issued licences, they were much more than simple money lenders (though they could do that, too, at an official interest rate). They were contract brokers, auctioneers and even acted as a sort of bank, guarding money for their customers (which did not attract a fee) or lending it to others at interest (which did).

The most public role, however, was – as the name implies – the changing and essaying of market coinage. Coin varied markedly across the Empire, but as long as it bore the Emperor's face it was valid currency, though the argentarius might be required to value coins or even weigh them, as in some provinces the quantity of metal was debased. (The same was true of local gold and silver coins, which might be filed by the unscrupulous!) Even foreign coins could be exchanged, the value being calculated on the weight of gold, while an argentarius was also licensed to supply the necessary small change for the market-stalls. There was a fixed fee for each transaction, and a money changer could become a very wealthy man, though – since every member of the guild was jointly and severally responsible for the losses incurred by any other member – he was also likely to be educated, honest and astute.

But at this period there were dangers in his trade. Pescennius Niger had been issuing coins in his own name for months. These might reach Glevum unobserved and circulate, though passing them on was a capital offence, along with falsifying coin or overstamping it – deemed treachery, like desecrating a statue of the Emperor. (Likenesses, in these pre-photographic times, had an almost mystic quality, like the famous wax death-mask images of ancestors which 'attended' high-class Roman funerals.)

Holders of all these civic offices were, naturally, men. Although individual women might inherit large estates, they were excluded from public office, and a woman (of any age) was deemed a child in law. Marriage and motherhood were the only realistic goals for well-bred women, although trade-men's wives and daughters often worked beside their men and in the poorest households everybody toiled. Celtic women, like the Gwellia of this tale might have more freedom of expression than their Roman counterparts.

The Britannia these folk inhabited was the most far-flung and northerly of all Roman provinces, still occupied by Roman legions, criss-crossed by Roman roads, subject to Roman laws, and administered – dangerously – by 'Caesar' Clodius Albinus, the Provincial Governor and one of the current claimants to the Imperial wreath. Around him life went on as usual. Latin was the language of the educated, people were adopting Roman dress and habits, and citizenship, with the precious social and legal rights which it conferred, was still the aspiration of almost everyone.

At the perimeters there still were small groups of dissidents who refused to yield to Roman rule. They were often associated with Druid practices, such as the sacred groves adorned with the trophy heads of enemies – in spite of (or perhaps because of) the old religion being officially proscribed. However, there is no record of any rebel activity occurring as far east as Glevum, at this period.

Glevum was an important town, built as a colonia for retiring veterans; and all freemen born within its walls were citizens by right. Most inhabitants, however, were not citizens at all. Many were freemen, born outside the walls, scratching a more or less precarious living from a trade. Hundreds more were slaves – mere chattels of their masters, to be bought and sold, with no more rights or status than any other domestic animal. Some slaves led pitiable lives, but others were highly regarded by their owners, and might be treated well. A slave in a kindly household, with a comfortable home, might have a more enviable lot than many a poor freeman struggling to eke out an existence in a squalid hut. Indeed, some poor free families were constrained to sell their elder children into slavery in order to feed and clothe the rest, though they became the outright property of their masters and could be used at will, like Iliath in this text.

For all classes, there were important rituals surrounding death. It was believed that, if these were not properly observed, unquiet spirits might return to walk the earth. Despite this slaves were often buried without any rites at all, unless the deceased had been a member of the Funeral Guild, which (for a regular subscription) would see that the proper rituals were observed – all matters integral to the narrative.

The rest of the Romano-British background to this book has been derived from a variety of (sometimes contradictory) pictorial and written sources, as well as artefacts. However, although I have done my best to create an accurate picture, this remains a work of fiction, and there is no claim to total academic authenticity. Septimius Severus and events in Rome are historically attested, as is the existence and basic geography of Glevum. The rest is the product of my imagination.

Relata refero. Ne Iupiter quidem omnibus placet. I only tell you what I heard. Jove himself can't please everybody.

ONE

It was a misty day in Februarius, a little after the midday trumpet call. I had been at the meeting of the Glevum curia – perforce, as the newest and most reluctant of all town councillors – but I had been astonished to be met by a pageboy afterwards and summoned to attend my patron, here at the public baths. A little apprehensive too, since he could have nominated his villa, just as easily – he was certain to return there, and it was barely a thousand paces from my roundhouse gates.

This must be some emergency, I thought, because this was a most unfashionable hour, when the women's session had barely ended for the day and any freeborn male with a *quadrans* in his purse can avail himself of the facilities.

Later in the day, of course, it would not have seemed so odd. There is a saying that 'the council meets officially in the basilica but does its business in the bathhouse afterwards'. I've never been a regular patron of the baths, so – until one of the new *duumviri* dropped dead and I was elected in his place – I had supposed that this referred to small groups meeting in the covered colonnade outside, where snacks and beverages are to be obtained and handsome young athletes, practising their sports, can be admired by those with a penchant for such things.

Now, however, I was learning otherwise – though I still found it bizarre, broiling naked in the steam room with fellow councillors, discoursing on the subject of town drains, or meeting hopeful tradesmen, similarly attired, who wanted a contract replacing gutter tiles. Roman males (whose attitudes derive from army life, I suppose) are not much given to prudery, at least among their peers.

Even so I was startled to find my patron now, lying on a massage bench, completely nude, in full view of any plebian who might happen by.

'Ah, Councillor Libertus, there you are at last! I was beginning to fear that my messenger had not located you, and you
had already left the basilica and were halfway home.' Marcus
Aurelius Septimus eased himself a little on the marble slab
and turned his head to look at me, as the massage slave rubbed
oil into his naked back.

'Excellence!' I murmured apologetically, and then said
nothing more, not certain what more he would expect.

Marcus was a man of high patrician rank, reputed to be
related to the Imperial house, and a stickler for proper etiquette!
Hence my predicament. I could not even kneel to kiss his hand
without endangering what little dignity I had. I'd had to shed
my clothes as I came in, of course, and – not having my
bathing *subligaculum* with me – had only a thin, hired drying
cloth to wind around my loins. It was embarrassingly small,
I had to clutch at it to keep it up at all, and here in the massage
area there was no steam or water to veil my nudity. But then,
my patron was not wearing so much as a ring that I could
kiss.

And I was already rather later than was probably polite,
although – not finding him out in the colonnade – I'd rushed
through the bathhouse with unseemly haste. I was almost
afraid that I had missed him after all – but he must have been
ahead of me throughout, because here he was back in the
tepid area. (In Glevum, one returns here last of all, so that
– having worked up a sufficient sweat elsewhere – one can
be strigilled clean and take a quick, cold dip to close the
pores before one leaves.)

But what was the accepted form for greeting a superior
when only a strip of fabric protects one's modesty, and he
himself is as naked as a slave for sale? I compromised by
bowing slightly from the waist. 'I hope I have not kept you
waiting, Excellence.'

'You're here now, that is the important thing. I wanted
somewhere to have a private word with you.'

'Private?' I glanced at the attendant who was pummelling
his back.

'One of my own slave boys,' Marcus said. 'Don't worry
about him. And I've arranged for a deaf-and-dumb slave to

attend to you. So we can talk quite freely while we are being strigelled clean.'

I stared. This was a new Marcus. Generally he thinks of slaves as human furniture and I have often had to remind him that they have ears and tongues. But his current caution was obviously wise. We were living in very troubled times.

Something I'd just seen on my way to the baths today was a sign of that. Workmen with ropes and pulleys were busy in the square, removing the bust of Didius Julianus from its niche, to replace him with a hasty statue of the latest Emperor (who came from the African provinces and was said to have dark skin and fleshy lips, though that was not evident from the images, nor from the new coins issued in his name which had just begun to find their way into Britannia). And this was the fourth change of Emperor within the last twelve months!

So when Septimius Severus had been officially proclaimed there was a feeling of general relief that the political upheavals might be at an end. But that had – emphatically – not turned out to be the case, because there were still two other pretenders to the purple – both of whom had claims as strong as his.

One, Pescennius Niger, would probably have been the people's choice. He was very popular, not just in Rome but throughout the Empire – from Dacia to Antioch, and had been proclaimed Emperor by his followers months ago, when Pertinax was killed. He had stubbornly refused to repudiate his claim, had issued coinage with his face on it, and was even now engaging Severus in active war.

The other potential rival was our own Provincial Governor. Clodius Albinus had claims of lineage, having been adopted into the Imperial family, (just as Octavius Augustus had been) and commanded considerable support. He had only been persuaded to give up his claim – for now – by being given the courtesy title 'Caesar', the doubtful accolade of 'co-Emperor of the west', and the still more doubtful promise that he would be next in line. (Especially doubtful, because Severus had children of his own.)

All of which meant that Severus certainly had paid informers everywhere. Especially in Britannia. And with reason, too.

There were already local murmurings in support of Clodius, with the legions ready to mass on his account. So it paid to be very careful what one said, to whom.

In fact the commander at our Glevum garrison, a shrewd and educated friend of Marcus's who had been denounced for having Clodian sympathies, had recently been relieved of his command and – though recalled to Rome – had deemed it more expedient to disappear to Gaul. (Where he had landed safely, a smuggled letter said, except for the loss of his favourite hunting dogs and two precious manuscripts, which had not survived the trip. He would not, he wrote, communicate again for fear of betraying his final whereabouts.)

And Marcus was his known associate! No wonder he was learning to be more discreet!

My patron must have seen that I was hesitant, and gestured that I should occupy the vacant bench nearby. I lay down gingerly, still wondering what this summons was about, whereupon one of the public bathhouse slaves appeared at once to whisk off my little covering with a deft and practised hand. This must be the deaf-and-dumb attendant that was promised me.

It still seemed improper to converse with His Excellence in this state, but I told myself that he had chosen both the time and place; he had a perfectly good private bath-suite in his country house, which we could both have reached within an hour or two. So this meeting was entirely of his own design. And I could hardly refuse an order from someone who was still (for now, at least) one of the most important men in all Britannia.

So there was no escape. I too was about to be pummelled, oiled and scraped, and then obliged to take that chilly plunge. Not that I fear cold water, but I generally prefer a simple rub-down at the spring, using the Celtic lye-and-goosefat soap that Romans despise so much. I'd already had more baths in this last month than in my life before. One of the disadvantages of rank! I must be the cleanest Celt in Glevum, nowadays, I thought, as the bath attendant began to rub my back and I lay and waited to learn why I was here.

I did not have long to wonder. 'That letter that arrived in the curia today . . .' My patron turned his face so he could look at me. 'You heard it read, no doubt. What was your opinion, my old friend?'

Old friend? That was ominous. Marcus only ever calls me 'friend' when he wants me to do him a favour of some kind – usually something which will take me from my trade for several days. I gave an inward sigh. I was rarely in my mosaic workshop these days, as it was – being a councillor left little time for that. I felt I was the prisoner of privilege, sometimes. But not even a duumvir can argue with a man of Marcus's rank, and he was waiting for an answer; I could see his eyebrows arch.

I made a non-committal noise, partly because the massage-slave was pressing on my lungs, and partly because I did not know what answer was required. I had heard the reading of the letter, naturally, but I'd not paid undue attention since it did not touch upon pavements, wells or aquifers, which were my areas of responsibility. (Though since Marcus had been presiding, as senior magistrate, it was not prudent to admit that I'd been daydreaming.)

My grunt had clearly not been good enough. 'Well?' The eyebrows rose again.

What I'd heard of the letter had seemed unremarkable to me. 'Some private visitor from Rome, presenting his credentials to the curia and hoping for patronage and entertainment while he was in the town.' Nothing at all unusual in that – it was a common practice for patrician visitors. 'He is a person of good family, I assume.'

'One could say so!' Marcus sounded wry. 'Laurentius Aurelius Manlius is a distant relative of my own. The youngest son of a half-cousin of Mother's, I recall, though that branch of the family has fallen on hard times! His father lost a fortune on imported grain.'

'I suppose that – as you're a relative – it's you he hopes to see? Though he writes that business brings him to Britannia?'

'Business brings him to Britannia? Laurentius Manlius? The fellow never did a day's business in his life!'

'Then you think he might be hoping for a loan from you?' I said. It would explain my patron's obvious irritation with the man.

Marcus snorted. 'No one in his senses would come all this way, simply on the off-chance of a private loan. It would cost a fortune just to journey here – and in the winter season, too, when any normal captain keeps his ship safe in port! And then he sends that letter in advance instead of merely bringing it, like anybody else. By the Imperial post, what's more. Does he think we have no power of reasoning at all?' He signalled that the slave should cease to scrape his back and should set to work to clean his legs instead. 'So, since it's fairly obvious what really brings him here, what do you think that we should do with him?'

It was not at all obvious to me – nor, whatever his purpose, what affair it was of mine – but Marcus clearly expected some response.

'You do still have an aging female relative in Rome, don't you?' I said, as the massage-slave made little chopping motions on my legs. 'So this might be a marriage offer, perhaps? Though she is almost thirty?'

Marcus had legal responsibility for this unfortunate, of course – since, as a woman she was still a child in law – and thus if a marriage was in prospect, his consent was formally required. If so, I could not see why it should irritate him so. The arrangement would be an advantageous one: Laurentius would get the dowry – or the use of it; the woman (who at her age had few choices left) would have a protector in the capital; and Marcus would no longer have to be prepared to provide for her in an extremity.

But that was not the answer. Marcus curled his lip.

'Of course it is some time since you were in the capital.' I was guessing wildly now. 'Is it possible that he has recently acquired a trade? An interest in some export enterprise, which might bring him to Britannia?'

'Trade? Laurentius Manlius? It's obvious that you know nothing of the man.' (That was a fair assessment – until today I had never heard of him! But, of course, I did not interrupt.) 'The fellow's a Praetorian – or used to be. Even you must realize what that implies!'

'Oh,' I murmured weakly, as my massage-slave stepped away and signalled me to turn onto my back. I had never met a serving Praetorian, myself, though I'd heard the outgoing commander speak of them – in no very flattering terms.

It was at a little feast at Marcus's, when he had been hunting with my patron for the day and I had been invited to make the table up. 'There's an Imperial tribune coming to inspect. They're all the same, these ex-Praetorians,' he'd told me, dipping his bread into the oil. 'Used to having the best of everything. Praetorian quarters in the Imperial palace itself. Distinctive uniforms, to ensure appropriate respect. They are supposed to be the absolute elite, but as the Emperor's personal guard, they very rarely fight – indeed they scarcely leave the capital at all, unless going into battle with the Emperor himself or escorting him on visits overseas. Yet they get better pay and better pension rights, and a substantial bonus when they leave! No wonder that the regulars resent them quite so much.'

However, that banquet was more than a moon ago, and the commandant was gone. Though – like everybody in the Empire – I knew the legends anyway: Praetorians were bullies, susceptible to bribes, who had made and unmade several Emperors within the last few years. Severus was rumoured to have disbanded them, as soon as his accession was assured, and replaced them with soldiers of his own whom he could trust. Though that was only rumour – like everything, these days.

'I know of the Praetorian by repute,' I answered – cautiously.

'Repute? You mean like assassinating the splendid Pertinax, because he would not give them the bonus they demanded – and then selling the Empire to the highest bidder?' He gave a scornful laugh. 'And later switching loyalties again when they found that Didius could not pay?'

I knew the story about Pertinax, of course. How one of his own guard had drawn a bow and wounded him. And then, instead of rallying to his defence, the rest of the Praetorians had joined in to murder him. Pertinax had been my patron's friend. Small wonder that Marcus had no love for them.

However, I didn't mention that, at least not in the presence of the massage-slave. It had occurred to me that even the dumb may learn to write, and the deaf (allegedly) to read the lips. The Imperial laurel wreath may have changed hands – recently – more often and more quickly than a forged *denarius*, but it's certain that whoever wears it still has paid spies everywhere. Who knows to whom the bath slave might be reporting every word?

'Well armed, well trained and very powerful, so gossip says,' I hazarded. 'Though it may be that rumour is unkind to them?'

Marcus had no such inhibition, that was clear. 'They are worse than their reputation paints them!' He waved his attendant impatiently away, then swung around and sat up on the marble bench, dangling his legs. 'They've so much power, they almost run the state – and no one, from the Emperor down, dares thwart them anymore.' He signalled for another drying cloth – but far from draping it across his loins he took it in both hands and rubbed his face and chest, spurning the slave boy's offers to assist. 'No wonder Severus had them all replaced.'

The public bath slave had begun by now to oil and scrape my chest, so my head was on a level with the bench that Marcus was sitting on. I averted my eyes. 'But Laurentius "used to be" a Praetorian, Excellence, I think you said? Was he one of those dismissed by Severus?' That sounded disrespectful, so I added hastily, 'Or has he moved on to a regular command somewhere? Become a tribune like the one who visited, perhaps?'

My patron shook his head impatiently. 'Naturally not – or why would he be writing to the curia? He would have informed the garrison and sought accommodation there. The fact is, Laurentius retired months ago. He left the army at the end of the reign of Commodus.'

How and why? I wondered. When a man enlists, he contracts to serve for a given term of years – or until his death, whichever's earlier – and he can't escape unless he's wounded, mad, or seriously ill, in which case he gets an 'honourable discharge' and is entitled to his pension rights. But clearly this Laurentius was alive and well.

'Was . . .?' I tailed off, as a group of chattering bathers came into the room, laughing and noisy as if they had (impolitely) eaten and drunk too well at lunch.

Among them I recognized the hairy, bearded form of Josephus Loftus, the official money changer from the marketplace –

banker, contract broker and occasional auctioneer – who was famed for knowing all the gossip of the town.

I was almost glad of the intrusion, appalled that I'd been ready to suggest that my patron's relative might have been dishonoured and dismissed. Though a possible reason had occurred to me, which even Marcus would understand, if not entirely condone. Laurentius had served until the fall of Commodus – and the Praetorians had (naturally!) been implicated in the plot to eliminate that cruel and half-crazed Emperor. But his successor, Pertinax, far from rewarding them as they had hoped, had set out to purge the guard of those who'd taken part. So was Laurentius one of the conspirators, perhaps? Not actually executed, but quietly removed? However, with our current audience, this was not the time to ask.

Marcus had recognized the money changer too. 'Enough!' He was clearly irritated by the interruption. 'Come, let us take the plunge. We'll speak about this further when we can be alone.' He strode across the room, and plunged himself into the chilly water with a gasp.

I was only semi-strigilled, but my slave could take a hint. He swiftly finished scraping me, and re-wound my woeful cloth round my nether parts. However, Josephus and his companions had moved away by now, into another room, so I trailed over to the plunge pool and stood at the edge.

'Your relative. He was not implicated in the Commodus affair?' I hazarded, when Marcus surfaced, blowing out his cheeks.

The cold prevented him from answering at once, but Marcus shook his dripping, curly head. 'Not he!' he said, when he had caught his breath. He signalled to his slave to bring a drying robe, and climbed out into it, still panting from the chill. 'Laurentius Manlius is too careful for such things.' He actually smiled, as the slave boy patted him with lightly-perfumed oil. 'He would not take the risk – especially against a madman like Commodus, who took such pleasure in devising interesting deaths. Though my kinsman may have known there was trouble in the air, and chosen to retire as soon as possible.'

'So he'd served his contract out?' I'd forgotten that praetorians serve for only sixteen years. ('Full seven years less than common soldiers do, who fight Rome's wars and guard her frontiers', was how the commander had phrased it, bitterly.) So this Laurentius might be relatively young, perhaps no more than thirty-two years old – not the aging veteran that I had been picturing.

'Exactly!' my patron said, reminding me. 'And if Praetorians don't rejoin the army and – as you say – rise immediately to command somewhere, they either retire to some family estate or seek other employment at the Imperial court, as my precious cousin obviously has, since he has no family estate to speak of, nowadays.'

'Other employment?' What could such a man do for the Emperor after he retired, especially a careful one who did not want to fight? 'In what capacity?'

'Serving as the Emperor's private spy, of course! Is that not obvious? It's clear Laurentius has an Imperial warrant for this trip – without one, at this season of the year, a man would have to bribe a captain handsomely! Much more handsomely than Laurentius could afford, even with his bonus! Now, are you going to plunge into that pool or not?'

I nodded – too astonished to reply.

'Then I'll see you later, in the colonnade. There is a pressing problem, councillor, which I need your help to solve.'

And he swept out, accompanied by his page.

TWO

For a moment I could only stand staring after him. It was very possible his cousin was a spy – especially in the current circumstances – but how did Marcus suppose that I could help?

I could understand his evident concern. There'd been already one visit to Marcus from a legate, late last year. It was pretended as a courtesy to Pertinax's friend, but it was almost certainly to check that my patron was supporting Severus – which of course he was, in public anyway. But – with insurrections everywhere – no doubt there was renewed Imperial interest now in discovering where his secret sympathies might lie. And what better way than to send a relative?

I was almost glad of the distraction of the pool. The water was so cold it took my breath away and I was panting as I stood up and clutched the side. My teeth were chattering from my unwelcome plunge, but the chill was not the only thing that left me shivering. My dip had obviously cleared my head, because a worrying idea had just occurred to me.

My patron had just addressed me, several times, as 'councillor'. Something which he had not done since I was first elected to the post – though I was there at his insistence, and as his nominee. So why would he suddenly have started doing that? To remind me, perhaps, that he'd backed me for a post for which – strictly – I did not qualify?

It was my turn to worry, now. True I was freeborn and was now a citizen, but otherwise I hardly met requirements. I was a Celt, a tradesman, and I had been a slave – any of which might normally exclude me from office. But when Marcus's previous nominee fell dead, barely a moon after election to the post, my patron had waved these details aside, arguing that I'd been of 'noble birth', since I had been a chieftain's son, that the town required my talents, and that if Caligula could make his horse a senator, then he could make me a simple councillor!

He had personally provided the necessary 'deposit' into the town funds, and even made certain that I met the property requirements, by 'gifting me' a town apartment which he'd recently acquired, complete with basic furniture and staff (though on condition that the flat went back to him, as soon as I no longer 'needed it').

I wanted the place as little as I wanted to be duumvir at all, but property of a certain size in town was a prerequisite and my patron made it clear that he would take offence if I refused. In the end I could resist no more and, with his backing, of course, I was duly elected by the populace – with a huge majority, though I had no promise of public works or games to offer them.

Was that why Marcus felt that the visit of a spy might be of consequence to me? It was more than probable. There were rumours that Septimius Severus, appalled at the laxity of Commodus's regime, was taking stern steps to see that Roman laws were properly enforced, especially in the field of local government. In which case, I thought glumly, it was the worse for me. Impersonation of a curial officer was a serious offence, punishable by exile at best – and if it were proved that I was not entitled to the post, that might be the charge. And it would implicate my patron too.

Yet it was not possible simply to resign! Without a pressing reason (such as death, the jesters said) leaving before one's term was up not only incurred a heavy penalty, but invited an investigation of one's suitability. So perhaps my patron wanted to suggest that I should consider leaving Glevum for a time, at any rate while the visitor was here.

'Councillor Libertus!' I recognized the voice. Josephus Loftus! I had lingered here too long. He and his companions had just come in again, preparatory to moving to the hot room nearby, but he'd clearly seen me in the plunge pool and come waddling across to speak to me. (He was clumsy in the fabric slippers one can hire to keep one's feet from burning in the hotter rooms.) 'Citizen, I thought I saw you earlier.' His voice was slurred and unusually loud – he'd obviously drunk even more good Rhenish with his lunch than I'd supposed. 'I'd be glad of your opinion . . . business matter . . . if you have a moment afterwards . . .?'

I shook my head. I always avoided Josephus as much as possible – though he was honest, as money changers go, and commerce obviously brought us into contact now and then. But conversation with him was at best a time-consuming affair, and today he was tipsy as well as garrulous. 'Another time perhaps. I am attending on my patron, as no doubt you saw, and he'll be awaiting me.' I gave him a brief, blue-lipped smile, and plunged back into the pool. By the time I came up spluttering, the man had gone.

A tap upon my shoulder. The massage-slave was handing me another drying cloth, so I permitted him to help me out and rub me dry, then (since my own budget did not run to costly perfumed oils) I hastened off into the robing room – anxious lest my patron had already left. I glanced round the room, where there were several servants sitting, bored and patient, on the benches and the floor, guarding their masters' goods. (Some such arrangement is advisable, otherwise one is likely to emerge to find that one's clothes have disappeared or – if one is luckier – merely taken in exchange for garments of lesser quality.) But there was no sign of my patron, or his massage-slave.

'Master!' My own attendant, Minimus, had leapt up from the stone bench opposite. 'Your patron has dressed and is awaiting you. I am to tell you that he's in the colonnade and is ordering some refreshments for you there.' He hurried over and began to help me dress, bringing the dry tunic that I'd left there in his care. As he leaned close to help me into it, he murmured in my ear, 'I expect he wants to talk to you about this visitor. You know he suspects the man is coming here to spy?'

I frowned at him, surprised. 'That is supposed to be a secret,' I hissed, speaking in an undertone myself and hoping that I sounded sufficiently severe. Marcus would be furious to learn that servants knew – though he'd clearly not been careful to ensure that they did not. 'Where did you hear of this? Gossiping with that massage-slave, I suppose.' (Minimus had been a slave of Marcus's before he came to me so he still knew many of my patron's staff.) 'Although I don't see how. He was with Marcus in the baths, throughout, and would not have had the opportunity for idle talk with you.'

Minimus grinned. 'I was speaking to your patron's other page, the one who was left here to guard the clothes! You will want your toga, too, now, I suppose?' He took it from the open locker space, where he had folded it away, ready to leave it at the town apartment overnight.

It was the only thing for which I really used the place, except once or twice to bring my wife to Glevum overnight, to shop the morning stalls and have new sandals made, while I met delegations from the populace, petitioning for market licences or complaining of the drains! But it was convenient to store my toga there. For one thing, each visit was officially an 'occupation of the property', so I complied with the legal minimum, and for another a toga is not a thing in which to walk for miles. As a duumvir I needed one, of course, and preferably one that was reasonably clean – not trailed down muddy lanes – to wear at meetings of the curia.

And I had a second, more elaborate toga, now – which, although the purple stripe around the hem was as narrow as the weaver's art allowed, had cost a fortune and was difficult to clean. It was, of course, considered a privilege of rank to be allowed to purchase one, though – being a junior magistrate of non-patrician birth – I was not required to wear it very much, merely for special occasions, like processions or appearances in court. A plain one was sufficient for most curial affairs – or for meeting my patron, formally, as now. And even that was wearisome enough!

'I suppose so,' I said glumly, and held wide my arms, so Minimus could wind the awkward thing round me and secure it with the shoulder-brooch. 'I hope you weren't gossiping where you could be overheard?' I added. 'I saw Josephus Loftus in the bathhouse, and if his slave was listening and told him what was said, it will be all over Glevum by the time the gates are shut!'

Minimus gave an unrepentant grin. 'There is no fear of that – Josephus Loftus did not bring a slave. In fact he offered me a quadrans to guard his clothes as well as yours, but naturally I told him that I could not stay – I'd have to leave when you did. So he gave me just an as and told me to watch his tunic for as long as possible. Though, who would want it, is another thing – a greasy Grecian tunic when there are cloaks and togas here.' He made the last adjustments to my shoulder-folds. 'Anyway the page and I were talking quietly – no one could possibly have overheard. And he was only saying that Marcus was worried about the visitor, and seemed to think that you could help. He couldn't tell me how.'

So Minimus had asked him! I suppressed a smile. 'I've no idea myself, but do up my sandals for me and I'll go and talk to him. In the meantime, you can stay and earn your as. On second thoughts, I'll ask you to run over to my workshop and tell my son Junio where I am. He's been working there since shortly after dawn, and I was due to meet him and travel home with him. He'll never guess that I am at the baths again – especially since I left my bathing loincloth with him only yesterday, to let it air beside the embers of the workshop fire.' (No doubt in Rome these things are easily arranged, but in damp Britannia wet clothes are hard to dry, especially at this season of the year.) 'Explain what's happened, say I've been delayed and tell him I will meet him at my town apartment when I have found out what my patron wants.'

'And not worry about Josephus's clothes?'

'We'll find an urchin to guard his things for him, and you go to the workshop. A better plan all round. Josephus says he wants to talk to me and if he comes out and finds you sitting here, he'll stay and wait for me – and I shall be already late setting off for home. Don't look so disappointed, you can keep your as, I'll give you another to pay the urchin with.' I took the small brass coin from my purse and put it in his hand. 'And come back here as fast as possible, I will need you to accompany me today.'

It was ridiculous – the apartment is not a hundred paces from the baths, but as a decurian it was not 'appropriate' for me to walk even that short distance without a slave attending me. Normally this did not concern me in the least, but there had already been veiled comments by other councillors – especially one of the younger *aediles* – and if this visitor was looking out for things to criticize I did not want to give him the opportunity. Even the threat of spies begins to alter how one acts.

Minimus, however, set off on his errand with a grin and I went glumly off to find my patron, who would no doubt not be in the best of moods himself. He does not care to wait.

I found him occupying one of the stone benches in the covered colonnade. He was sitting, idly watching a young athlete practising with weights, with his slaves behind him and a table of light refreshments spread in front. I made to kneel, as usual – but he gestured me to sit.

'So, Councillor Libertus,' he began, breaking off a piece of bread and dipping it in cheese-curds as he spoke.

There it was again, that uncomfortable allusion to my rank. 'Excellence?' I murmured, taking my place beside him on the bench – though ensuring that my head was lower than his own. 'You wished to talk to me? About this visitor?' I glanced towards the slaves. 'A private matter?'

Marcus caught my glance. 'Slaves, go and order us some watered wine. Tell them that I'll pay them afterwards. You need not hurry back.' Then, as the slave-boys moved obediently away, he added with a smile, 'I hope that allays your anxieties, my friend?'

I did not say that it did nothing of the kind, or that his page had already been gossiping with mine. It would earn him a flogging, and it was hardly the lad's fault if his master had been indiscreet. Instead I murmured, 'You suggested, Excellence, that I could be of help?'

'Ah, indeed!' He shifted on the seat. 'The problem is, as I said earlier, I'm quite sure that he's a spy. Of course he has written to the curia not to me, so this visit could be seen as a matter for the town. Yet, as a relative, I shall obviously be expected to arrange for his accommodation while he's here, and provide appropriate entertainment, banquets and the like. I might have asked the garrison to entertain him at the military inn – the best room and food and all that sort of thing – but he is a kinsman, and it might cause offence to send him there. Anyway the new incumbent sends word that the rooms are often occupied. I'm not sure I believe him. But I do not wish to have Laurentius in the house.'

I was astonished. 'You dislike him as much as that, Excellence?' Marcus, to my certain knowledge, had across the years entertained many people (including relatives and legates) that he did not like – and entertained them very handsomely – yet I'd never heard him express a sentiment like that.

'It's not entirely a question of dislike,' my patron said. 'Though, true, he's a fellow for whom I don't much care.' He beckoned me closer. 'The problem is, I may have spoken carelessly. I entertained the former camp commander several times last moon . . . and we may have touched on what would happen if Severus should fall . . . or fail to defeat Pescennius, perhaps . . .'

'And you fear that Laurentius may get to hear of this?' I said, with some relief. Perhaps after all I would not be required to leave the town. 'Excellence, I am sure that – when your safety is at stake – your staff can be relied on to be utterly discreet.'

Marcus looked at me as though I'd gone insane. 'Naturally, Libertus, I would expect no less. But my young son Marcellinus is of an age to talk, and he has no concept of being circumspect. And I may have had him in to banquets once or twice – as a kind of entertainment when the wine was being served – although his mother does not much approve. She even warned me that it might be dangerous – but Marcellinus loves it, and he can be very droll. I've had him in my town apartment, recently, as well.'

So Marcus had been showing off his son, in adult company – no doubt encouraging the child to 'play the man', by strutting with his little sword and tasting watered wine – and imitating what was said in front of him. It was so like Marcus that it made me smile. I thought I had merely done so inwardly, but my patron said, 'I see you understand me.'

And suddenly I did. I let out a sigh of pure relief. Marcus wanted me to give him back the flat – it would be officially a loan, of course – but it was unthinkable for him to ask for it outright. No well bred Roman would ever sue to have a gift returned – it was worse than bad-mannered, it was almost certain to incur bad luck. The trouble was, of course, I could not offer it – at least not instantly – for fear of implying that he had requested it.

'So you'll want a town apartment, suitable for a man of

substance?' I said, frowning as though this were a problem which required much thought. 'I have not heard of any which might be to let. I'll be sure to keep a listening ear alert and let you know at once if I learn of anything. Or . . .' I allowed my face to brighten, as if inspiration had just occurred to me. 'Your visitor could have the use of my apartment, while he's here.'

'Councillor, you are too generous!'

I knew by my patron's smile that I had guessed aright, but I hurried to qualify the offer, before I found that the visitor was here at my expense. 'Though it might not be entirely suitable. It is sparsely furnished – just sufficient for my needs – and I have merely the two slaves to keep it warm and clean. I fear my purse won't stretch to any more. And I don't run a kitchen worth the name. But if you'd care to arrange some extra staff for him, it might be possible . . .?'

'Never fear, Libertus, I will see to everything. Since he is a relative, I could do no less. And I'll organize a public banquet for him too – the guild of vintners have a hall that we could use, they are happy to lend it for civic feasts if they provide the wine. Your generosity will solve this splendidly. But you're taking no refreshment – please, do help yourself.' He gestured to the tray of salted snacks. (No pies or sausages, I was glad to see – in my current state of nerves I could not have eaten them.)

I took a pinch of salted lupin seeds, while he dipped his bread in oil and burbled on, making more plans for how Laurentius could be entertained – 'perhaps even a visit to the chariot race?' – and after a little while his two slaves reappeared. Obedient to their orders they did not approach, but loitered at a little distance from the bench – one with a small jug of watered wine and the other with a pair of goblets in his hand. Marcus looked up and gestured them to come.

'Let us drink, then, to the gods and to a problem solved,' he said, and that is what we did. I was still smiling when I went back to the locker room, where Minimus was waiting with my cloak.

He fixed it round my shoulders and nodded to a ragged urchin sitting near the door. 'I hardly needed to have spent your as so soon,' he said. 'Josephus hasn't come back for his garments yet!'

'Talking the ears off his companions in the plunge pool, I expect,' I said, unkindly. 'But whatever he wanted with me I'm sure that it can wait. And I need not have worried about my patron's visitor. He is going to use my town apartment, that is all. Let's go there now and meet with Junio.' I led the way outside. 'I wish all problems were as simply solved.'

I could not guess how wrong I'd prove to be.

THREE

The next day was officially *nefas* – ill-omened – on the calendar, and therefore all courts and theatres, and many businesses, were shut. So I did not go to Glevum but stayed at home to make some overdue repairs to the stockade around our roundhouse. This was to propitiate my dear wife, Gwellia, who had been asking me to attend to it for half a moon (a high wind before the Kalends had blown down an outer section nearest to the lane), and who – to my surprise – was not happy that I'd offered our town apartment to the visitor.

'Typical of your patron,' she grumbled, lifting the morning oatcakes from where they had been baking in the embers overnight, and passing one to me. 'Gives it to you one moment, to suit his purposes – and wants it back, when that is convenient to him!' She handed me the water jug so I could pour a drink. 'And don't keep saying that he didn't ask for it – we both know that's, effectively, exactly what he did. And if we can see that, no doubt the gods can too! I'm surprised he isn't worried about bringing down a curse.'

'But we hardly used the place, in any case,' I said, pacifically, biting into my fragrant breakfast as I spoke. 'And as official hosts of this Laurentius we will certainly be asked to one of these banquets that you've been wanting to attend!'

She was not mollified. 'Banquets? And what, exactly, do you imagine I should wear? You've got your councillor's toga with a fancy purple stripe but, as your wife, I can hardly attend a formal civic feast dressed in homespun Celtic plaid! I was going to buy a proper Roman *stola* and *tunica* – or at least some fine-weave fabric so I could make my own – but thanks to your patron that won't now be possible, I suppose. I can't even get into the market easily, from here!'

There was no reply to that, so it was at that point that I went out to mend the fence, accompanied this morning by my small slave Tenuis; Minimus having been sent to fetch new bedding-reeds and water from the spring.

It was a cool fresh day, but the sun was peeping through, so the chore of disentangling the errant stakes and then replacing them proved quite a pleasant one – a welcome change from civic duties in the town. Nor was it especially difficult. Despite the tangled pile which confronted us, the stockade had merely been blown inwards in one area and only a small portion was actually destroyed. So by the time the sun was setting we had all three rows of palisade securely back in place.

I said so, rather proudly, to my wife, as I sat on a stool beside the fire and enjoyed the bowl of steaming stew which she'd prepared for me. (I'd thought it more expedient not to stop at noon.)

I was not quite forgiven, as I realized from her sniff. 'At least we can have the poultry back again, without the worry that they might escape!' She spoke as though we'd sent a whole flock half the way to Rome, rather than simply driving our half-dozen geese and chickens through the gate into Junio's enclosure next door.

All the same I recognized the promise of a thaw. 'I'll make sure to take you on the mule to town, before this fellow comes,' I said. 'And you can have your Roman gown. Though you look well enough to me in what you spin and weave.'

It was not altogether flattery. Gwellia is no longer young, of course, and – having, like me, been captured as a slave – her life has not been easy, so her face is lined and worn, but she is still handsome. Especially when she smiles, as she was doing now. 'You are foolish, husband! But, speaking of Glevum, I understand from Minimus that Josephus Loftus was looking for you yesterday, again, when you were at the baths?'

I was about to nod vaguely and keep on eating stew, but suddenly I saw the force of what she'd said. 'Again?'

It was her turn to sound apologetic now. 'Perhaps I should have mentioned it, before. But you know what Josephus is like – always looking for a reason for a chat. It must have been the last time I was in the market square. You remember that you gave me that foreign coin, to have it weighed and proved?'

I nodded. It was a *tetradrachm* from the African provinces, which a customer had given me, among a purseful of other coins, in payment for repairs. It was official coinage – one side of it showed Commodus himself – but the quality of silver in Egyptian coins is so debased these days, that nobody will take them, and one has to have them changed. 'I should have spotted it at once,' I said. 'Was there a problem?'

Gwellia shook her head. 'Not exactly, though it fetched less than I supposed, and then he charged commission of a tenth – although you always say he's honest.'

'For a money changer, so he is!' I said. 'And you spoke to him, direct? I understand he's got a young assistant now, because he's getting older and his eyes are failing him.'

'I dealt with Josephus, since you recommended it, though I had to wait for him. The new man was on duty at the booth when I first arrived.' She gave a sudden grin. 'Handsome looking fellow, with a charming smile – and less inclined to chatter, which will no doubt be an asset in attracting customers. I gather he is taking over more and more.'

'Which no doubt explains why Josephus was free to use the baths that afternoon,' I said – adding to moderate her animated praise. 'Though I understand he goes to the booth each day to supervise. He's training the new man himself, to join the guild of *argentarii*, and he takes the responsibility seriously.' As he should, of course. The guild is a very exclusive one, with strict admission rules – since any member is legally responsible for losses incurred by any of the rest.

'Then they can have the licence formally transferred?'

I nodded. In Glevum there's only one official money changer at a time – though of course there are private money lenders by the score. Josephus will lend you money (if you have collateral), but he has other duties too – testing coinage and providing change, as well as assaying foreign coins like mine. He'll take gold and silver on deposit (and lend it for profit – at a fee), or arrange an auction of goods or property. A man with a finger in every deal in town. 'So what did the old rascal want with me?'

She made a little face. 'I'm not entirely sure. You know how much he talks, and I'm afraid I wasn't really listening

by the end. Something about some coins which didn't weigh
the right amount. It was the assistant who first noticed it,
apparently. Josephus was worried that he might have missed
a few, because he couldn't see the scales – and he might be
called upon to pay the difference, if the error ever came to
light. Though I don't know what he thought that you could
do to help!'

'Everyone assumes a councillor can help with anything,' I
said. 'Someone filing pieces off the coins, again, I expect. But
it's not my area. Really he should take this to the aediles,
they're the ones responsible for enforcing market rules. I'll
tell him so tomorrow – I'll go and talk to him, though they
won't be sympathetic if he's made mistakes. But I can't take
you to buy your cloth as well, in that case, I'm afraid. Junio
and I already have a customer to meet and nothing with
Josephus is ever very quick.'

She gave me a ready grin. 'The clothes can wait if they are
to be purchased ready-sewn. And it is probably better that
tomorrow I should fetch the poultry home . . .' This really
meant that she would spend a happy day with Junio's wife
and our little grandchildren. 'Now, would you like a little
bread to mop your plate?'

So that is how I came to be in the marketplace next morning
before noon, in search of Josephus. There was no curia meeting
for me to attend, and after a brief visit to the workshop, (during
which I was invited to admire the extensive pavement-patterns
which Junio had designed for a brand-new country house, and
to witness the first contract, ever, in which I'd had no part!)
my adopted son had volunteered to come with me to the booth.

'It would be wise to take these coins for Josephus to guard,
in any case,' he said, waving at the bulging money sacks
the contract had produced. 'It isn't safe to leave them in the
workshop, overnight, and there is far too much to carry home
on foot – pity we did not bring the panniers for the mule today.
So I'll come with you, if you're going, in any case.'

I nodded. I'd hardly expected our client to pay us in
advance – I'd rarely managed to wring that out of customers
before. But I did not say so. 'A good idea. There won't be
any charge for simply leaving it – we're not requiring him

to lend the money out. I can help with carrying the bags, so Minimus can stay and mind the shop for us, in case another potential customer arrives.'

'Though it's unlikely we'll find another one like that!' Junio was almost hopping with delight. 'What a splendid contract! I am glad we managed it.' He meant of course that he'd secured it – and it was churlish of me not to share his pride, though it was painful to discover that I could be done without.

'I don't believe I could have done it any better,' I replied, and was relieved of the necessity of saying more by being handed a pair of bulky money sacks, each sealed with one of Josephus's own tags to show that the contents had been checked. The bags were very heavy and I was glad to reach the forum and the money-changer's booth – though it was the assistant who rose to meet us from the stool.

'Greetings, good sirs. Can I assist you in some way?' The voice was civil and the Latin excellent, but I could see at once what Gwellia had meant about his looks. He was as handsome a young fellow as I have ever seen – tall and bronzed, with high cheekbones and dark hair: slim, yet muscular enough that even his long-sleeved, full-length tunic did not look effeminate. 'You have some money to deposit with us, would I be correct?' His tanned skin was made more striking by the whiteness of his smile, though I detected a slight tone of mild surprise as his brown eyes flickered from our humble working tunics to Junio's money sacks.

I gave him a half-nod. 'But we'd like to speak to Josephus, if that is possible.' I glanced around the busy forum for him, but without success. 'If he's not here at present, we are prepared to wait. I have other business with him.'

The perfect features took on an expression of dismay. 'Unfortunately, sirs, I cannot help you there. I have not seen Josephus all day. Or yesterday, in fact, though I did not expect him then – we do not open on inauspicious days. I fear the fall that he suffered at the baths may have been more serious than was at first supposed.'

'He had a fall?' I echoed, though, looking back I was not entirely surprised – the baths were slippery and he had seemed much the worse for drink. 'I saw him there myself, but I had not heard of this. Though I was surprised to find that he'd not returned to claim his clothes before I left. Where did he take the fall?'

The young man frowned. 'In the hot room, according to his slave – and not so much a fall as a collapse, though it seems he struck his head. Overcome by heat, or something, it appears – and his companions either did not realize, or had moved on by then. And when they did notice that he wasn't with them, they thought it was a joke, supposing that he had stopped to talk to somebody. Apparently he'd mentioned to them earlier that he had seen a citizen he knew, with whom he wanted to exchange a word or two – and with Josephus that was apt to mean at least a half an hour.'

'That was me,' I told him, and saw a strange look flicker in the eyes. This assistant was no idiot – and, charming though he seemed, I realized I might be in danger of him reporting me. I'd just told him I was a citizen, and all citizens are technically required to wear a toga in the forum at all times, on penalty of a fine – though in muddy, damp Britannia in the winter months this regulation is not rigorously enforced. Unless one is a councillor, of course, or a complaint is laid. Or, in this case, both.

I had neglected this regulation so often and for so many years that I hardly thought of it. Yet we were anticipating an Imperial spy, who might be charged with seeing that such laws were obeyed – and all fines collected.

'I am a citizen,' I hastened to explain. 'But I am a tradesman too, and today I came to the colonia to work – that's why I'm not wearing formal dress. I have a mosaic workshop just outside the northern gate.' I was about to add that Junio was a citizen as well, but the young man interrupted me.

'Ah!' The tone had suddenly become obsequious. 'Then you must be the duumvir Libertus. I have heard Josephus speak of you. Forgive me, councillor. I am fairly new to Glevum, and I don't yet know which customers are which. I don't believe I've had the honour of meeting you before. Allow me to introduce myself. My name is Graeculus Properus – an odd name hereabouts, but my father was a freeman from the Eastern provinces. He called me Properus – "hasty" – because I was early born.'

'But it means "dextrous" also,' I remarked. 'No doubt you earn that, too.'

He acknowledged the compliment with a little bow. 'My father would not think so. He was hard to please. He did not forget a grudge – nor a favour either, which is why he was a friend of Josephus. Josephus once arranged a private loan for him, when he first moved to Britannia years ago – and set up a little business in Corinium, making salves for eyes. He needed money to buy ingredients.'

I nodded. Corinium is famous throughout the Empire for treatment of the eyes. 'He prospered?'

'So much that he had clients from abroad and served the governor. Dead now, I fear, but he never forgot to whom he owed the fact of his success.'

He must have prospered very much, I thought, for the family to afford the placement fees for this apprenticeship, though no doubt Properus hoped to rise still more. Obviously he was not yet a citizen but with good contacts he might hope to win a nomination for that privilege, for 'service to the state'. And acting as a money changer was a useful start – it would introduce him to the wealthiest men in town, who might be willing to act as guarantors if he could offer little fiscal favours in return. Not strictly legal, but it's the way these things were done.

'And you are the duumvir?' He was awaiting my reply.

'I am Libertus,' I agreed, 'and this is Junio, my adopted son. Can you tell me where Josephus can be found? I believe he hoped to talk to me.'

Something unfathomable – it might have been amusement – moved in those dark eyes but the voice was courteous. 'I imagine, councillor, that he will be at home. I had planned to go and call on him myself, if he did not appear, but that won't be till dusk. I can't leave the booth here unattended until business is over for the day. I can give you directions, if you wish. Though, from what I learned from his servant yesterday, he may have a headache and not welcome visitors – not even gentlemen of high rank, like yourselves. Can I take a message for him?'

I shook my head. 'I know the house,' I said. 'We'll call and visit him – if only to enquire about his health. In the meantime, we can deposit these with you?' I gestured to the money sacks which Junio was piling on the counter as I spoke. 'No more than overnight. We have Josephus's own statement here of what is in the bags.' I handed Properus the piece of bark-paper.

The white teeth flashed again. 'With pleasure, councillor. I'll give you a receipt – or these two citizens can act as witnesses.' He gestured to a pair of purple-stripers – both senior members of the curia – who were approaching us. 'I'll even weigh the coins, to double-check.'

I shook my head. 'No need for that,' I told him, hastily. I had no wish to be recognized while incorrectly clad. 'There's no need to break the tags. I trust Josephus. A receipt will be enough. You can simply add your mark to his account of what is there!'

'Naturally, duumvir, if that is what you wish.' He sounded disappointed, as though I'd spoiled his chance to show his expertise in using the steelyard in the booth. (The councillors had turned away by now and were talking to a third – one of the market aediles.) 'Furthermore, I'll lock the bags into the money-chest tonight, and accompany them to Josephus's residence myself – the money is taken every evening under guard. Please tell his servant that I'll be sure to come.'

I nodded and was about to take my leave when some impulse made me check. 'You don't know, I suppose, what it is he wants me for?'

The striking face became a mask of courteous puzzlement. 'I fear not, citizen. Josephus did not discuss his private plans with me.'

That was a wonder then, was my unkindly thought. Josephus was not known for reticence – though it might be different in business matters, where discretion was almost a requirement of the job.

Junio was clearly echoing my thoughts. 'Not personal, I think. Something about some coins which were underweight?'

The handsome shoulders shrugged. 'Ah, those!' He rummaged in a wooden chest beside his feet, produced a shining silver coin, and handed it to me. 'You can see it for yourself. We have had one or two in recent days. Inferior forgeries of a denarius. Most imitations that we see are better ones – sometimes produced from real official dies that have been stolen from a mint – and those are very difficult to spot. But these are very crude.'

'I can see that the details of the Emperor are blurred,' I said, passing it to Junio.

'And more overweight than the reverse,' my son observed, judging it in his palm before returning it to me. 'Though I would have accepted it, I think.'

Properus laughed. 'Then keep it, citizen, as a gift from me. It is virtually worthless, anyway. No value beyond the thinnest sheet of silver plate – which is the concern for Josephus, of course. But more a matter for the aediles than for a duumvir, I would have thought?'

I could hardly argue – I had thought just the same. 'Then here is your opportunity, Properus,' I said, as an aedile began to move towards the booth.

As he approached, I recognized the man. It was Rufus, a chinless and ambitious youth of wealthy stock who did not care for having a pavement-maker as his supposed superior on the curia. (Being an aedile used to be a necessary step to civic power – still can be, in the provinces – but the role has little power, nowadays, whereas there is a lot of status in the title 'duumvir' although the post is not important here as it would be in Rome.) Nothing would give him greater pleasure than reporting me for 'inappropriate dress'. Junio had seen him too, and was already in retreat.

'Thank you for your help,' I said to Properus over my shoulder while moving hastily away. 'We will be sure to pass your message on to Josephus.'

I made the casual promise with a smile. But as it happened, I was wrong again.

FOUR

Despite my confident assertion to Properus, I had only ever called on Josephus once before, and I couldn't remember exactly where he lived. However, I knew that his apartment was in the Street of the Gold and Silversmiths, and it was certain that someone there could direct us to the place – everybody in business knows an argentarius. There was no shortage of potential informants, either – from the moment that we turned into the street we were accosted on every side.

'Silver serving platters, or gold necklets for your wives? Travelling images of the household lars – or a nice pair of goblets for yourselves? Special price to you!' Young men crowded round us, plucking at our cloaks, each trying to persuade us to inspect their family's wares.

We brushed them all away, and hurried on, though several times we had to step into the road to avoid the glittering displays which spilt out from the front of every shop. Most establishments had living quarters at the back, but in every block there were also public staircases leading to other apartments on the upper floors. But which one was it? I could not recall.

I seized on a youngster, more ragged than the rest, who was loitering by a display of silver plates. 'Can you tell me where Josephus lives?' I had to raise my voice above the incessant rhythmic hammering from the workshops on either side. 'The money changer from the marketplace?' I added helpfully.

The child looked doubtful, but a proffered quadrans prompted him to point to a staircase opposite. 'Up there, first landing, second door.' He seized the coin and disappeared inside, before I had time to ask him any more.

I was a little doubtful of his veracity, but we followed his directions and climbed the narrow stair (past the inevitable crowd of idlers playing illegal dice, who stopped to stare at

us). But our informant was correct. Once on the landing, I
recognized the door and the watchers lost interest when they
saw us rap on it. All the same, we had to hammer twice, and
I was almost persuaded there was nobody at home until I
heard a shuffling on the other side.

At last the door was opened – a thumb's-breadth, hardly
more – and through the chink a pale suspicious eye looked
out, while a cracked voice demanded, 'What is your business
here?' It was hard to know if the speaker was a woman or a
man. 'If you want my master I'm afraid that he's asleep. He
took a nasty tumble in the baths the other day and he is not
to be disturbed.'

'I was hoping to hear that he'd recovered,' I replied, looking
politely at my feet so as not to confront the eyeball. 'I saw
him at the bathhouse, before he had the fall. He asked to speak
to me. I am the councillor Libertus – I have visited before –
and this is Junio, my adopted son, also a citizen.' I flinched
as a fat housewife shouldered past, carrying a pair of flapping
fowls in either hand, on her way to one of the meaner tenements upstairs. 'Could we come in and leave a note for him?
You could supply a writing-tablet, I assume?'

'I suppose so, citizen – since you're a friend of his.' The
eye drew back and there was the rattle of a chain before the
door was opened wide. Before us stood an aged, withered
crone. She wore a simple brown tunic, like any slave, but
around her head and shoulders there was draped a woollen
cape, from which a few white wisps of hair escaped, and which
she held in place with one thin blue-veined hand. I wondered
for a foolish moment if this might be Josephus's mother, but
she had called him 'master', so this must be a servant. I
wondered what had happened to the dignified old attendant
who'd admitted me the last time I was here.

'This way, citizens.' She stood back to let us in, then put
the chain back on the hook to seal the door. 'I'll fetch a
writing-block, he keeps one on his desk.' And she hobbled
off, with an alacrity surprising for her age – despite her
bandaged feet.

While she was gone I looked around the flat. It was much
as I remembered: quite a modest one – half the size of Marcus's

(or even mine) – but this central room was square and spacious, with two large windows which would overlook the street, if one could have seen out through the thick glass windowpanes (which must have been expensive, but did keep out the draughts, though letting a little amber light into the room). There was not much furniture, just a table by the wall, a couple of small cabinets and a pair of folding stools. There was also a brazier alight – whatever cookery went on must be conducted here, as a bubbling pot of something on a gridiron testified – but an altar niche with the usual statues of the household gods showed no sign of recent sacrifice.

A narrow doorway led off to either side: one to the bedroom and study, (which – as I knew from my previous visit to the place – contained the weighty iron-bound strongbox where Josephus kept his cash) and the other presumably to the slaves' room and the storage area. Not a mansion, but a pleasant place to live – apart from the constant hammering from the street.

I was about to make a wry remark to Junio, when the old servant came back with the writing-block. She set it on the table, fetched a stylus and stool, and motioned me to write. But I had hardly started when she began to talk – evidently she'd decided that she could confide in us.

'I am sorry you can't speak to him in person, citizens. But he's been asleep since all day. And I am glad of that. He had been restless ever since he got home from the baths, until the *medicus* arrived late yesterday and, despite it being a nefas day, gave him something to assist.'

'No doubt he bled him first, and prescribed a cabbage diet?' I said, more sourly than I ought. I have no high opinion of the public medicus in Glevum. 'That seems to be his remedy for almost anything. And then he asks for an enormous fee.'

But the woman shook her head. 'Nothing like that, citizen. Master had always refused a medicus before – he'd had an argument with some member of the profession once. He was rude and violent with this one too, but the man was not deterred. Soothed the master and gave him something to help him to relax. And certainly it worked. Half-an-hour later he was sound asleep.'

Perhaps it was the assistant medicus, I thought – most public

phsyicians have one, officially to accompany and observe them
in their work, and thus to learn the trade. If so, this fellow
was outshining his instructor. 'A younger man, perhaps?'

'Not an old one, certainly, but he was very good coming
on a nefas day like that. He even called this morning with
another dose, and looked in on Master, but he was still asleep.
I asked him then about the bill – a little worried because I
don't have access to the purse – and he was very kind. Said
that he would call back in a day or two – to see if anything
further was required – and we could pay him then. I haven't
heard a murmur from Master ever since. I almost wish I had.
I've made this soup for him. But the medicus was adamant
that first he needed sleep and must not be disturbed.'

'He will have given him poppy juice, of course?' Junio said,
making it a question, though it did not need to be – poppy
juice is the standard treatment for sleeplessness and stress.
'That can make you sleep for hours.'

'I gave him that the first night,' she replied. 'One of his
visitors brought a phial for him. But it hardly seemed to
help. He dozed a little but soon awoke again and was shouting
and half-delirious all day yesterday. But the medicus knew
exactly what kind of draught to give. I don't know what it
was – some kind of soothing medicine he said. Certainly my
master needed it – perhaps he was knocked stupid by the
fall, but I have never known him like it. Shouting, raving,
and all nonsense half the time. I blame those friends of his.
They said it was the heat, on top of all the wine – but I think
they gave him something very strong to drink. On purpose
probably – as some kind of a joke – because Josephus has
always been careful and waters everything. He says a money
changer must be sober all the time. He would never deliberately drink enough to make him lose control – let alone
enough to make him fall.'

'Perhaps he missed his footing because he couldn't see,' I
said, pacifically – though without much confidence. Josephus
had certainly seemed drunk enough to me. 'And he was wearing
fabric slippers, which can be slippery. And, as you say, he hit
his head – that can make people act in most peculiar ways.
Though you would be wise to keep a careful eye on him for

a day or two, when he does start waking up. There can be damage which isn't evident at first.'

She made a scornful noise. 'If so, it will be the fault of those so-called friends – and I shall tell them so. Slipped and fell, indeed! They were clearly worried that they'd had a hand in causing it. Not only did they bring him back here on a litter from the baths – just as well, I doubt he could have walked – but they paid for it themselves. Then one of them sent the medicus the next day, apparently, and another made a point of calling in as well to find out how Master was – even bringing little gifts of food and drink to tempt his appetite. It did no good – he wasn't well enough to eat. But they would not have done all that, if they weren't feeling guilty, I am sure.'

'So Josephus was not really improving since the fall?' If this were delayed concussion, as I feared, it was clearly serious.

She shook her head. 'Worse if anything. He was delirious and shouting half of that first night – and he looked so bad at one stage, I was afraid for him. Until the medicus arrived. He was so clever, he set my mind at rest. Once that draught had taken its effect he assured me that the master would be all right – with rest. There wasn't any bruising and he hadn't fallen far. He even suggested a calves-head soup to give him when he wakes, so I have made a start' – she gestured to the pot – 'though it isn't easy, we're not properly equipped for cooking here. And no doubt he will be hungry. He won't have eaten since he left here for the baths – apart from whatever snack he might have had with those so-called friends of his. But I need some leek and turnip to put into the stew.' She looked at me, imploringly. 'Advise me, citizen. I don't know what to do. Do you think I could leave him for a little while? I could do with fetching water, too, if he is well enough to leave.'

'So you are here with him, entirely alone?' I said. 'What happened to the manservant Josephus used to have?'

She made a little face. 'Isn't that always the way the Fates arrange these things? Semprius would normally be here, of course, but my master sent him on a mission just two days ago – some urgent letter that he wanted him to take.'

'Your master could see well enough to write? I understood his sight was failing him.'

'Not easily, but he's taken to sending a lot of messages of late – wanting to write them while he was able to, I think. This one must have been an afterthought. He turned up here before he went to bathe – only a little after noon, I'd just heard the trumpet sound. He scratched the note and nothing would do but Semprius must go with it at once. It was something private or he'd have used a public messenger – he usually did – and it was obviously not to anybody in the town, because he gave Semprius a purse of coins, so he could hire transport if he needed it. I don't know when he is expected to return.'

I frowned. 'So you don't know what the letter was, or where it was to go?'

She shook her head. 'My master would not have told me, anyway – and when he got back from the baths he wasn't making sense. Kept on burbling about the Emperor, but he did not even seem to know which Emperor it was. And when I tried to ask him he just threw things round the room.' She looked at me and I saw that her eyes were full of tears. 'It isn't like my master, citizens. He's a dreadful talker, on any subject but his work – he can keep you standing up for hours, telling stories about people you have never met – but apart from that he is the best of masters and the gentlest of men. So I'd like to make his soup. But I don't like to leave him, in case he wakes while I am gone.'

I glanced at Junio with my eyebrows raised and was rewarded with a nod. 'One of us will stay here,' I promised, with a smile. 'I don't suppose that you'll be very long. Meantime I'll write this message, for you to show him when he wakes.'

The old slave smiled, showing empty gums. 'Councillor Libertus, you are very kind. I'll hurry to the marketplace and come straight back again.' She burrowed into one of the little cabinets and produced a cloak, a woven basket and a drawstring purse, the last of which she looped onto her belt. 'There! I've got enough small coins to buy what I require, so I'll take the smaller water jug' – she put it into the basket as she spoke – 'though perhaps, before I go, I'll take a risk and just look in on him, to make sure that he isn't likely to wake and want something while you're here. I wouldn't like . . .' She did not finish, but hurried – hobbling – through the door towards her master's room.

She hadn't closed the door, so we waited silently, not wishing to disturb Josephus as he slept. I resumed my letter and had just begun – 'To the most esteemed Josephus' – when there was a scream, a bang, a clatter and the slave woman came back into the room.

Her face was ashen and her pale blue eyes were wide. 'Citizens – oh, citizens – you'd better come and see. The master's turned a funny colour and I cannot feel his breath. And he's as cold as snow. I think he might be dead.'

FIVE

'Dead?' Junio glanced at me, looking as astounded as I felt. I started to my feet but he was already following the servant through the door, and there was nothing for it but to hasten after them.

Past the study – which I had visited before – there was another open door. Junio and the woman were staring into the little room beyond. The old slave was trembling and it was evident that she was reluctant to go in there again.

'I can't believe what I am seeing, citizen! Come and look at him yourself.' She stood back as I approached.

Even from here a frame-bed was visible. One human arm was dangling from under the woollen blanket and furs which covered it, and beneath which one could see the outline of a form.

Josephus the money changer might have been asleep, if it were not for the colour of the face, which lolled grotesquely off the pillows, and the open, bloodshot, blankly staring eyes. It was quite evident that the man was dead, but – since something was clearly expected of me – I crossed the room and raised the arm, as if to check there was no warmth in it. There was none, of course. In fact, I noticed, the limb was already getting stiff. He was not only dead, but he had been dead some time.

Junio meanwhile had espied a mirror, a disc of polished bronze which stood on the clothes chest on the far side of the room. He glanced at me, I nodded, so he went and fetched it and handed it to me so that I could hold it in front of those bluish open lips. But there was no breath to mist it.

That seemed to be the final proof the slave required. She let out a wail – almost as if she'd been hoping I might work a miracle. 'But he can't be dead. He can't be.'

I shook my head at Junio, and he gently took her arm and led her to a nearby stool, murmuring, 'I fear that fall proved fatal after all. Does he have relatives?'

She shook her head. 'He never married, and he was an only child. His father is long dead, so there is only me. They call me Florea. I was his nurse, you see – his mother died when he was very small, and his father kept me on to care for him. I've done so ever since.'

'Then, in the absence of his manservant, you are the senior mourner in the household, Florea. You must be the one to come and call his name – to make sure his spirit's flown. Then you can go and find some herbs to purify the room.' Junio clearly understood that it would comfort Florea to have work to do. 'We'll close his eyes and do what's necessary here. And – if Semprius does not return today – we'll need to find which undertaker's company the guild employs, to come and have your master washed and fitted for a proper funeral.'

He helped her to her feet and stood politely back until she had called her master's name three times – in a voice so faint that it seemed a ghost itself. Then, taking the woman's skinny arm again, he led her back outside, where I could hear her sobbing into the corner of her shawl.

I brought the stool across and sank down for a moment beside the lifeless form, so that I could close the eyes and rearrange the lolling corpse more fittingly. Corpse! It was singularly shocking, when I'd seen him – lively and particularly loud – just two days before. And I'd been too discourteous to stop and talk to him. I could not shake the feeling that I should have done – surely I had not managed to contribute to his fate? Could he have known then there was a problem with his health, and wanted to alert me that he was feeling odd?

I shook my head. He had mentioned business, so that was not the case. And he had been clearly drunk. Probably, as his friends had said, he had been overcome by heat and the resultant fall had caused some damage to his brain – damage that proved fatal. Such things were not unknown – though there was not the slightest sign of bruising on the head that I could see.

Except perhaps a little around the nose and mouth? It was hard to tell – the pallid skin was slightly blue in any case. But surely a blow there, on the upper lip, even if he fell against the stone rim of the bath, could not have killed him? It might have loosened his front teeth, perhaps, but I had never heard of a fatality resulting from that kind of injury. Unless he'd bitten off his tongue. For a moment I entertained that horrid possibility – one could slowly drown in one's own blood from such a wound. But surely, then, there would be bloodstains visible? And according to Florea, he'd been talking freely since – which obviously disposed of that hypothesis.

Though since I was going to rearrange the corpse and close the eyes it would do no harm to check. It was not my place to slip a coin into the mouth to pay the ferryman, but I put a tentative finger inside to check the tongue. It seemed quite swollen but it was intact, and there was not even any sign of movement in the teeth, although . . . I sat back upright, frowning in surprise.

The front teeth were rammed so hard into the lips that they had left an indentation. I'd actually had to prise the lip away to test if they were loose. Obviously he'd hit himself much harder than I thought. And there was something adhering to the ridge inside the mouth – though not a piece of tooth. It was something soft. I'd felt it brush my hand.

Perhaps, in retrospect, I should have left it there. Gwellia certainly thought so, when I told her afterwards. But at the time I was merely curious, so I put my finger back and gently extracted the offending thing.

It was a tiny feather, and initially it did not surprise me over-much. My first thought was simply that it must have come from the downy bottom section of a goose's quill. Perhaps the medicus had used one (as they sometimes did) to tickle the inside of the patient's throat and so cause him to vomit up whatever substance might have disagreed with him – in this case, alcohol. Though there was no sign or smell of vomit on the body now.

I shrugged. No doubt the slave had cleared it up. I was inventing things. I would ask her about it later on, perhaps, when she was less upset. Meanwhile she would be waiting now, for the signal to arrange her master's funeral. I leaned across and closed the bloodshot eyes. I also made a senseless effort to close the gaping mouth, at least a little, so he did not look so dead. But – like the arm – the face was stiffening and I desisted, half-afraid that I would break the jaw.

I got quickly to my feet. How typical of a medicus, I thought, to give Florea such bad advice and keep her from the bedside when she was needed most! However sound asleep he had been earlier, obviously now he had been dead for several hours. No wonder she was shocked. And I was not helping things. After my exploration efforts in the mouth, the head was now lolling more grotesquely than before. I tried to rearrange it, raising it to lie gently back onto the pillow, which had slipped down badly out of place. An expensive pillow – goosedown, I realized, when I found a tiny feather lying on my hand. Obviously Josephus was prospering, if he could afford such Roman luxuries.

I had almost reached the door before suspicion dawned. A second feather!

I wheeled around and looked down at Josephus again, suddenly seeing a pattern which I did not like. The bloodshot eyes, the imprint of the teeth, the bruising round the nose and lips and the presence of the feather in the mouth – any one of these alone was quite explicable. But taken together? It came to me, with shocked astonishment, that this death might not be as natural as it had been made to seem.

Though the feather was not poisoned, by the look of it. There have been incidents where people have been murdered by such a means, of course – in fact I was once witness to such a case myself – but there were no signs here of any poison which I recognized. No arching, no discolouration, no foaming at the mouth. No sign of agitated movement. Quite the opposite. Rather the indications were that Josephus had been murdered while he slept. Suffocated, if I was any judge.

Indeed, once the idea had occurred to me, I realized that the position of the pillow should have alerted me before: it was lying where it could neither have fallen by itself nor smothered the sleeping man by accident. Someone had pressed it over his nose and mouth until he ceased to breath, then stuffed it roughly underneath his neck.

And therein lay a problem. Dare I voice my doubts? Normally I would have had no hesitation in fetching Junio in as witness and explaining what I thought. But what would it mean for Florea, if I did?

She was already stricken with grief and shock, and of course the thought of murder would be a greater blow – but that was not the worst. The law is not kind to any slave who is so much as present in the house if the master is the victim of a homicide – the theory being she should guard him with her life.

So even as I framed the thought, I knew what I must do. Unless I could discover who had murdered Josephus and prove it to the satisfaction of a court, I was condemning the poor woman to a painful end. In the meantime, it was best to hold my tongue. So I composed my features and went back out to help.

It had occurred to me that Properus might know which undertaker's company was favoured by the guild – and also that he might have a strongbox of his own, in which the takings could be kept until more permanent arrangements could be made.

And so, indeed, it proved when Junio went to ask. I, meanwhile, assisted Florea to find the herbs and candles to set around the corpse, and by the time that Junio returned with the women from the funeral house everything was ready for them to start their work.

'Then we must leave you,' I murmured to the slave. 'When they have finished you can start up the lament – unless of course Semprius has returned by then.' A manservant would naturally take precedence, of course, and there were no relatives. 'Though when Properus arrives he may wish to claim the right – I imagine he will call. I'll let him know he shouldn't bring the treasure here tonight.'

'No need,' Junio murmured. 'It was arranged that he would not. He didn't come here yesterday, of course, because it was nefas and the booth was closed. But he came the day before – bringing the takings under guard, in the usual way, and very surprised that the old man had not come back from the baths to escort it himself. But when he heard that Josephus was injured and in bed, they decided not to bring the cash upstairs that night. It would have been discourteous to stop and count it here, trailing all those armed men in to witness it, while the sick man was lying right next door. And a kitty would be needed for the booth again today. So he took it home with him. And as a trainee, waiting to take over one day soon, he obviously has a strongbox of his own. He's quite prepared to do the same again.'

I nodded. 'I'm sure his licence will be expedited now –
Glevum cannot be without an official money changer very
long. And, meanwhile, I will ask the watch for news of
Semprius.' I meant, in case his corpse had been discovered
anywhere – he was an aging man and running all these errands
might have been too much for him. 'It may be that he has
been taken ill, and not identified,' I added, for Florea's benefit.
'They'll look out for him. If there is any news, I'll have them
bring it here to you.'

I was talking to myself, though. Florea did not care.

Junio, too, was pensive as we went to pick up Minimus and
the mule, and – after I had given my message to the watch
– we began to make our way back down the forest track to
our respective homes.

We went some way in silence, but after a little – when
Minimus's young legs had taken him some way ahead – my
son burst out, 'What is it, Father? Can you tell me now we
are alone? Something has disturbed you, I can see it in your
face. Something more than unexpected death?'

I outlined my suspicions.

It was late by this time and the day was drawing in, but
Junio stopped dead and turned to look at me. 'Murdered?
Smothered? You really think he was?' There was no one on
the forest path but us, but he kept his voice low as though he
might be overheard. 'I had not guessed at that.'

'With his own pillow, by the look of it, and there was no
sign of struggle, so it was almost certainly while he was asleep.
Under the influence of that "soothing draught", I think.'

'You blame the medicus?'

'That was my first thought, certainly – he, after all, administered the sleeping potion – but now I'm not so sure. He
would hardly want his well-known patient dead, in circumstances which might point to him. Rumours like that could
ruin such business as he has – and the gods alone know that
it isn't thriving as it is. And why should he want to murder
Josephus, who'd never been a patient, so the woman said . . .?'
I put a warning finger to my lips as Minimus appeared.

'Is there a problem, master? I was waiting down the path.'

'Shocked by the news of the money-changer's death, that's

all – and chattering too much,' I said. 'You can run on and tell your mistress we are on our way.'

The boy nodded and sped obediently away.

Junio did not speak till he was out of sight. 'About the medicus. Florea was sure he'd never treated Josephus before – I see that line of reasoning. But a money changer can make many enemies. And Florea did speak about an argument – there may have been a professional grievance that we don't know about. Though Josephus was generally honest, I believe.'

'Famously so,' I answered. 'But even with a private motive, why take the risk of smothering Josephus today, when he could simply have given a lethal mixture at the start? And further-more, why forbid all visitors? That only ensures that no one else could be suspected, if any question ever did arise.'

Junio shook his head. 'But why should it arise? It was supposed to look like natural death. Perhaps he simply wanted time before the news got out? And it's hard to know who else would have the opportunity – unless you think that Florea was involved?'

'I am quite sure she is not. Her reaction could hardly have been feigned, and she had no need to ask us in to see the corpse at all – especially just before she planned to leave the flat herself. If she had killed him, surely, she would have left us there, and not "discovered" he was dead till she returned?' I urged Arlina into a shambling walk and moved on down the steep and winding track.

But Junio soon caught up with me again. 'And we would have been suspects, if anybody was? But as it is . . .?'

I nodded. 'And what motive might she have for killing her master? She seems to have loved him. She did not even need us to witness he was dead. Properus, for instance would have called in later on, if we had not ourselves prevented it.'

'He told me he had been planning to do so when I called on him. Possibly accompanied by members of the guard, to see if Josephus was well enough to keep the cash again.' He took Arlina's rein. 'More potential witnesses! And ones who knew that Josephus was injured at the baths and would not have questioned the fact that he was dead.'

'Certainly they would never have looked closely at the

mouth – only the funeral women were likely to do that, and they do not ask questions. It is only chance that I did so myself.'

'But if you had suspicions, why not voice them then?'

I gave him a wry look. 'And condemn poor Florea? You know what happens to a slave whose master is murdered while they are in the house.'

'You might persuade Marcus that she is innocent. And the laws are not as sweeping as they used to be. There have been cases recently where there has been a trial, and the slave has been reprieved.'

'Only if physical coercion can be proved. I doubt we shall find that Florea has a single bruise. Though she's likely to have plenty, if she is called on to give evidence. They will give her to the torturers.' I meant it. It is what they do to slaves – especially where testimony about their master is concerned. 'I doubt she would survive the questioning. So unless I can prove who did it . . .' I shook a rueful head. 'Better let this seem a natural death.'

'So Josephus will be cremated and no questions asked?' Junio said, surprise and disappointment in his voice. 'That is not your usual way of doing things.'

'Nor is that exactly what I said!' I pointed out. 'Tomorrow I propose to go and see that medicus – and, I assure you, there will be questions then. But don't tell your mother – not about my doubts. We'll have to let her know that Josephus is dead – she is bound to hear that from Minimus, in any case.'

He nodded. 'The news will be all over Glevum by this time, anyway.'

'She will be shocked – because she knew him – naturally, but, if I am any judge, once she hears about the fall, she will be too anxious about our coming visitor to give it further thought. Though we'd better hurry home before it gets too dark and she starts asking what has caused us to delay!' I picked a switch from a nearby bush and urged my poor old mule into a trot.

SIX

The next morning it was raining – hard. And it was unusually cold. Normally I would have cursed the Fates, but today I felt they were rather on my side. I had expected to have a long discussion with my wife, dissuading her from travelling to town today to order her new clothes – on the grounds that I'd need the mule and panniers to bring home the money bags. True, of course, though not insurmountable – but the fact was that I wanted to go and ask a few questions of the medicus, and I could not do so if she were there, without raising all sorts of fears about my health. But the weather removed the need for argument.

'Husband, I think I will delay my trip to town. It is too wet to go today. It's only a pity that you have to go yourself. Junio could man the workshop – he's clearly capable. Look at that wonderful contract that he won yesterday.'

'Unfortunately, I am obliged to go. There's no general meeting of the curia today, but there's a hearing about this civic contract for the sewer repair, and as presiding duumvir, I shall have to wear my toga with the stripe today.'

I was aware of sounding jaded but this was the tedious truth, although the hearing was a pure formality. (The bestowal of the contract had effectively been settled long ago, by councillors more senior than myself, but sewerage was officially within the remit of the two duumviri – a shared responsibility – and today it was my turn to attend.)

'It is a nuisance, but unavoidable,' I added, thinking that it really was a nuisance, too, because it delayed the opportunity for me to find the medicus. 'Though I need to go, in any case, to bring that money home. Minimus is putting the panniers on the mule.'

'It will be strange to go to the money-changing booth, and not see Josephus,' my wife said, thoughtfully, as she helped me wrap my thickest cloak around myself. 'Poor fellow, it's quite sad to think that one will never hear him chattering again. Call in at his home again, if you have time, and make a duty visit of respect. You needn't stay there long – I presume there won't be a formal lying-in-state or anything, it's not as if he were of patrician stock.'

'Or even a citizen,' I said. 'He only lives in a cheap apartment block. But I'll do as you suggest.' I had intended to do so anyway, for reasons of my own. 'There'll no doubt be professional mourners provided by the guild, so I will not be expected to lament. But I can take some funeral herbs to offer before the household gods with a prayer to smooth his passage to the afterlife.'

That seemed to please her. 'Then make sure you get fresh hyssop from the market stall – don't let them sell you dried. Then, since I won't be there myself, don't forget to give my instructions to the slaves when you go to the apartment to put your toga on. And don't get any wetter on the way than you can help!'

I promised. She'd reacted to the news of Josephus's death exactly as I'd hoped. I could only guess how worried she would be if she knew I had suspicions of the death, and – worse – was proposing to investigate without so much as Marcus's authority. Feeling slightly guilty for not consulting her, I gave her a parting squeeze, then pulled my hood up round my ears and went out to brave the wind and driving rain.

Minimus and Arlina were waiting at the gate, both of them looking as despondent as I felt.

'No Junio, this morning?' I enquired as I approached.

'He has set off already, master,' the slave explained. 'Before this rain gets any worse, he says. Those clouds on the horizon are looking very dark and he thinks there may be hail later on – though if we hurry we will miss it and may even catch him on the way.'

I nodded glumly as Minimus helped me up onto the mule. 'Perhaps.'

But of course we didn't. The track was slippery and even for a mule the going was treacherous, especially when it did begin to hail: small, hard hailstones which stung one as they hit, and piled like little frozen rollers on the road. By the time we got to Glevum I was drenched through to the skin and cold enough to be mistaken for a ball of ice myself. I was glad to reach the building where my apartment lay and hand Arlina over to my slave.

'Make sure that she's kept inside today, and see that the fellow rubs her down and feeds her well,' I said. (We had an arrangement with a friendly stableman, these days, instead of tying her to a ring outside the shop – now that I was councillor these things were easier! And generally free, I am embarrassed to report.) 'Then come back here quickly and you can help me dress – and we'll try to get you dry, yourself. With luck there'll just be time before I go to court.'

Minimus nodded and led the mule away, while I went in and climbed upstairs to the apartment, looking forward to the dry clothes which would be awaiting me – not only my elaborate toga but a fresh tunic too: I'd sent one to the fuller's and it should be back by now. The sewerage question was the final item for the day – the licence court closes when the midday trumpet sounds and does not reconvene – so I calculated that I would be free to call on the medicus shortly after noon.

I knocked on my door and waited to be admitted by my slaves. There were two in residence. They were not the liveliest of lads – Marcus had lent me those that he could spare most easily – but they were pleasant and willing, in a plodding kind of way. They were going to be unusually busy for a day or two, I thought! Gwellia had given me a lengthy list of tasks, all of which she wanted done before Laurentius arrived – sweeping, cleaning, setting blankets out to air – I only hoped I could remember all of it.

But when the door opened, I was in for a surprise. I was greeted, not by either boy, but by a hefty doorkeeper whom I did not recognize – and his unfamiliar ochre uniform did not suggest he was a slave of Marcus's. He had a head and shoulders like a battering ram, with muscles in his arms and legs that bulged alarmingly, and the look he was giving me was not a friendly one.

What was he doing here? I looked up at this giant with a nervous smile, and was met with a suspicious frown. My first thought had been to challenge him, but when I tried to speak I found that my throat had suddenly turned dry, and all I managed was a strangled croak.

His voice on the other hand, was loud and threatening, and – bizarrely, since this apartment was officially my own – demanding what *my* business was in calling here! I was stammering some inanity in reply, when to my amazement a familiar voice boomed out.

'Dear Jupiter, fellow, have you no sense at all! Let that man in at once. That is Libertus, the landlord of this place, who has been kind enough to offer it for my kinsman's use. You'd better hope that he's disposed to be forgiving, too, because he's technically your owner for a little while, at least!'

For a moment I could not believe my ears. But it was indeed my patron. I could see him through the – now – fully-opened door. He was sitting on a stool, but he rose to meet me as I was ushered (by a very flustered and apologetic slave) down the passage to what was – theoretically – my own reception room.

Although I would scarcely have recognized the place. When I'd left it – only yesterday – it had been simply and basically equipped. Now it was full of handsome furniture. There were tables, rugs and gilded ornaments – some of which I felt I'd seen before, though I could not remember where. They certainly weren't mine. Nor were the two extra burning braziers. Nor the table and reclining-couch which transformed the small *tablinium* recess into a dining area again. I stood at the inner doorway, totally bemused, as Marcus came towards me with both hands outstretched – a sure sign that he was feeling particularly friendly and self-satisfied.

'Libertus, my dear fellow, I must apologize – that wretch was only purchased earlier today, and so he couldn't know . . .' He broke off, as the slave relieved me of my dripping cloak and I came into the room, my sandals squelching water with every step I took. I had brought no softer house-slippers to wear.

'Excellence!' It was my turn to be flustered as I knelt to kiss his ring, acutely conscious of my dripping hems. As an ex-slave myself I was vividly aware of all the work which had been done, and which I was now undoing with every move I made. The floor, like every cranny of the room, had been cleaned and polished to a state of spotlessness – except where I had left my trail of muddy footprints from the door, and the little pool that was forming round my knees.

Perhaps it was the chill of my lips against his hand, but even Marcus seemed to realize how cold and wet I was, and he signalled me to rise. 'Slaves! Attendance on your temporary master here!'

At least a half a dozen servants hurried in, none of whom I recognized but all of whom had clearly been hard at work elsewhere. They were dressed in an assortment of tunics of every length and hue. Most of them were male, and all looked bronzed and strong, including the pair of lissom-looking girls who had doubtless been chosen for Laurentius's delight. Of my previous two serving-lads there was no sign at all.

'A drying cloth and blanket are required at once, and stoke up the brazier so he can warm himself. Then fetch his robes and set his shoes to dry.'

'The purple-striped toga from the chest beside the bed,' I had the wit to add, before the servants hastened to obey.

'And when they have finished they can clean the floor again.' Marcus was chuckling at my evident surprise. 'Meet your brand-new household, my dear councillor. I bought you this whole lot from the slave-market today. I know the dealer – I have dealt with him before – and I caught him shortly after dawn before he'd set up stall. He assures me these are the very best he had for sale. Freshly on the market this very day, so I had the pick of them.'

Or so the dealer claimed, I thought sceptically – but all I said was, 'To wait upon Laurentius while he's here?' I've never been afraid to ask the obvious.

Another chuckle. 'Exactly, my old friend. Not cheap, but I'll move them to my own flat afterwards. If they prove satisfactory, that is. Otherwise, I've warned them, I shall send them back. They'll be lucky to find a good position next time round – rejects never do. I've already traded in that pair of useless boys – they escaped a flogging for their indolence. It would have been deserved. But these new purchases have done a better job, so far.'

As if anxious to prove it, they swarmed around me now. In an instant they had stripped me deftly and borne off my dripping clothes. Before I knew it, I was dry and dressed and sitting by the brazier being offered cheese and figs – like any patrician in my purple stripe. Someone had clearly warned them about my Celtic tastes as well, since I was handed a goblet full of warm, spiced mead – in a handsome silver cup that I'd never seen before. Meanwhile the floor was miraculously shining clean again.

My patron, who was sitting opposite and watching all this with some amusement, judging by his smile, forestalled my thanks with a reassuring hand. 'No need for thanks, Libertus. You are the one who has been generous. Though no doubt it came as a surprise to find the place so changed.'

My mouth was too full of cheese to answer properly, but I managed to mumble, 'All this furniture . . .?'

'The contents that were in the place before – seized when the previous owner died, with the rest of his effects. Fortunately very little had been sold and it was still in store in a warehouse not very far away. I've provided you with a chestful of his silverware, as well.'

I nodded. Of course, that was where I'd seen it all before – no wonder it filled the space so beautifully. 'It must have taken quite a time to move it all back here – and in this weather too.'

'Two hours at least – though we had extra hands,' he said. 'I persuaded the garrison to send some troops to help.' He made a little face. 'The new commander was not easy to convince and I was obliged to make a contribution to the legion's funds. But something of the kind was necessary, as I'm sure you will agree. Fortunately I held a little banquet for him yesterday – I wanted to establish good relations with the man. One cannot be too careful with the garrison.'

Especially when you are expecting an Imperial spy, I thought, but I simply nodded.

'I took the opportunity to introduce him to some visitors of mine – a decurion from Corinium and his wife. And it was just as well he knew that I was here, in my town apartment, overnight. It seems that when he got back to the garrison, he found there'd been a courier at dusk. The previous commander would have sent to me at once, of course, however late it was. But this one does things strictly by the rules. I was awakened at first light by a message from the fort, saying that my relative, Laurentius Manlius – far from spending time with the Provincial Governor as everyone assumed – has already left Londinium and is on his way.'

SEVEN

stared at my patron, almost more astonished by the news than I had been by the transformation of the flat.

'On his way? So soon?' I blurted. 'But, Excellence, if you are correct and this fellow is a spy, one would expect him to spend more time than that with a rival claimant to the Imperial throne!'

'Clodius Albinus was anxious to be rid of him, no doubt. Get him out of Londinium as soon as possible – which makes me even more certain I am right. Laurentius has been provided with the Governor's fastest gig, and a mounted escort – while his effects and his servant are following by mule. So despite the weather we can expect him very soon. Possibly tomorrow, if the roads are not too bad.'

'Not today? You don't suppose . . . since the message came last night? Saying he was already on his way?'

My patron shook his head. 'I doubt it very much, but it is just pos—' He broke off as there was a rapping on the outer door. There was a silence as we exchanged a startled glance.

Beyond the inner door, which had been closed again, we could hear the giant hurrying to greet the visitor. A moment later he reappeared, alone.

'Well, fellow?' The barking tone showed Marcus was alarmed.

'It appears to be an urchin, Excellence. Says he wants the duumvir and will not go away.'

'Probably my slave,' I muttered, in relief. 'You'd better let him in.'

The giant shot me a doubtful look, but Marcus snapped, 'Obey!' and he hurried off to do so.

My patron turned to me. 'I didn't think that it could be Laurentius yet,' he said (although I'm sure that – like me – he'd been afraid it was!). 'That message to the fort was sent by the Imperial post, and official couriers hardly stop to rest

– they only pause to change to fresher horses now and then. If I know Laurentius he will do the opposite. He'll stop at every military inn, waving his warrant and demanding food and drink, and the use of the finest room and horses in the mansio. But one must make preparations just in case . . .' He broke off, as the doorkeeper came back – unaccompanied.

'The lad is unwilling to come into the flat. Too wet and dirty to sully it, he says, but he has a private message for the duumvir. And no one but the duumvir, apparently. Those were his instructions and he will not pass the message on to anybody else.' He'd been addressing Marcus chiefly, but now he turned to me. 'I am sorry, citizen, but you may wish to come and hear. He says it's urgent. From somebody called Florea. Perhaps you know the name?'

I was already on my naked feet and making for the door – my sandals were still drying by the brazier. 'I do. Excuse me. She is the money-changer's slave.' Then, seeing that some explanation was required, I added hastily, 'I presume you had heard, Excellence, that Josephus was dead? He fell that day we saw him at the baths. Hit his head, it seems. They took him home, but he has not survived.'

Marcus was frowning. 'I'd heard a rumour. It's very sad, of course. But how do you come to know his maidservant, and why should she call you?'

'I called there yesterday – not knowing he was dead – to ask after his health. I helped the slave to call the funeral house. Perhaps she wants advice.' I went out to the door. Behind me I heard Marcus make a disapproving noise.

Outside on the landing I found a dripping child, clearly one of the urchin boys that haunt the streets, looking for casual errands or messages to run. He looked suspiciously at me – especially my feet. 'Are you the duumvir?'

'I am. You have a message from Florea for me? About her master?' I spoke sharply, half-afraid that she had read the signs of suffocation – or that one of the undertaker's women had – and so the funeral was about to be postponed.

But the lad was shaking his bedraggled head. 'Nothing about her master. This is about a slave. She says you'll understand. They've found a body in a ditch not far outside the town, she says. It might be the one you know about. He'd been attacked and robbed while on the road and what should she do now.'

For one idiotic instant I thought of Minimus, but then the boy went on, 'She seems to think she shouldn't have it in the house, not with her master dead.'

'They think it's Semprius?' I murmured, ashamed of my relief.

'I couldn't tell you, councillor. I never heard the name. The army death cart picked the body up today, but did not put it in the common pit because you'd asked for news of any aging slave answering that description to be conveyed to her.'

'So it was discovered on the public road?'

He shook his head. 'They found it on a country track, apparently. Some gooseboy happened on it, and reported it – worried that its presence might bring down a curse. So the soldiers went and brought it in, though it was off the normal route of their patrol. But now they want her to collect it – what do you advise?'

I thought a moment, wondering if the two deaths could be linked. But then I shook my head. Is this were Semprius – which was probable – this had to be a sad coincidence. Though if so, Semprius had chosen not to hire transport, after all – or simply could not find a cart to carry him. Unwise, to say the least. A solitary, unarmed walker on a lonely road, especially an aged one with a heavy purse, would be an easy target for ambushing by thieves. (Such things do happen, more often than the authorities would like. Indeed the savage penalty – highway robbers are routinely crucified – may actually explain why so many bandits murder those they rob. Dead bodies tell no tales.) Poor Florea, I thought. This would be a double blow.

Meanwhile the grubby messenger was awaiting a reply.

'Tell her to ask the slave guild,' I supplied at last. 'They have a place for bodies, I am almost sure, and if this is Semprius, and he was a member of the guild they will arrange the funeral. Florea will know if her master paid the dues. If not I will pay the fee myself – even if it isn't Semprius – and you may tell her that. I'll call in later to find out what arrangements they have made – both at the apartment and the headquarters of the guild. You understand the message?'

He nodded but he made no move to go. I realized that he was waiting to be paid.

'Wait a moment. I have left my purse inside.' I went to fetch it. 'I need some money for the messenger,' I said, hunting through my wet clothes for the leather bag. 'Ah!' I found it and produced a coin. 'Here is a quadrans – that's all that I can spare. I promised to buy some funeral herbs to take to Josephus. I am planning to call in at the money-changer's booth and pick up what I left there yesterday, but the bags are sealed and it's better not to open them until we've got them home – I don't want money spilling because the panniers bounced.' I stopped, suddenly conscious that I was talking to myself and the doorman was watching my every move. I handed him the coin. 'In the meantime, give this to the boy.'

The giant sighed, but hurried off with it. After a moment I heard the front door close.

His Excellence was looking quizzically at me. 'Something of importance?'

'Nothing that can't be dealt with by the funeral guild,' I said, hoping that was true. I forced a cheerful smile. 'So let's return to the arrangements here.'

Marcus nodded. 'We know that Laurentius is travelling by gig. If he arrives in daylight he can't drive into town, so will naturally present himself to the guardhouse at the gate. I did suggest to the new commandant that, if by any chance he does arrive today, they should offer him accommodation at the mansio tonight, like any other official visitor. Though Laurentius may not want it, and the fellow seemed unwilling anyway – he shares my opinions about Laurentius, I suspect. Though he did agree to try.'

'But he was not unhelpful?' I supplied, 'He provided the manpower to move the furniture?'

Marcus gave me a wry look. 'He does not want Laurentius talking to his men. At one time that legion was ready to march for Clodius – why do you think the last commander was recalled? And Laurentius is, after all, my relative. So I agreed that when he does comes, they'll send word straight to me. Meanwhile I shall stay at my apartment – it's fortunate I have that visitor from Corinium there, it removes any question as to why I could not accommodate Laurentius myself. But I can be ready, at any time of day, to go and greet him at the fort and then escort him here, if that's what he prefers. Though, obviously, you will have to vacate this place and take those wet clothes away as soon as possible.'

'Today?' I stared at him aghast.

'Of course. I will present you to Laurentius in due course and introduce you as his official host – but you do not need to meet him straight away. I'll see that you're invited to a civic feast – I'll hold one for him in a day or two – that would be an appropriate occasion. I'll arrange one that includes the ladies too, so you can bring your wife.'

'Dear gods!' I muttered, thinking of her hopes for Roman clothes.

'There is a problem?'

I outlined my anxieties. To my relief, my patron simply laughed.

'That problem can be easily resolved,' he told me, airily. 'My wife has many garments which she does not wear. I'm sure that something suitable can be arranged. Your Gwellia is very useful with a needle, I recall.'

'You are too generous, Excellence,' I said, though I had private reservations. Julia is kindly to a fault, and would no doubt be happy to assist. But she is a good deal younger than my wife, and Gwellia – though comely – is no longer slim. I doubted any of Julia's stola-and-tunic combinations could be made to fit, however talented the needlework.

Marcus, however, was warming to his theme. 'I'm sure we can even find a veil for her to wear – since you'll have to travel by litter from your roundhouse, I suppose. Unless you stay at the workshop overnight. I can hardly invite you to my flat, as you will understand.'

I sighed. Gwellia had never veiled her face. Yet she was as much a prisoner of my newfound rank as I was, and she would have to behave like a modest Roman matron in public from now on. But as for sleeping at the workshop! That was laughable. The room upstairs is uninhabitable, since the fire, and we could hardly bed down in our finery amid the stonechips on the workshop floor! But I did not want to start discussing that. I had already delayed for far too long.

'Thank you, Excellence,' I said, again. 'And now, if I'm to go to court, I'd best put my sandals on. My cloak, too I suppose, though it's so wet it hardly helps. I'll come back for the other things this afternoon. And for my slave as well, though I'd expected him by now.'

Marcus gave me his most gracious smile. 'My dear fellow, you cannot walk to the basilica in this. Not in your formal clothes. We'll send for a litter – I will bear the cost. And don't bother to protest, I heard what you were saying to the urchin at the door.' He pulled up his toga-folds around his shoulder, to reveal a coin-purse strapped around his arm and tossed me a couple of denarii. 'Take these – they should be more than sufficient for the fare, and leave enough to take another litter to your roundhouse later on. You'll need one, if you are going to carry all your clothes from here, especially if your panniers are full of money bags. Get your son to take the animal, you ride home in comfort like the councillor you are, and you can repay me when it's convenient.'

It was a sensible suggestion, though typical of Marcus to spend a fortune on the slaves and then require me to repay a litter-fare. But it was getting late and I accepted gratefully. One of the servants was dispatched to find a carrying-chair, putting on a dry plaid cape before he left, I noticed with surprise. Slaves are sold entirely naked, as a rule, so that the purchaser can have a close inspection of the goods and make sure there's no disease, and though the tunics that they came in may be supplied, it is rare that cloaks are included in the price.

My patron must have noticed my surprise. 'I daresay you could borrow one of those yourself,' he said. 'I insisted on the slave-trader providing cloaks and a change of tunic each. Only the Dacian came with any possessions of his own, if you can call them that. His master had just died, apparently, and the heir just put him on the market as he was – complete with heavy sack, containing his old bedroll, and a change of clothes, among other bits and pieces he somehow had acquired. Which saved the cost of new things for him, at least!' He paused, so I could laugh at this economy. 'The others we equipped from the second-hand stall in the marketplace – though in the time available I could not make them match. But it hardly matters. All these things are yours, officially – so you can use a cape, and your Minimus can have dry clothes when he arrives.'

Minimus did not come before the litter did, but there was no time to wait. So – in a borrowed cloak and accompanied by a borrowed slave – I made my way across the town to the basilica. It was as well I had the litter and that the boys were fast. I got there just in time to attend the hearing about that contract for repairing drains.

EIGHT

The hearing was every bit as tedious as I'd expected and the outcome entirely predictable. However, it was mercifully quick – though all the time my mind was less occupied with sewers than with the deaths of Josephus and his unhappy slave. However, I had done my duty and it was not yet noon as I came out into the portico, feeling slightly awkward in my formal toga and ill-fitting cape. The rain had ceased – another mercy, I thought happily, as I started down the steps into the busy forum, where I hoped to find Properus at the money-changing stall.

'Master? Councillor Libertus?'

I whirled around, startled to find the borrowed slave who'd been attending me. I had forgotten all about him, though obviously he'd been waiting somewhere dry till I emerged.

'Do you wish another litter?' His Latin was spoken with a foreign lilt, but the voice was melodious and the grammar excellent, if a little quaint. This man had been well educated at some time in his past.

I looked at him with interest. This was clearly a very high-class slave indeed. He had run behind the litter, as the custom was, and naturally he had helped me down when I arrived, but we had not exchanged a word and in the rain I'd hardly seen his face. Now that his hood was back, I got a better view: a youngish man, perhaps twenty-five years of age, with a bronzed and earnest face, framed by a mop of red-brown hair, while beneath the heavy cloak the limbs were long and muscular. Very much the type that Marcus always liked. This one would certainly be kept on afterwards!

'No litter yet, thank you. I am not carrying sufficient cash with me – at least until I've visited the money-changer's booth.' I gestured towards the alcove in the forum wall, where Josephus had always had his niche – and realized it was empty and the shutters closed. Properus was not there.

For one brief moment my imagination raced. Could it have been Properus who held the pillow across his master's face? Had he now panicked and escaped to flee the law? Taking my money with him, probably?

But, of course I realized that it wasn't possible. The day that Josephus was killed Properus had been working here in the marketplace since dawn, under the watchful eye of the duty aediles – and Junio and I had seen him there ourselves. And I was certain that no mere apprentice (who would not even earn a proper wage) could afford to engage the Glevum medicus, whose fees were almost as painful as his cures.

I shook my head, abashed. I was too ready to be suspicious of poor, hard-working Properus – simply because Gwellia had praised his youthful charm! Besides, what could he gain from the death of Josephus? Without a patron his promotion to the guild would simply be delayed.

My new servant saw my gesture, and misinterpreted. 'Your pardon, master, but the booth is closed. I used it as a space in which to shelter from the rain, in fact. Several people have been looking for the man, and I overheard them talking to the aediles. There is some problem with the licence – apparently the previous holder died quite suddenly.' He broke off, giving me a smile that showed his perfect teeth. 'Although you are already aware of that, I think. I believe I heard you speaking of it to His Excellence.'

I nodded, smiling in return, but inwardly alert. In front of this slave I should have to guard my tongue – the man was clearly both intelligent and very alive to what was said and what was happening. The threat of spies had made me vigilant. 'You said there was a problem?' I was thinking of my missing money bags.

'No serious one, master. Simply that there has not been sufficient time to notify the guild and have his successor ratified. There's been an application, which is being dealt with now, but which may take some time. That is my understanding.'

I should have realized it was something of the kind. (I'd even thought of it, a moment earlier, without connecting it to why the booth was closed.) Of course there'd be a delay. A nomination by Josephus would certainly ensure that Graeculus Properus was eventually installed – but there were not enough members of the guild in this colonia, so supporting votes would have to be canvassed from elsewhere. Corinium, at least. And, of course, until he was granted a licence of his own, Properus could not operate alone.

I began to say, 'Thank you,' but realized that – bizarrely – I did not know my own slave's name. 'What do they call you?'

He looked at me, wryly. 'Master, I see that you select your words with care. The slavers call me Fauvus – the tawny one. My real name I left on the battlefield in Dacia. I shan't dishonour it by using it in slavery.'

So this was the Dacian that Marcus had remarked upon. And one of rank, no doubt – which explained the signs of education, as well as the accent and the youth and vigour of the man. 'A rebel warrior, then, captured and enslaved?' I realized I had been startled into saying that aloud, and I added hastily, 'I understand, Fauvus, more than you suppose. I too was a free man – a chieftain's son, in fact – seized and sold to slavery in my youth, though in my case it was raiders and not the Roman army who imprisoned me. Sometimes in my dreams I still see them roaring in, killing the old and dragging off the young . . .' I tailed off, embarrassed at having said so much. Baring one's soul is not the Roman way, but Fauvus only smiled.

'Citizen, I have no need of dreams. I carry a constant reminder of that day. That's why, when the trader who had owned me died, his son made the decision to sell me on again. The family did not deal in heavy merchandise, only luxury items like exotic perfumes, herbs and silks, but all the same he felt that this impeded me. As my new master it is only fair that you should know.' He extended his left arm and pushed back the tunic sleeve.

I thought for a moment he was hoping I'd admire the wonderfully detailed dragon tattooed on his skin, but as he turned the limb to show the inner side I saw what he had meant. A long jagged scar that ran from shoulder to elbow showed where a sword thrust had almost taken his arm off, and left it maimed and weak. I could see it would enormously decrease his value as a slave – which is no doubt why he had been so readily available. 'Struck with my own falx,' he told me bitterly.

There was a moment's awkward silence, then I said, in an effort to be brisk, 'So now we know each other, Fauvus, thank you for your helpful vigilance. But I have urgent business with that would-be licensee – his name's Graeculus Properus and I deposited some bags of money with him yesterday, before his sponsor's death was known. I'm sure there is no problem in retrieving them, but he won't have left them in the house of death. I'll have to call on him. See if you can find out where he lives.'

Fauvus looked around the forum in dismay. 'Your pardon, master, but where should I begin? I've never been in Glevum before the slave auction today.'

'Try the forum stallholders,' I said. 'One of them might know. Otherwise find one of the market police and ask.' This was rather a wicked afterthought. I had spotted the aedile Rufus by the fish market, though he affected not to notice me today, dressed as I was in my full curial robes. I was not sorry to have him learn that I had bags of silver stored. I gestured in his direction. 'There's one over there. Say that the question is on my behalf, and why. When you have the information, come back and meet me here. Oh, and buy me some hyssop from the herb stall too – fresh if they have it.' I fumbled in my purse and handed him a coin. 'Meanwhile, I have another call to make.'

He nodded doubtfully. He was clearly uneasy at leaving me unattended, toga-clad in the forum as I was, but after a moment he went loping off towards the stalls. I saw him hesitate outside the fish market and, after a moment, disappear inside. When I was satisfied that he was out of sight, I hurried around the corner to the narrow lane where I knew the public medicus had his premises.

I rapped the door and it was opened by a scruffy slave, who did not ask my business or address a word to me, but simply led the way inside, along a narrow ill-lit passageway. Halfway down he thrust aside a door, revealing another gloomy room within.

'A caller, master!' the boy announced, and scuttled off again.

The medicus was sitting at a table, where – by the light of a flickering oil lamp – he was poring over a section of a scroll. Behind him an open cabinet held phials and cupping bowls, a range of wicked looking saws and knives, and pots which might be full of anything – herbs, or leeches, unguents or maggots for cleaning out infected wounds.

If it was intended to impress and terrify his customers, it would have worked for me. I cleared a nervous throat.

He looked up, saw me and gave a sigh. 'Citizen Libertus!' he said heavily, letting the document roll together with a snap as he looked at my curial toga with ill-disguised disdain. 'Now councillor, I see. How may I have the honour of serving you?' He did not deign to rise.

He was a short fat balding fellow with a warty nose, and a high opinion of his own abilities, which he knew I did not share. However, he forced his face into a smile – revealing the famous imitation two front teeth that he'd had the goldsmith fashion when the natural ones decayed. They were doubtless intended to display his affluence, but the effect was sinister.

I refused to be intimidated. I was a councillor! I sat down, uninvited, on a stool. 'I want to talk about a patient that you called on yesterday. Or, more likely, your assistant did.'

He raised his eyebrows and looked amused, I thought. 'The lady Ursulina? I bled her in the morning and prescribed some cabbage soup. She assured us all that she felt better afterwards. Are you here to tell me that she's been taken worse?'

I shook my head. 'I'm talking about Josephus the argentarius,' I said, testily. And then, when there was no response at all, I added, 'I understand that one of his companions fetched the medicus for him, after he had fallen at the baths and hit his head.'

'Well, I did not attend him, councillor. Unfortunately so. We had our differences, but I might have saved him all the same. As it is, I hear that he has died. I trust that isn't why you thought I was involved?' He gave me that disturbing metal smile again. 'If so, I have to disappoint you, councillor. I did not poison him.'

I backtracked hastily. I was raising the very suspicions I

was seeking to allay. 'There is no question of poisoning,' I said. 'But the doctor who attended was not paid.'

He shook his head. 'Then perhaps it is a pity that I did not visit him. But I certainly did not. If you doubt me, ask the Ursulinus family – they will confirm that I never left the lady's side. All day yesterday and the day before. She had a fever and I stayed with her all night. You come upon me calculating what the fee should be. So . . . if there's nothing else that I can help you with?'

I struggled not to bridle at the condescending tone. 'I believe – from the description – that it might have been your assistant who attended on Josephus, rather than yourself.'

The medicus looked up sharply, in genuine surprise. 'Not my assistant, councillor. I don't have such a thing. The fellow I was training was dissatisfied, and persuaded his family to pay for him to travel all the way to Gaul – if you can believe it – and attach himself to an army medicus who had studied under one of Galen's protégés.'

I frowned. 'That's very curious. If you have no apprentice—'

He misinterpreted. 'It's more than curious! It's inexplicable. Said that my methods were outdated – by the gods! – and even applied to get his money back, although he did not get it, you may be sure of that!' His pale eyes flickered angrily, and then he pursed his lips. 'So it was not my assistant – and it was not me.'

'Someone's private medicus, perhaps?' I said, thinking aloud. 'You don't know who keeps one, I suppose?'

He shrugged his shoulders with pretended disdain. 'It's become a fashion for the rich to have their own. Patricians, on the whole. As a member of the curia you may know who they are. But I don't move in such exalted spheres. Now, I don't think I can assist you any further, councillor. So, if you will excuse me, I have work to do.' He was about to summon the boy to show me out, but I held up a hand.

'There is one more thing, you might assist me with,' I said. 'It's just occurred to me. You know a little about herbs I think? This unknown physician prescribed some kind of unusual sleeping draught – which was most efficient and seemed to do him good. If I can find out who supplied the herbs, they may lead me to the medicus. What might you give a man to make him sleep, apart from poppy juice?'

'Aside from mandrake juice and sorcery?' I did not smile and he shrugged, impatiently, but could not resist the appeal to professional vanity. 'Vervain, probably, or valerian. Or even a distillation of strong wine. Though I'd choose poppy juice above them, every time.' He gave me a mock-bow. 'I will not charge you for this consultation, councillor, but if that is really all . . .?' He rapped his knuckles sharply on the tabletop. 'Slave, bring a taper here!'

The ragged servant hurried in again.

'The councillor is leaving. Show him to the door.' And I was unceremoniously ushered out into the street.

I was thoughtful as I made my way back to the forum to meet my temporary slave. It had been a disappointing interview, but there was something about it which did not ring quite true – the man was hiding something, I was almost sure of it – although I could not identify what made me feel that way. The way that he'd been so anxious to get rid of me, perhaps? Or his eagerness to offer me – unasked – an account of his movements for exactly the period when Josephus was ill and could have been drugged and smothered in his bed? And he'd known about the death before I mentioned it. Was it likely that he'd simply heard the details on the street?

My preoccupation must have made me frown, because as soon I turned into the forum Fauvus was at my side, bearing a huge bunch of aromatic herbs. 'Do not be anxious, master. I have obtained directions to the young man's residence. I've memorized them all most carefully. If you are ready I could take you there.'

He was so solicitous and proud to be of use that I summoned up a smile, though I was hardly dressed for strolling round the town. 'Then lead the way. And when we have finished with Graeculus Properus, you can find that litter you were talking of – I wish to pay a visit to the dead money-changer's house.'

He gave a little bow. 'Ah hence the herbs, of course. No doubt there will be other mourners too – members of the guild of argentarii?'

'Indeed,' I murmured, though I hadn't thought of that. If there were people calling from the collegia, then the body would be no doubt laid out on display and I would be expected to oblige by offering a few words of praise and at least a short lament. Which meant I'd have to wear my toga after all. I'd wondered about taking the opportunity of removing it in the carrying chair, and leaving it – together with the money bags, if I'd collected them – in Fauvus's care while I went up to the flat to talk to Florea.

This was no disrespect to Josephus. Quite the contrary. But I wanted to find out who his bath companions were, and which of them had called the medicus – and if possible refresh my memory about what Semprius was like, so I could identify him at the slave guild later on. Without his tunic, I was not sure that I could pick him out. And for that I needed Florea, to help.

She had talked to me, freely and willingly, only yesterday – but I was wearing my working tunic then. I'd warned her that I was a councillor, but turning up in my curial toga was quite another thing. Formal dress can be intimidating for a slave.

However, that was for later. First I would try to get my money back.

'Lead on,' I said again, and followed Fauvus down the street towards the alleys that led to the river and the docks.

NINE

'Can this be the right direction, master, do you think?' The area to which Fauvus's instructions had been leading us was the unfashionable quarter of the town, behind the docks (though still in the shadow of the creaking wooden derricks on the quay) where – as well as warehouses – there are brothels, soup kitchens, bars and shady inns for the entertainment of visiting seafarers.

I nodded. The alleys in this area are notorious at night for thieves and drunkenness, but rent is cheap and there are lots of rooms to let, because people do not stay there very long. 'I'm sure that we will find the place. Lead on.'

He did so, though looking more and more uncomfortable. We were now shouldering through a noisy alley full of seedy hot-soup stalls – and seedier customers – and past a brothel with a series of painted signs above the door graphically advertising their specialities. Clearly he had not been accustomed to such things.

At last he burst out, 'Forgive me, citizen. I thought that most apprentices lodged in their master's house – if not actually in the shop itself. Obviously nobody could live in that small market booth, but . . . this?' He tailed off, embarrassed. 'I am sorry, master, I am speaking out of turn. But I am worried that I might have been misled.'

I shook my head. 'I don't think, so, Fauvus. Of course the majority of apprentices do live on their master's premises. But Properus (whom I forget you have not met) is not a slave, like most of those who are apprenticed to purely manual trades. He's an educated man. To be an argentarius one must not only read, but write – preferably in several languages – and be an adept with an abacus.'

'I misunderstood. Josephus was his master, I believe you said?' Fauvus skirted round a pile of anchor stones, roughly drilled to take a rope and heaped outside a scruffy booth for sale.

'His master – but in an educational sense. He was teaching Properus his craft. His family will no doubt have paid a handsome premium for him to learn.' I waved away an aging prostitute, who was wiggling her skinny hips at us – under the give-away 'whore's toga' – in what she clearly hoped was an alluring style. 'Though Properus is much older than you might expect.' (Slave apprentices often start at fourteen years or less, especially if they are purchased specifically for the task.) 'He is well into his twenties if I am any judge. An argentarius needs maturity – even a trainee.'

Fauvus nodded. 'Rather akin to being assistant to the medicus?'

I hadn't thought of it, but the comparison was apt. 'Exactly,' I replied.

'So he'll earn a little money of his own?' He looked around at the enticements to spend it locally.

'Not a wage, exactly,' I agreed. 'But a professional *discipulus* is allowed to keep a small proportion of what his labour earns. But, even if he is among the small elite trusted to rent himself a private residence, he is unlikely to be able to afford much more than this' – I gestured up towards the attics in the crumbling blocks around – 'though his master will be bound by contract to provide his food and drink.'

Fauvus nodded glumly. 'And we are getting close. Just around this corner . . . and the second left, I'm told.' He led the way again. 'And this must be the building!'

'Dear Mars and Juno!' I spoke with some surprise. The directions had brought us back into a major thoroughfare, and the block in question was a substantial one. Still noisy, because a crudely painted sign directed one through the building to what was clearly a little blacksmith and iron-smelter's forge behind – evidently specialising in making nails for ships – but otherwise entirely respectable.

The little workshop – from which a dreadful hammering emerged – seemed to interest Fauvus and he was inclined to pause and watch, until he saw me waiting by the public stairs. 'I'm sorry, master,' he said humbly, hurrying back to me. 'My family worked in metal – though we were silversmiths.'

I nodded. Dacians were famous for their silverwork, not

only those elaborate spiral bracelets for which the race is known, but able to take ornaments made from baser things and weld on thin silver coating with such skill that no naked eye could see the join.

'No silver-working, here,' I told him, and he looked rebuked.

There was a little wood-turner, open to the street, whose bow lathe gave off an everlasting whine, but both that and the neighbouring rope-maker – slowly walking backwards in his narrow shop, painstakingly twisting his triple cord of hemp – were respectable, thriving businesses.

Even the crowded, hot-food stall next door, selling chunks of fried river fish and eels, looked fairly civilized – though its clamouring customers (mostly warehouse slaves and sailors by the look of it) were too intent on their strong-smelling snacks to pay any heed to us. The whole building was clearly a recipe for conflagration – given all those workshop fires – but if this was really where Properus rented rooms, it was a different proposition from what I had supposed.

And when we enquired more closely for the exact address (from an urchin so like the one that directed me to Josephus that he might have been his twin) we found that Properus's residence was not a garret in the warren of attic rooms upstairs, but was a proper flat.

'On the second floor, masters. Safer than being immediately above the street, if you live here, citizen,' our informant told us, pocketing his tip. 'Quieter, too,' he added, and I could see that this was true, though the second flight of stairs was narrow and steep.

It must have been inconvenient, I thought, for Properus and the guard to have carried all the money from the booth up here, as presumably they had done since Josephus fell; we were empty-handed and even we were squeezed against the wall by a fat, frowsty woman with a basket, and her squalling brood.

We fought our way up the crowded staircases to the indicated door. That was surprising too: a handsome wooden one, equipped with several locks and opened – not by some scruffy slave-child who was still learning what to do – but by an equally handsome, olive-skinned servant in a Grecian robe who looked no younger than Properus himself. Now, though, he was scowling ferociously.

'Well? State your business!' It was so unexpected I was almost wondering whether we'd come to the wrong place, but then he saw my toga underneath my cloak and his whole manner changed. The glower vanished and he said, with more civility, though there was still no vestige of a smile, 'Your pardon, citizen, I was expecting someone else. To what do we owe the honour of your visit here?' He bowed, but he made no move to ask us to come in – as would have been considered normally polite.

'My business is with your master, Graeculus Properus,' I said, stung into severity by this reception, but adding the name in case it was the wrong address.

But it seemed not. He acknowledged my statement with another little bow. 'In that case, citizen, I fear you come in vain. He has gone to the house of his former tutor to pay funeral respects. And to speak with other members of the guild, he says – they will doubtless have been contacted and so come to view the corpse and honour Josephus.' He gave me a speculative look. 'You heard what happened to him, I suppose? An accident at the bathhouse which proved fatal in the end.'

'The news had reached me,' I agreed. 'And it's that which brings me here. So perhaps you can assist me? I left some money with Properus yesterday, while he was working at the booth. He gave me a receipt and we agreed that I would pick it up today. I'm hoping to collect it. I'll have a litter waiting. There are several bags.' I was looking past him as I spoke and I could see a whole array of bulging money sacks heaped on a large table in the reception room beyond. 'Among those, I expect.' I gestured with my chin as I fumbled underneath my toga folds to find my drawstring purse. 'Four leather money bags, all sealed by Josephus himself. Ah, here's the document.'

The civility had vanished as quickly as it came. 'There I'm afraid I cannot help you, citizen. You'll need to speak to Properus himself. I am merely his personal attendant – Scito is my name. He does not entrust me with the details of his business affairs. I am not authorized to give you anything – for fear of a mistake.'

It was my turn to frown. 'You can't make a mistake with these. They're quite distinctive. Sealed with blue seal-tags – with my name and my son's scratched into the back. If you can't take responsibility, I'm sure that I could pick them out myself.'

He shook his head. 'I'm sorry, citizen. My master's adamant. If you would care to call back later on, I'll try to find the bags that you describe and see that your money is put aside for you.' He gave a final half-bow and made to close the door.

I put my foot against the door jamb and stopped him doing so. If he'd been more apologetic I might have gone away as he suggested, but there was something in his manner which I did not like. I had been slightly jealous of Gwellia's enthusiasm for Graeculus Properus, but now I would have welcomed just a fraction of his charm – this slave was as inflexible and rude as his master had been obliging and polite. I had been humiliated, in front of Fauvus too!

I lost my temper slightly. 'So, Scito, you refuse to part with it? When it's my money and I have shown you written proof? Is this the answer that you give to all his customers? And I am clearly a Roman citizen. I've a good mind to complain about this to the aediles – and certainly I shall tell your master what I think. In the meantime, I'll leave my servant here. I'll give him the receipt, and he can wait for Properus. Then he can bring the money to my flat.' I turned to Fauvus who had been standing at my shoulder all this time. 'Get one of those urchins on the stairs to run and find a carrying-chair for me. I'll take these herbs and go to pay my own respects to Josephus. With luck I may find Properus while I'm there, in which case I'll come back to collect you with the chair. If he gets here before me, engage one for yourself and go straight to my apartment with the gold. Marcus will reimburse the litter boys. The money is too heavy to carry on your own.' Especially in view of that damaged arm, I thought – but did not say.

Fauvus acknowledged this instruction with a little bow. 'You do not need attendance, duumvir?'

'Not with a litter,' I told him with a smile, and he hurried off. I turned to Scito, who was still standing so that he blocked the entrance to the flat. 'I presume it is convenient for him to come inside? It is hardly courteous to make him wait out here. Perhaps he can help you guard those moneybags!'

I meant to be sarcastic but it made him blush. 'I was merely helping Properus with his accounts.'

'Despite the fact that he does not entrust you with his business affairs?'

That seemed to humble him. He looked discomfited. 'Not the details, councillor, which was all I claimed,' he muttered, so hastily and apologetically that I almost felt ashamed – until I realized what had caused the alteration. He'd taken me for a patrician of no special stripe, but Fauvus's mention of my decurion role had changed his attitude.

Indeed now he was positively eager to explain. 'Forgive me, councillor. I am not privy to the details of the accounts, of course – who owes what money, and who deposits it – but of late we've had a lot of extra money here and my master was anxious to get everything correct. I was to help him double-check – weigh the bags, and sort and count the coins which were brought in for exchange. And obviously when there's so much money in the flat we don't encourage visitors. But give me one moment and I'll clear it all away, and your slave will be welcome to come inside and wait.' He sounded almost abject as he bowed himself away.

For a moment I thought he was going to shut the door, but he seemed to think better of it, and left it half ajar, so I could see him moving money bags, disappearing in and out of sight. The bags were heavy and there were a lot of them, so it took him several trips, but Properus's strongbox must have been not far away, because by the time that Fauvus came to tell me that the litter was downstairs, Scito was hurrying back to greet us at the door.

'He may come in now, by all means, citizen.' He was slightly panting and red-faced, from his exertions. 'And you, yourself, of course – if you are so inclined.'

I shook my head and gave him a disapproving stare.

This time there was almost the suspicion of a smile. 'If I had realized that you were a duumvir, I should, of course, have invited you to come in earlier but we've had several callers since Josephus died. People demanding to have their coins assayed or their deposits back – some of them quite threatening – but Properus has not received his licence yet and . . .' He waved a hand at the empty table where the bags had been. 'He warned me not to admit anyone at all, while he wasn't here himself. Normally, of course, all this cash would have been with Josephus. So I ask for your indulgence, councillor. It was not my intention to offend.'

Put like that, I could almost sympathize. I nodded. 'Very well. We'll say no more about it. But I shall not come in. I have much to do before I leave the colonia tonight. Fauvus, I will see you later, either here or at my flat. If you arrive there before me, please tell Marcus Septimus that I will not be long. He won't be leaving until he's sure that I've cleared all my possessions from the place – just in case this guest of his from Rome arrives. So please assure him I will come as soon as possible.'

Fauvus said, 'At your service, master,' and repeated the message back to me with the intelligent certainty of a well-trained slave. I went down the stairs, confident that my communication would reach my patron word-for-word.

The litter was still waiting. I had been a little afraid that the carriers would have found another fare and left, but a stripe (of any width) confers its privilege, and they were there, leaning listlessly against the wall. When they saw me, they leapt upright at once and rushed to help me climb into the seat, gabbling that my servant had described me perfectly. I settled on the cushions and pulled the curtains shut.

'Where to, citizen?' they asked as they hoisted me aloft.

I gave them directions and they set off at a lope. If you have ever ridden in a litter you will know how much it bounces as they bear you through the streets, but as a mode of transport it can be very quick. It seemed no time at all before I found myself in the Street of the Gold and Silversmiths again, drawing up outside of Josephus's apartment block.

I left the litter there to wait, and went up to the flat.

TEN

The staircase was unnaturally empty this afternoon and for once there were no idlers on the landing swapping tales or gambling at dice, though when I saw the money-changer's door I realized why. Someone – probably a servant from the undertaker's house – had nailed a piece of cypress over it, signifying that this was a house of death. No wonder the other inhabitants were keeping well away.

Romans are famously superstitious about corpses of all kinds, and it is especially ill-omened to linger near the newly-dead, whose unquiet spirit might yet be hovering! (Even when the deceased is laid in state, as regularly happens with the rich and powerful, the mourners who come to pay respects often wear protective amulets (available at any undertaker's shop) to keep the ghosts at bay.) So the sprig was clearly having its effect.

The only person in evidence was a skinny little slave – he could not have been more than eight or nine years old – who had been squatting by the wall, and who leapt up to his feet as I approached. He was a bony child with red hair and pallid face, who wore a skimpy ochre tunic that scarcely reached his thighs and a pair of sandals half a size too big, and he generally looked ill-clad and badly fed. From this, and from the guilty expression on his face, I took him to be a servant of the undertaker's firm, supposedly on duty at the door – as would be usual if a lying-in-state was taking place.

I was surprised enough to ask. I had not expected Josephus to have merited, or desired, such extensive obsequies. But the slave-boy shook his head. 'An undertaker's slave? Not me, citizen. I'm waiting for my master, that is all. He's gone in there to pay his personal respects.'

'Your master? That's not Josephus's assistant, I suppose?' It was a foolish question, as I realized even as I uttered it. I'd just met Properus's impressive servant, at his flat – and few

apprentices could afford to keep a slave at all, much less a
second one. I amended my enquiry. 'Or one of the college of
argentarii perhaps? I was told I could expect to find them
here.'

Another headshake, more vigorous, this time. 'Well, if any
of them came, he isn't in there now. There's no one here except
my master. Comux, his name is. A trader in the town.' He
spoke with pride. 'You may have heard of him?'

I frowned. I had done, vaguely. Some sort of importer of
dried fish, furs and smelly pigments from somewhere frozen
like the Scandian Islands. 'I think I know the name. He once
supplied some exotic pelts to a tanner who has a workshop
next to mine. From giant Northern deer, or something, I believe
– and very tough, hard-wearing ones they were, though they
were silky to the touch.'

Now the boy was nodding, sagely, pleased to demonstrate
his knowledge of the trade. 'They will have been *tendandro*,
I expect. Great shaggy creatures that are used for pulling sleds
– like we use horses. It's always icy there, so they don't have
chariots and carts, apparently. My master does import their
skins from time to time – and their antlers. The horn is very
good.'

I did not want a lecture on the Scandian trade so I said,
hastily, 'And he was a good friend of Josephus? Or a customer?'
That was more probable. What could an importer of smelly
skins and horn have in common with the argentarius?

The slave-boy shuffled, as though this troubled him. 'I could
not tell you, citizen. I never met the money changer in my life.
You would have to ask my master that yourself.' He brightened
suddenly. 'He must be nearly finished by this time. Even if he
isn't, there is an aged maid inside. If you knock, I'm sure she'll
let you in. In the meantime, I should be on watch for his return
– so if you will excuse me, citizen.' He bobbed me a brief
bow, then turned away and – quite politely – took up the age-old
stance of waiting slaves: feet apart with hands behind his back
and a gaze fixed on the middle-distance.

There was clearly nothing more that I would glean from
him, so I took his advice and gently tapped the door.

A slow shuffling and rattling on the other side suggested

Florea, and shortly afterwards she opened the door a cautious crack. As soon as she saw me, her face lit up in a smile, and she unchained the door – obviously I need not have worried about her being overawed by my attire! But instead of ushering me in, she came outside to me and gently closed the door; from the wailing ululation from within, I deduced she did not wish to interrupt the trader's lamentation for the dead.

She was wearing more formal clothes herself, I saw – a dark mourning tunic of great antiquity, her swollen feet were thrust into ill-fitting sandals now, there were ashes in her hair, and funereal dust was rubbed onto her face, where tears had made little runnels on her cheeks. But I had won that toothless smile.

'Citizen Libertus! I hoped that it was you. I thought at first it might be Properus – he said that he would call again, today. But it is you, and that is good. I wished to speak to you. Though . . .?' She glanced towards the slave, but he was still staring into nothingness.

'Just waiting for his master,' I said, cheerfully. 'But he won't be long, I think?'

She made a doubtful face. 'I hope not, citizen,' she murmured in that cracked old voice of hers. 'It's not for me to say, but for a casual acquaintance, I don't think so much lamentation is appropriate. You must have heard his wailing for yourself?' She cast her old eyes upwards, as if appealing to the gods. 'Anyone would think he was a lifetime friend!'

'And he isn't?' I dropped my voice, aware of the presence of the slave nearby.

Her voice was never strong but she did not lower it – quite the contrary – almost as if she meant the boy to hear. 'Not as far as I know, citizen. Of course my master did not tell me everything, but I never saw Comux here before that fateful fall. Though the way he is lamenting now, would befit a member of the family.'

A guilty conscience? I wondered privately, but I did not speak the words aloud. Instead I made a sympathetic face, and murmured, 'Perhaps he simply did not want to be outdone? I imagine someone from the college of argentarii has already called today?'

'Indeed, two of them came a little after dawn – the funeral women were still working then. But they were dignified, did not make a show – just scattered herbs and told me that the college would take care of everything. The cremation is to be tomorrow night, with a small procession and musicians too – all taken care of by the funeral fund. And that is what I hoped to talk to you about.' She dropped her voice now and glanced towards the slave.

I could not imagine what more she had to say, or why – in any case – it demanded secrecy but I could see what was required. 'Boy,' I told him, 'this is private. Go and wait downstairs. I'll explain things to your master.' I could see that he was still unwilling so I rummaged in my purse and found a single quadrans. I held it out to him. 'I noticed there's a hot-pie seller in the street. If you are quick you might have time to eat. And you need not worry too much about speed, I have business with your master before he looks for you.'

I had judged aright. The boy was frightened, but hunger is a stronger spur than fear of punishment. The quadrans – and the slave boy – disappeared at speed. I listened to the outsized sandals clattering downstairs, then turned to Florea. 'Now what was it you wished to speak to me about?'

'Firstly, to thank you, citizen, for your advice. Regarding Semprius, supposing it was genuinely him.' She was speaking in a croaked whisper as it was, but she beckoned me nearer and dropped her voice to such a conspiratorial wheeze, that I had to bend low to make out the words. 'You were right about the slave guild.'

'They took the corpse for you?'

She nodded. 'And they're making arrangements for cremation too. Nothing like the argentarii provide, of course. But he will be treated with a certain dignity. They even have a small niche in a *columbarium* reserved for member slaves, where the ashes can be put. And there's nothing more to pay, so there's no problem about that.'

'But . . . ?' I prompted. 'There is a problem about something, clearly.'

She nodded. 'The trouble is, I've begun to wonder if it's really Semprius they found. They could not produce the slave disc and that troubles me. It was on a chain around his neck, and I cannot imagine that the robbers would want that. I'd be glad if someone could identify the corpse, and then I'd know for sure. And I can't go myself. Somebody must stay and keep a vigil here.' She looked at me.

I nodded. 'I'll go.' I wanted in any case to interview the guild. 'But I'm not sure I'd recognize his face. I only saw him once, and that was long ago.'

She gave her toothless grin again. 'I'll tell you how you'd know him for certain, citizen. He has a burn scar, here' – she pointed to her right leg, high up on the thigh – 'did it when he fell against the brazier once. Shaped like a turnip – the size of a small coin – but you couldn't miss it, if you got a sight of it. I only know because I helped to dress the wound.'

She was so anxious to assure me there was nothing intimate, that I actually smiled. 'You didn't ask the guild to check for it?'

'I didn't think of questioning the disc until it was too late. And once they'd gone, I could not get out to ask them anything. And that's another thing. They have other slaves to deal with, they told me, and they want the space. There's no family to consider and Semprius – or whoever it is – has already been dead a day or two. So they are arranging for the funeral to take place this very night.' She raised her faded pale-blue eyes to mine. 'The other thing is, citizen – once we are sure it's really him – would it be in order for me to attend? I would not like to think of him without a single mourner at the pyre.'

'But surely the slave guild . . .?'

She shook her head so violently that ashes fell from it. 'Oh, they'll provide a weeping woman to fulfil the rituals. But it's not like having someone whom you knew in life. On the other hand, I don't like to leave the master's corpse. Someone should keep a constant vigil here.'

I frowned. Surely she wasn't hoping that I would volunteer for that? If so, she would be disappointed. For one thing the funeral would happen in the dark (cremations in Britannia generally still do, though Marcus assures me that the ancient custom has died out in Rome) and by that time I intended to be safely home, sitting by my roundhouse fire with Gwellia, out of the reach of wolves and bears and other hazards of the woods at night. Furthermore this was really none of my concern: Josephus was no especial friend of mine in life and I had hardly met his manservant at all. Most of all, with this visitor from Rome expected very soon, I had more pressing matters to engage my time.

'What about the funeral women who came for Josephus?' I enquired. 'Or one of the undertaker's slaves? Could they not stay and watch your master's corpse?'

'The women have finished with the body now, so they've long packed up and gone. And they did not leave a slave. I was here to keep the vigil on the corpse, and I didn't hear the details about Semprius's pyre until after they had left. I can hardly fetch them back. Besides, they have done everything that they were contracted for. They won't be here again until tomorrow night at dusk, when my master's funeral procession is scheduled to begin. Though they are going to make the usual announcements in the street – they think that many people will attend. Josephus was well known in the town.'

'Though there will be professional mourners?'

She nodded. 'The argentarii have arranged for that – four mourning women to shriek and tear their clothes, and a funeral pipe and drum to play a dirge. They've been most generous. But I can hardly expect them to hire a slave for me, to take my place here while I go to Semprius's funeral, tonight. I'm just a slave myself. They would think it was my duty to remain.' She sighed. 'Perhaps it is. And I have no access to any of my late master's funds to hire anyone myself.'

As deft a plea for alms as I had ever heard, I thought. The old servant had more guile than I'd supposed. I was once more reaching for my slim purse with a sigh, but she shook her head again. Her eyes were full of tears.

'I'm not asking you to lend me money, councillor. I could not repay you – where should I ever get the means? And I do not wish to beg. But there is no one else that I can turn to for advice. What do you think is proper, citizen?'

ELEVEN

I looked at her, with pity. Her whole life had shattered in the last few days: both her master and her fellow slave were dead, and who knew what would now become of her? Josephus had no natural heirs to whom his slave would pass. So technically she would be sold as part of his estate. But who would buy her now? Too old to be useful, and no ornament – it was doubtful that any slave-trader would even add her to his stock, it would just be another mouth for him to feed. More likely she would be simply turned out on the street. Of course it was distinctly possible that Josephus had bequeathed her freedom in his will – such things were not unknown with lifetime slaves – but even so it was hard to know how she'd survive for long. And without a master to pay her slave guild dues, how many mourners would attend *her* funeral?

I toyed for a moment with the thought of buying her myself, but of course that was absurd. I already had more slaves than I could comfortably support. Hard enough to feed and clothe the ones I usually kept, and they were young enough to be of use. That thought sparked another – there was, of course, one thing I could do for her. A wonder that it hadn't occurred to me before!

'As it happens I have an apartment full of slaves. Tomorrow I'm expecting an important visitor from Rome, but tonight they have nothing particular to do. I am sure that one of them could easily be spared to come and keep vigil on your master for an hour or two. I will see to it. Expect someone at dusk. On second thoughts, I'll send two slaves, in fact. It will seem more respectful and it's safer for them too. I'll give them a taper, to light them home, if you will see it's lit.'

I think she would have fallen to the floor to kiss my feet if age and disability had not prevented her. As it was she grasped my toga-hem and pressed it to her lips. 'Citizen –

councillor – you are very good. I can never repay your kind-
ness, but I will pray the gods for blessings on your head.'
She was so grateful that I was embarrassed at having
misjudged her earlier.

'It's nothing,' I said, gruffly. 'Now don't you think it's time
to go inside? I have brought herbs to make a little sacrifice and
pay homage to the dead – and my appearance may induce Comux
to desist!'

She hobbled to the door and placed a hand upon the latch,
ready to open it and let me pass. 'Should I announce you,
citizen?'

I shook my head. 'I'll introduce myself, when it's appropriate. If you're expecting Properus, perhaps you should stand
by to let him in. He could even assist me with my offering,
and I would be glad to speak to him. I was rather expecting
to find him here, in fact – though I'm surprised he did not
call in yesterday to pay respects.'

She was anxious to defend him. 'But he did come, citizen,
after you had gone, though it was very brief – and he under-
took to call again today. It wasn't suitable to linger then, he
said, because he had to get back and deal with the accounts.'

'I suppose that had to take priority?' She was speaking of
Properus with the same eagerness I'd seen in Gwellia, and I
was ashamed to realize that it irritated me.

She nodded, oblivious of any irony. 'It was a requirement
of the guild – he explained that at the time. He was most upset
that he could not stay and make proper lamentation. But the
records for the last few days must all be double-checked for
the college of argentarii. They require that everything has been
accounted for, down to the last bronze quadrans, before they'll
grant a licence to anyone at all – as it is, Properus thinks
there'll have to be a temporary appointee, till he is voted in
and can carry on himself.'

'Though, surely, that should not be very long?' I had
expected a delay, but the idea of a different appointment
startled me. 'Josephus had already put it all in hand.'

'Of course. But he had just begun the process when he died.
Apparently it might take a moon or so to get sufficient signa-
tures. And obviously the town can't wait as long as that! How

would the fishmonger get enough small coins, or foreign traders get their money changed?'

'I see!' But it was like having a sore tooth, I kept prodding at the thing. 'Does Properus worry about who will take his place, meanwhile? Lest his replacement decline to step aside?' I saw that Florea was hesitating to reply. I forced a smile and added, 'As a duumvir I may be able to use my influence, and expedite affairs on his behalf.' Or rather Marcus could, I amended inwardly.

She returned my smile with evident relief. 'Well, I know that he'd be grateful if you could. And, I admit it, citizen, I would be grateful too. He was always kind to me.'

'I did not realize that you knew him well. Surely he is generally at his booth, or at his flat?'

'Naturally, citizen. But he lived here for a day or two, when he first came to the town. You did not know that?' Her feeble voice was filled with sudden warmth.

'But he did not choose to stay here?'

'It was not convenient – there was not sufficient room, we had to put him in the study on a sleeping mat. He had a little money – from his father, I believe – so he found himself a place. I've never seen it, but my master did. It is respectable, I think – he even has a slave.'

'And an expensive one!'

She shook her head. 'Not to Properus, citizen. The slave is from his father's household, I believe, so he is well provided for.' The lined face glowed again. 'But it was good to have him here. Sent from the gods, I think. Such a help to my poor master. Even Semprius liked him, and he was hard to please – Properus gave him a used tunic, once, as I recall. But that was typical.'

'A perfect lodger?' I was aware of sounding sour.

'Too impatient, so Master used to say.' Her reply was so indulgent that I felt ashamed. 'Like that tunic, which was not really an appropriate gift, though Semprius treasured it. And Properus was always asking questions, my master said, and then not waiting for a full reply.'

I had to smile. 'Which Josephus generally liked to give – at length?' I saw her expression and added, hastily, 'But one must not speak unkindly of the dead.'

A rueful nod. 'Indeed, especially when their spirits may be close nearby. And generally my master thought highly of Properus, I know – said that he was very quick to learn and had lots of clever plans for how to attract more money for the booth. I've heard him say he wouldn't be surprised if Properus rose to be a citizen of influence one day.'

'Neither would I,' I acknowledged, adding wickedly, 'I am sure that he's always charming to important customers.' (Ambitious and knows whom to flatter, in other words.)

'But Properus was also very kind to lesser folk, like me. Even gave me a quadrans tip while he was here. But I'm standing gossiping instead of serving you. I was asked to let you in.' She opened wide the door. 'I will not introduce you, since you prefer it. Or is Comux known to you?'

I shook my head, then wished that I had not. When the slave had mentioned it, I had recalled the name, but when I came into the flat I recognized the man.

He had been kneeling by the corpse and was now struggling to his feet – a big, jowl-cheeked fellow with a shock of thick brown hair. He had a girth that suggested far too many greasy pies – unlike his wretched slave boy – and a reddish complexion round the nose and cheeks that spoke of too many amphorae of imported wine. Not a person that I'd had dealings with, but I was sure I'd seen him somewhere, fairly recently.

For a moment I could not place where that had been. The episode with the tanner had been years ago, and in any case I had only seen the skins, not met the man who had imported them. But then it came to me. It was the garments which had defeated me at first. Last time I'd seen Comux, he wasn't wearing much – he had been at the baths that day with Josephus.

Now, though, he was dressed, and with a show of grief. I could see what Florea had meant about it being quite extreme for a 'mere acquaintance'. He wore a long black tunic, unbelted and reaching to his knees, and the cloak that lay beside him was of a similarly funereal hue. His hair and face was streaked with dust and ashes. No toga, since he was obviously not a citizen, but otherwise in keeping with the strictest kind of Roman mourning dress.

But the features were Celtic, and the name was too.

I took a chance. 'You are grieving, townsman Comux?' I greeted him in what I guessed to be his native tongue.

The grey-green eyes looked startled, but I had guessed aright. 'You speak Celtic, citizen?' he replied, in kind.

'I should do, since I am Celt myself,' I said. 'Our dialects are different – naturally, since I wasn't born round here – but it is possible to understand each other, I believe? I do not want to cause upset to the slave.' I nodded at Florea, who was standing mystified, clearly unable to comprehend a word.

Comux frowned. 'There is a problem, citizen? Or do I recognize you as a councillor? I believe I saw you in the forum on election day?'

'The duumvir Libertus,' I acknowledged, with a bow. 'But here I am merely a mourner like yourself. Though I do have a question, about the medicus who came. Was it you by any chance who sent him, or do you know who did?'

'I'm sorry, councillor. I fear I cannot help. I've no idea who sent him. It was certainly not me.' He kept his eyes averted as he spoke – no more than my rank deserved, Marcus would have said, but it discommoded me. I had hoped to build a bridge between us by a common tongue, but I could not do it if he would not look at me. 'Is there some problem with him?' he went on. 'I heard from the servant that he was excellent. Surely there's no question of a poisoning – or any accidental overdose?'

His sharp intake of breath, when this occurred to him, reminded me that I must be very careful what I said.

'There's no suspicion of anything like that,' I answered – with truth – then repeated the excuse I'd used before. 'Only that the man has not been paid,' I said. I glanced again at Florea, who – like any well trained servant, was standing by the wall, staring at nothing and waiting to be called. 'I would be glad to do so, if I could find him out, since Florea does not have the wherewithal and I do not wish her to be embarrassed by his calling with the bill. I called on the public medicus, but it was not him, it seems.'

Comux advanced towards me, in evident distress. 'I cannot

help you, as I said before. But if you find him, councillor, please send me the account. I should be the one to pay. It would help me to atone. It is my fault Josephus is dead. My partners will tell you that I killed him, councillor.'

TWELVE

For one wild moment I could not believe my ears. Was the man actually confessing to having murdered Josephus? When everybody knew the penalties for such a crime?

I looked at Comux, but he had dropped his gaze determinedly to the floor again – though not in an embarrassed sort of way, as one might expect. Rather, he seemed shifty, like a man with things to hide.

I had been conscious from the first of his marked reluctance to look me in the eye but – since he had just apparently admitted everything – I was astonished now. One would have expected an unburdening of guilt, or at least some explanation and beseeching looks! But there was no sign of either. He was still avoiding letting his gaze meet mine, and he clearly had no intention of saying any more.

So what was he expecting me to do? Of course it was not as if the old argentarius had been a Roman citizen – but Comux did not have the protection of that rank, either, so this was still likely to be a capital offence. Though it occurred to me that he would probably deny in court that he had admitted anything – since we were talking Celtic there were no witnesses and he was likely to argue that I'd misunderstood. Though (being not only a citizen but a councillor) my word would outweigh his.

Perhaps he realized that I was protecting Florea. He would know that his confession did not exonerate the slave, unless he would also swear – not only that she'd had no part in it – but that he'd actively ensured she wasn't present at the time, and could possibly not have prevented it. And it hardly seemed likely that he'd agree to that – yet I shuddered to think what the implications were for her, if he did not. That must be what he was relying on. But, as a councillor, I could hardly ignore the statement he'd just made.

'I'm not sure I understand what you are telling me,' I told him, trying not to look too anxiously towards the aged slave.

Comux misinterpreted, or affected to. He said immediately, in Latin, 'Then ask the servant. She was the one who pointed out my guilt. When she first accused me, I was furious, but when I considered further I could see that she was right. And my partners both agree. If I had not persuaded Josephus to come into the baths, he would not have fallen and he would not be dead. I killed him as certainly as if I'd poisoned him.'

'Ah!' I heard myself breathe out. 'Hardly murder, then!' Not a genuine confession, that was what I meant. I must have sounded as irritated as I felt, because he gave me a sharp look.

For an instant I caught those grey-green eyes and was surprised to read the expression in their depths: not gloating, but a mixture of guilt, embarrassment and shame. As quickly as he'd glanced at me, he looked away again. He may not have smothered Josephus, I thought, but the man had something on his conscience – I was sure of it.

A thought occurred to me. 'You did not set out to give him too much undiluted wine, as Florea thought?'

He shifted uneasily, but answered readily enough. 'Not I, citizen. We did invite Josephus to eat and drink with us, but he said that he would snatch a snack in town and meet us afterwards. There was urgent business to attend to before he bathed, he said.' He was giving more information than I had asked him for, as though glad to have something safe that he could talk about.

Florea, however, had shot him a disbelieving glance – though as a well-trained servant she did not interrupt.

I gave her the opportunity to speak. 'Your master did not often buy from the pie-sellers?' I asked.

She shook her ancient head. 'I have never known it, citizen, in all my years with him. He'd take a piece of bread and cheese with him, or cold cooked meat and fruit. I used to put it in a little pouch for him. But he did not take one that day – I would swear to that. He did not want one. He had other plans, he said.'

And he'd certainly been drinking when I saw him at the bath. I frowned at Comux. This was puzzling. 'Plans?'

The trader shook his head. 'I cannot answer as to that. But the maidservant is quite right about one thing, councillor.

The whole visit to the baths was my idea. The others were in favour of inviting him formally to dine—'

'The others?' I interrupted sharply. 'Your companions at the baths?'

'My two business partners,' he said quickly. 'Brokko and Boudoucus – you may have heard of them?'

I shook my head. I hadn't.

'They are traders – with me – with a warehouse at the docks. Anyway they favoured turning on a feast for him one night – but I argued that he might have seen that as extravagance. Counterproductive, as we were looking for finance. A visit to the baths was more relaxed, I said – more likely to make him think of us as friends and accept the business offer we were going to put to him. And, when they agreed to this, I personally persuaded Josephus to come.' The pink hands fluttered. 'So the whole tragic business was entirely my fault. I feel it very much. He was not a bad old fellow – even if he liked to talk.'

'And quite famously an honest one,' I said. 'Hence this "business offer"?'

I must have touched a nerve. Comux looked sheepish, as though he'd talked too much. 'Just a little proposition we hoped to put to him, since he was planning to retire as argentarius. Though we never did, because he had that fall and died.' He glanced down, uneasily, towards the corpse. 'So perhaps this is not the time and place to be discussing it.'

For fear of offending the spirit of the dead, he obviously meant – though he did not seem to know that the money-changer's death had been anything other than a tragic accident. Or did he? All this deep mourning and ashes – much more than convention would require for someone (other than a town dignitary, of course) who was neither a relative nor a personal friend? And Comux did not qualify on either front, it seemed – even the 'business partnership' was a potential one.

So far from being satisfied that he was not involved, I began to wonder if his whole 'confession' to an imitation crime had been purposely offered in order to mislead. I could not see how Comux could have smothered Josephus himself – when he left the old man was still alive, according to Florea's account. But I only had his word for it about the medicus: that mystery figure whom I suspected more and more, and was becoming more and more anxious to locate.

So had Comux sent that medicus, in fact, or did he know who had? One of those two 'colleagues' he had spoken of, perhaps? It was beginning to be clear that I would have to talk to them if I ever wanted to find out the truth – whether or not I made it public in the end.

I thought quickly and (taking a cue from Properus) decided that this was a moment to try charm. I favoured the trader with my broadest smile.

'Then allow me to offer up this sacrifice of herbs and perhaps we can continue this discussion somewhere else. Perhaps, in fact, you'd care to help officiate?'

I said this, not because I wanted any help, but because I did not want to let him go and I did not trust him to wait outside for me. Without his help, I might never find his friends – if he warned them of my interest they might disappear and not be seen again until the funeral. And – worse – they would be sure to warn the medicus, if one of them had sent him. And he'd been provided by a 'so-called friend' according to Florea's account.

'I am a little uneasy about unquiet ghosts myself,' I added, stripping off my cloak. I did the smile again. 'Two sets of prayers are more acceptable than one.'

A little blandishment can have remarkable effects. I half-expected Comux to excuse himself and leave, but instead he looked flattered and – I thought – relieved. In any case he set to work at once, helping me spread my offering before the household gods while Florea lit a taper from the brazier for me. I set the herbs alight, sending the aromatic smoke spiralling upwards to please the deities. Then, as the embers flickered, I knelt before the altar and muttered as much of the ritual formula as I could recall, to speed the old man's spirit on its way. Comux and Florea seemed impressed enough, although I cannot answer for the gods.

When I had finished I turned to Florea. 'Do we have a little wine or perfumed oil to pour on the remains?' It is usual to sprinkle something of the kind, since it is – of course – unfortunate if any part of the offering is not entirely consumed.

She shook her head. 'I have lamp oil, citizen, but that is all, I fear. Master was frugal when it came to wine – and did not keep much in the house, unless he was entertaining visitors.' She gave me that smile again. 'If Properus had been here, he could perhaps have helped. He always kept a small amphora of Rhenish in his room – some special vintage which his father liked, and very fine he said – though master was rather contemptuous of the expense and would never taste it, though Properus urged him to. But of course that isn't here and all I can give you is a little cooking oil, or something from the lamps.' She frowned. 'Though there is that phial of sleeping mixture the doctor left for me. I think that might have wine and herbs in it.'

I gazed at her. Of course, she had mentioned that the physician had left another dose – how could I have been so stupid as to have forgotten that? I was about to speak, but Comux chimed in eagerly.

'But wasn't there something supernatural about it? Brokko was here when the medicus first called, and he says that the potion had amazing qualities – almost as if it were dragon's blood or mandrake root.'

'Magic?' Florea looked alarmed – and well she might. There were laws against employing sorcery, and such potions would not soothe the ghost. 'There were no spells or incantations, I can promise you. Just the medicine. But wait a moment and you can see it for yourself.' She shuffled off and reappeared a moment later with a leather pouch, from which she drew a little stoppered phial. 'Here it is. I'd put it on one side. I was going to pour it on my poor master's pyre – it was the only thing that gave him comfort in the end – but there is very little left. And the guild will make provision for an oblation at the funeral. This might be better offered here and now.'

I was thinking furiously now, trying to find a reason for not parting with the phial. Meanwhile I lifted the stopper to smell the contents of the flask. There was a smell of wine, but was there something herbal which I did not recognize?

'Do you wish to sprinkle that yourself, councillor, or shall we share the task?' Comux's voice cut across my thoughts.

I looked at him sharply, but the florid face was bland and innocent.

'Neither, at this stage, possibly,' I replied. 'Since we do not know exactly what the flask contains, it might be better not to pour it out. If there is any sorcerer's ingredient, it may not have the effect that we desire – it might cause a flare up in the ashes or burn with acrid smoke. Better to check it first, rather than send it with him to the pyre – Florea can pour it as an offering afterwards, when the ashes are interred.' I looked at Comux, who was nodding gravely at all this, and added daringly, 'I imagine the medicus could tell us what it is?' I pushed the stopper back into the phial, made sure it did not leak, then slipped it back into its pouch and put it carefully in the money purse which dangled from my belt. Fortunately it was almost empty now and there was just sufficient room.

I glanced at Comus to see what reaction there would be, but the tradesman's expression did not change a bit. He went on nodding. 'A wise notion, councillor. I should like to find this medicus in any case. As I say, I ought to bear the cost. If that potion is exotic it will be costly, too. I agree with you, I should not like him to call back here, demanding money, with Josephus lying there.'

It was exactly what I'd said, of course, but I was beginning to doubt that the elusive man would really come, largely because – as far as I could see – he was the only one with the opportunity to smother Josephus. Though who he was, what his motive could have been and why he did not choose to poison his victim when he had the chance – were questions to which I could see no logical reply. But if he was the murderer, he was unlikely to return.

Florea did not think so.

'Your pardons, gentlemen,' she broke in in that quavering voice of hers. 'May I have leave to speak? The medicus did promise to come back, within a day or two, to see how master was progressing and collect his payment too. If you are willing, Townsman Comux, you could reward him then. He did his best, and I was glad of it – though nothing can bring my master back to life.'

For a moment, I stared at her, surprised. I had forgotten that we'd been speaking Celtic earlier, so Comux's offer was a new idea. Clearly, too, it had sounded to her – as it had done to me – that the suggestion was somehow born of guilt, not generosity.

Comux, though, acknowledged her rebuke with another of his sober nods. 'That visit should be prevented, while the corpse is in the house. It would show disrespect. The fellow must be found as soon as possible, to stop him coming here. He may not even know that Josephus is dead – although I suppose the rumour will be all around the town.'

'Then help me look for him. One of your companions might know where he is? I understand from Florea that he was sent by one of you?'

The trader raised the dark shoulders of his tunic in a shrug. 'Not that I know of, councillor – but we could go and ask. I think I know where we might find them at this hour.'

It was more than I had hoped for. My visit to the slave guild and Semprius's corpse would have to wait a while, but I did remember what I'd promised Florea.

'Expect two servants from me later on!' I said to her. 'And if Properus arrives, please tell him that I need to talk to him – a question of some money that I left at the booth. You may tell him where I've gone.' I turned to Comux, pulling on my cloak. 'I believe you have a slave boy waiting at the door. Perhaps he could be spared to take a message to my flat – I'll direct him where to go – telling the servants there that I have been delayed and that two of them are wanted over here at dusk. They are to be ready with a taper and a cloak, because I want them to hold vigil on the corpse of Josephus from their arrival until they are relieved. He can give them directions as to how to find this place.'

Comux looked flustered, but he could not well refuse. 'With pleasure, citizen.' We stepped outside. The boy was standing there – looking a little greasy round the chin – and I listened as his master barked my commands at him. The slave boy looked at me shyly, grinned and hurried off.

'Excellent!' My smile was wholly genuine this time. 'Now, Comux, I have a carrying-litter waiting in the street. You lead the way to your companions and I will follow you.'

THIRTEEN

My litter boys were waiting patiently, and soon we were following Comux. He led us back in the direction of the docks. The trader moved at a surprising speed for a person of such corpulence, and he did not glance back once. I almost thought he meant to lose us in the press, but my carriers were easily a match for him. So when the black-robed figure paused in an alley beside a warehouse door, the litter came to rest beside him even as he knocked.

He did not look, I thought, especially pleased to find me there, but as I paid off the litter he said, cheerfully enough, 'Here we are then, councillor. My friends should be here somewhere at this hour. Ah, and here's our servant, Iliath, come to open up.'

The servant in question was an awkward girl, in a short ochre tunic which hardly hid her scrawny, budding form. She might have been pretty if she were not so pale and thin, and if her face had shed its sullen, haunted look. In fact, as she gazed silently from me to Comux and back again, I realized there was something oddly familiar about her – though I could not place where we could possibly have met. I assayed a smile, but there was no response.

'As you can see I've brought a visitor,' Comux said, loudly, as though talking to an idiot. 'A decurion, no less. So let us in, at once.' He turned to me. 'Sister of that useless slave boy who was with me at the flat,' he said. 'Got them from their father in payment of a debt.'

Of course, I thought! That was why I felt I knew her face. She looked like her brother – the same red hair and pale complexion, thin limbs and hungry eyes. How desperate must their family have been, I wondered, to have been obliged to sell them both?

But Comux was still speaking. 'No bargain, really, because they've not been trained, and have not the first idea of what's expected of a slave. The boy, Gwengor, is not much use for anything but running messages, he's too small to lift and carry any weight, and so nervous that he keeps on dropping things. But the girl has talents.'

I saw the flicker of distaste in Iliath's eyes at that, and the way she flinched as he reached out to slap her skinny rump, and I realized that her duties might be very varied ones – and not to her liking. My heart went out to her: my own wife Gwellia had been taken as a slave, and – though she never spoke of it – I knew that she had suffered the same way. Though there was no recourse. Not then, and not now. If these men owned Iliath, they could use her as they pleased.

She said dully, 'A visitor? You'd better come inside.'

She led the way, through a sort of anteroom, to the interior. The warehouse was dark and gloomy and malodorous. There were window-spaces high up in the walls but the neighbouring buildings crowded in on either side, so they did not admit much light. The space below was narrow and unlit, piled haphazardly with containers of all kinds: boxes, crates, sacks, amphorae and – in one shadowy corner – something dark that might be skins or rugs. Skins, more likely, given what I knew: and indeed l recognized the powerful smell of fur and animal, mingling with the musty damp, stale spice and the faint but persistent lingering smell of fish.

There seemed to be little organisation in the storage here (unlike any warehouse I had visited before) or even any clear route through the random piles: but there was obviously both, since Iliath led us quickly and confidently on, though – since she carried no taper – even she had to pick her way with care. As she walked ahead of me, I was surprised to notice that she moved quite sharply now and then, until I realized this was a trick that she had learned to keep out of reach of groping hands.

The idea displeased me – I do not like to be suspected of such things – and I turned to Comux, who was bringing up the rear, but he forestalled any comment by addressing me. 'Councillor, with your permission, you had better let me go in first and tell the others what you're doing here. The servant ought to do it, but she's an idiot, and in any case it will disturb them less if the information comes from me.'

The others? I peered around but there was nobody in evidence. There were faint sounds of movement somewhere to the rear, but that was merely a scuffling, as though there might be rats. Some warehouses kept guard slaves (or even dogs) to protect their goods from them, but evidently nothing of the kind was managed here.

Meanwhile Iliath was leading us on towards the further end, where in the gloom I could gradually make out a frowsty curtained area (probably a makeshift office for keeping inventories and interviewing clients) and next to it a wooden door which clearly led to some living-area beyond. The slave girl raised a timid hand to rap on it, but Comux shuffled past me and opened it himself.

The action revealed a poky little room, where two men were seated together on a bench before a smoky fire, so engrossed in playing a game of 'heads and ships' that at first they did not glance up as we came in.

I had expected Iliath to announce us, at the least, but Comux waved her impatiently away and as she closed the door behind herself, he coughed, as if to warn his friends that I was there.

There was no response from them, they were too engrossed, until he said, very loudly, 'This is the duumvir Libertus, from the Glevum curia.'

At this the two men stopped their gambling and whirled round in alarm, so suddenly that the coin they had been tossing in the air fell between them and rolled beneath the seat.

'No need to worry,' he added hastily. 'There has been no complaint. It's not about the warehouse. He just wants to talk to you.'

I was asking myself why they might be fearful of complaints, and whether they'd had visits from the curia before, when the larger of the gamblers got slowly to his feet.

He was a gigantic man whose thin cheeks bore the signs of recent barbering, and whom I half-remembered seeing with Josephus at the baths that day. Apart from his great height, it was his eyes I recognized: they were set in drooping sacks, like a woeful puppy's, giving him a melancholy look, and his wispy hair was short upon his head.

His companion was a short, fat, bearded man, so

unremarkable that I could have passed him half a dozen times and never noticed him. Like his companion, he wore a long-sleeved Grecian robe – which might have been ochre, red or brown; in this light it was difficult to see. (This was presumably to mark them out as tradesmen of substance rather than mere slaves, but the effect was rather spoiled by greasy stains that marred the fronts of both and the rough leather apron tied around each waist. It seemed to me they would have been much more at ease – and looked a good deal more respectable – in the Celtic plaid breeches and tunic to which they had, presumably, been born.)

The tall one with the mournful eyes regarded me for a long moment, and then his thin lips parted in a smile, showing a crooked row of yellow teeth. I preferred him doleful, I decided, it was not a pleasant smile.

'Councillor, is he? By grace and favour only, judging by the stripe. Well, so what does the toga-licker want?' he said to Comux, in a growling Celtic that he clearly did not think I understood. 'You have not found us another candidate to fund our little scheme?' He turned towards me as he spoke and sketched a little bow, which might have passed for deferential if I had not heard his words.

'No such luck!' I answered, using the same tongue, and saw the look of panic flit across his face. 'Though I will be very interested to know exactly what that little scheme might be. But first I want to speak to you about your visit to the baths the other day. I am speaking to Brokko and Boudoucus, I think? I understand you were the ones who invited Josephus?'

The two men exchanged a glance, then glared at Comux as if to blame him for all this: both for having brought me there at all and for not having warned them that I was a Celt.

Comux merely shrugged. 'This is my uncle Boudoucus, councillor,' he said, gesturing to the melancholy one. 'Whose warehouse we are in.'

Uncle? I must have looked surprised. All three men looked roughly of an age to me – though perhaps on reflection Comux might be younger, by a year or two.

'My eldest brother's only son,' the one called Boudoucus explained, growling in Latin now. 'Asked me on his deathbed to take him on and that's what we have done. By "we" I mean me and my partner, Brokko, there.'

The latter stood up and came across to me, grasping both my forearms warmly in the Roman style as though I were a friend. 'You want to talk to us regarding Josephus?' He stood aside and indicated that I should take his seat upon the bench. 'A dreadful business. Regrettable, of course. But it was not our fault, councillor, genuinely not.'

He nodded to Comux, who brought out a pair of folding stools, which had been stacked against the wall and he and Boudoucus each sat down on one – leaving poor, stout Comux, in his fancy mourning clothes, standing behind us like a wretched slave. I could see that the nephew – for all his pompous ways – had little dignity in this establishment, and was probably held at fault for everything.

Boudoucus's next words confirmed it. 'It was Comux's idea, as usual. And a most ill-omened one it proved to be. Brokko and I regret it very much. But we have insisted that he make amends. We hired him proper mourning dress to go and pay respects, and even gave him herbs to sacrifice.'

'On behalf of all of us, of course.' Brokko put in, with a smile (more charming than his partner's, in spite of several broken teeth). 'Of course it does not bring Josephus back – if there'd been any way of doing so, you may be sure we would have tried – but as it is you'll agree we have done everything we could.'

'You did not think to go and pay respects yourselves?' It was provocative, quite deliberately so. From the moment of Boudoucus's opening remarks I had begun to suspect that they were rogues. At the very least they were looking for a substantial loan to finance their 'little scheme' – the one they'd tried to lure Josephus into. I suspected they were looking for a dupe.

My challenge had brought another exchange of troubled looks, then Brokko said, still pleasantly enough, 'We did go to see him, councillor, while he was still alive – though, regrettably, he did not seem to know us, then. When we heard that he was dead we thought it was enough to send Comux as our representative. Especially as we had urgent business to attend to here.'

'Of course,' I agreed, sarcastically. 'You were engaged on it when I came in, I think. You'll find the coin underneath this bench.'

Brokko was clearly a little roused at this, though he did not reply. He simply stooped and snatched up the fallen coin, and even Boudoucus's droopy dog-eyes sparked a little fire.

The big man jumped up to his feet again, saying testily, 'We do have business, councillor – whatever you may think. Some, even, with the army. We have a contact with a shipowner who moves their animals about – mules, horses, oxen and the like. We often act as agents – make the arrangements and when the beasts are in transit we provide the feed.'

I did not doubt the contact, but I was not impressed. In my experience, if the army wants a boat they requisition it, and the same for any feedstuffs they might need – though it is possible a little money changes hands for information about where such things might easily be had.

'You have an arrangement with the quartermaster?'

'Among others.' Boudoucus was stung. 'We have many important customers.' More important than you, his tone of voice implied.

Brokko was more emollient. 'And as regards paying respects to Josephus, we cannot simply leave the warehouse unattended, Duumvir. At the moment we are short of slaves, and until we have replaced them we must man the place ourselves.'

'Though if there are no customers, you play at toss?' I said.

'Only for wooden counters, councillor,' he replied. 'Or – as today – to determine which of us should . . .' He hesitated. 'Well, go down to the dock and supervise the unloading of the ship.'

I did not believe a word of that – though I knew, of course, why he was so eager to explain. Betting for money is a technical offence, except during the month of Saturnalia – though everybody knows that it happens all the time, and people are only ever charged and fined when someone in authority is seeking an excuse, and nothing else illegal can be proved. I was not interested in such trivialities, but I did not say as much. Anything which gave me an advantage over these three doubtful traders might prove to be of help in making sure they answered my enquiries truthfully. I did not trust them to do so, otherwise.

I tried to take command. 'Before anyone goes to oversee unloading anything, there are some things I have to ask – in a professional capacity.' That was daring. I was suggesting that I had both some formal right to question them and the authority of the curia, when in fact I had neither. If they had protested – asked for my warrant, or to see my seal – I would have had to leave. But they were suddenly so anxious to co-operate, that I was strengthened in my feeling that there were things they hoped to hide! However, my immediate interest was in other things.

'My concern is Josephus,' I said and was aware of a ripple of anxiety. 'So, it was Comux's idea to ask him to the baths? Was the argentarius willing and happy to accept?'

Brokko looked startled, but he'd regained his pleasant calm. 'Councillor, it is hard to answer that. Josephus was naturally a cautious man. He seemed pleased enough, but only to a point. We had invited him to lunch with us as well, but he refused – saying he had other business at that time.'

'Wherever he ate he must have drunk too well – so, if that is what you are concerned about, the fault is not with us,' Boudoucus said, sharply. 'He was acting strangely from the time that he arrived. Shouting and laughing and swaying on his feet.'

'You all seemed rather merry when I saw you,' I said.

'Of course, I had forgotten you were there,' Brokko said at once. 'I'm afraid I didn't notice your presence at the time. When he told us that he'd seen a friend, I'm ashamed to say we thought he had imagined it – he'd already shooed away a flock of non-existent pigs and been talking to the air!'

'And you were not disturbed by that? It was not like him, surely, to be the worse for wine – especially not in the middle of the day?'

Brokko had the grace to flush. 'We concluded that someone must have played a prank on him – given him something much stronger than he was accustomed to. But of course he was our guest and we tried to match his mood – perhaps a little louder than we need have been. And the hotter the room the worse he seemed to get. We thought it was a joke.'

'Not much of a joke when he fell and hit his head,' I said.

'But nobody could guess that he would die!' Comux sounded stricken. 'Though you no doubt blame us, since he was a friend of yours.'

That was not true, on several counts, but I could almost feel sorry for the man. 'I don't blame you, in particular. But I suspect that your companions do, because it spoiled their plans. They could hardly hope to secure a major loan, or talk about investment when he was in such a state.'

The three of them exchanged an anxious glance. Then Boudoucus said, 'Councillor, there must be some mistake . . .'

'Oh come! You can't deny it now. Comux mentioned something of the kind.' I saw the furious look that he directed at his corpulent nephew, and was pleased to have the opportunity to add, 'And you yourself confirmed it when I first came in. You're still looking for investment, I believe you said? What was the scheme in fact?'

FOURTEEN

There was a moment's silence, while they looked wildly at each other, clearly wondering how they should reply. None of the three found anything to say.

'Come,' I urged briskly. 'You must know what you were trying to interest him in, and equally obviously you have not yet found the money that you need, since you were hoping I might be encouraged to invest. So what was it? An opportunity to finance some kind of import, I presume?'

Comux said instantly, with evident relief, 'Exactly, citizen. My uncle and his partner are astute. They often see opportunities which other people miss.' The others – far from being complimented – simply glared at him. He sat down sulkily, where Boudoucus had been, but his uncle and partner proffered nothing more.

'What commodity are you hoping to find a market for?' I persisted. 'I should perhaps remind you that I am a duumvir.'

I was hoping that a mention of my curial rank might awe them into speech, but I was disappointed. On the contrary it seemed to have the opposite effect. Even the affable Brokko had now lost his smile and all three were tight-lipped and staring at the floor. There was another long, long pause. I had achieved nothing to the purpose by my questioning, I thought – and now they were unlikely to tell me anything at all.

Then I had an inspiration.

I managed what I hoped was a knowing sort of leer. 'I mention this because – although I can't afford to offer anything myself – as a member of the curia I might know people who would be interested, if there is a profit to be made,' I said. It was true, there are members of the council who are not averse to dabbling in speculative deals, on the expectation of a quick return – not that I had any intention of involving them! Besides, some goods require a licence or are taxable, in which case the

curia might have an interest of a different kind. 'Though don't
say I told you so.'

Another quick exchange of glances. Boudoucus looked
doubtful and shook a warning head, but I'm almost certain
that Brokko was about to speak – and then I spoiled it.
'Supposing that it's honest,' I added with a smile.

It was intended as a jest, but the effect was instantaneous.

Boudoucus said, with indignation (or a good pretence at it),
'Why should you suppose it isn't honest, citizen? We are
humble traders, trying to make a living, that is all. You come
here asking questions – uninvited, I might add – and then cast
doubts upon our probity.'

'But what am I to think? When you will not tell me what
this honest trade is in?'

Another look passed between them – almost imperceptibly
– then all three spoke at once. Brokko said, 'Spices,' just as
Comux murmured, 'Furs,' and Boudoucus was growling, 'Fine
Falernian wines.'

Brokko recovered his composure first. 'Mixed cargo,
councillor – as you probably deduce.' He gave me his winning
smile.

What I deduce, I thought, is that you are telling me untruths.
Trading in all these things is commonplace – no one needs to
make a special effort to woo a possible investor by personal
invitations to the baths, not unless their credit is very bad
indeed. Besides, I'd just walked through a warehouse where
all these things were already clearly stored. These men would
hardly need finance to purchase any more!

But all I said was, 'In that case, gentlemen I don't think I
can help. My contacts would be hoping for something more
unusual – something the market had not seen perhaps – in
which a quick initial profit could be made.'

Boudoucus was looking savage now – though whether
because he thought he'd lost his chance with me, or because
he realized I had not believed a word, I could not tell. For
two quadrans I believe he would have sworn at me, but instead
he rounded on his nephew, giving him such a savage push that
Comux almost toppled off his stool, 'This misunderstanding
is your fault, as usual. You are the one who brought him here

without a word of warning, and left us unprepared. What did you tell him about our business? Don't shake your head like that. You must have told him something or he would not come here asking questions and casting doubts on our integrity. Where did you meet him, anyway?'

Comux hung his head unhappily. 'He was at the money lender's paying his respects when I was there. I brought him because he wanted to ask you about the medicus – whether one of you had sent the man to tend to Josephus. I said I didn't think so, but he wanted to be sure. Or that is what he claimed.'

'And what's that to do with us?'

'He wanted to find out where the fellow could be found,' Comux sounded thoroughly dejected now, 'because he'd not been paid and the money-changer's servant had no cash to do it with. I even offered to pay the bill myself, to save there being any disrespect to Josephus, but with no address that was not possible.' He shrugged. 'So I agreed to bring him. I did not expect all this.'

'Well, if that is what he wants, it is easy to resolve,' Brokko said, reverting to his genial tone again. 'I was there when the medicus arrived, but I had never seen the man before. Certainly I did not call for him. Did you, Boudoucus?'

Boudoucus shook his head. 'Whoever summoned him, it wasn't me. I've never had dealings with any medicus. I don't have the money for such extravagance – a wise woman with herbs is good enough for me. I'm rather surprised that Josephus didn't feel the same.'

Brokko nodded. 'He was a frugal man. In fact, when the medicus arrived, that maidservant tried to turn him from the door. Said the household hadn't sent for him – and he told her one of the visitors had done. And whatever you think of physicians, Boudoucus, it seemed to do him good. Josephus somehow agreed to see the man and was much less agitated after he had been – in fact when I called in later he was fast asleep. I thought that he would rally, after that, but obviously there was some deep damage to the brain. Strange how such a little fall can cause such tragedy – a warning to us that we are all mortal, I suppose.' He got slowly to his feet. 'Well,

I'm sorry, councillor, that we have been so little help. I hope you manage to locate this medicus.'

Boudoucus said, sourly, 'Doesn't he have an establishment in town? With advertisements painted so that he can be found?'

'This was not the public medicus,' his partner said. 'I would know him anywhere. A useless fellow – cabbage diets and carriage rides and blood-lets for everything. One of my aunts was ill and insisted he was called. She recovered – but no thanks to him, I'm sure. Besides, Josephus would not have had him in the house. Those two famously fell out years ago.'

'I'd heard as much, though not the reason why,' I interposed.

Brokko smiled. 'It is no secret, Josephus told me the tale himself, once when I was changing money at the booth. You know how he always liked to talk. It seems the medicus had incurred a debt he couldn't pay (for expensive false teeth, I believe it was) and applied to Josephus for an official loan. But Josephus thought that the debt was frivolous and refused to give him one – so he was forced to money lenders who almost ruined him. Though of course all this was long ago and the man has prospered since.'

'Josephus told you this?'

A nod. 'Because I'd mentioned what happened to my aunt. I think he was rather proud of having made a stand, though he confessed he feared to have the man attend him, ever since, because not only was he useless, he might try to take revenge! This other medicus was quite a different sort of man – youngish and good-looking and very competent. He might even have been Greek – he had the skin for it. In any case he's clearly skilled. His potion had immediate results. Someone's private doctor, I would judge – there is quite a vogue for them. One of the other argentarii, maybe?' He gave me another of his smiles. 'If you could trace the other visitors to Josephus, perhaps you'd find out who he is. And won't the friend who called him be prepared to meet the bill?'

It was a reasonable question – providing one did not secretly suspect the doctor of suffocating Josephus – and I was just considering how I could reply when there was a tentative tapping on the door. A moment later Iliath opened it.

'Your pardon, masters.' Her voice was as anxious as her face. 'I know you ordered that you were not to be disturbed, but Gwengor has come back with a man who says he has an urgent message for the councillor. I have left them waiting at the door.'

'Stupid child! What will the duumvir think of us? When people come, you are supposed to show them in.' Boudoucus sounded simply furious. I pitied the girl for what might happen after I had gone.

'I was leaving anyway,' I put in hastily. 'So you can lead me back to them.' I got to my feet and made a little bow. 'Thank you for your assistance, gentlemen.' If there was irony, they seemed oblivious.

Iliath, however, did not escort me out. Instead she looked at Brokko, making some sort of mute appeal with her eyes. 'Your pardon, masters, but should I take him round the other way?' She gestured to the doorway to the rear.

Brokko looked astounded. 'Through the midden heap? Whatever for?'

She seemed to be searching for a way to phrase her thoughts. 'Master, I didn't think you'd want people walking through the stock, just at the moment,' she ventured, finally. 'That lot that arrived yesterday require attention, urgently – or they will spoil and be no use at all.'

This time Boudoucus lost his temper utterly. He raised his hand and gave the slave girl such a slap that he left five red marks across her cheek. 'Stupid child, speak when you're spoken to. When will you learn to hold your stupid tongue? What happens to the stock is none of your affair.'

Brokko turned to me with an apologetic smile. 'Forgive my partner, councillor. Another delivery of untreated skins. If we don't get them to a tannery, or find a buyer for them very soon, they'll make a stench that gets in everything. A worry, naturally – but that's a matter for my partner and myself. Iliath's intentions are no doubt of the best, but she has yet to learn how a slave girl should behave. But enough – allow me to escort you to the door myself, through the front entrance, naturally!'

He smiled and stood back in the doorway to allow me to

come through, then led the way briskly through the warehouse to the street. He did not, I noticed, need a taper either – yet he found his way, so quickly that I struggled to keep up with him. I could see almost nothing. But I still have ears. And there was something living stored here, I was almost sure. I could hear it making almost – though not quite – a human sound. But I could not linger. Brokko hurried on.

The front door wasn't open, but he pulled it wide, so that the sudden daylight almost blinded me.

'Master!' It was Fauvus.

Brokko interrupted, raising a warning hand. 'Your slave, councillor, I see. And here is mine,' he said expansively, reaching out to pull Gwengor towards him as he spoke. 'Come, Gwengor, I have a little task for you.'

Gwengor nodded, and replied in babbling Celtic, 'Iliath told me, master. Should I fetch some water from the pump? The big one will need—'

'Silence!' Brokko also could be forceful when he chose. 'The duumvir has no wish to hear your wittering, even if you're talking in his native tongue. Now, make your bow, we'll deal with this inside! Farewell, councillor. Good luck with your enquiries.' And before the slave could say another word he had been pushed into the warehouse and the door was firmly closed.

Fauvus looked at me with astonishment, but being well trained he made no remark except, 'I bring a message, master, from the garrison. Your visitor from Rome is there, and is expecting you.'

I stared at him. 'Already? Does Marcus Septimus know that?'

A little bow. 'A message came to your apartment, where your patron was awaiting you. He's gone to meet the Roman visitor – it seems the man is a distant relative.'

I nodded. 'So I understand. So why did Laurentius not come to meet him at my flat? It is to be at his disposal while he is in the town.'

'He prefers to stay at the garrison tonight – matters to discuss with the commander there, he says. He seems suspicious of the arrangements which have been made for him. With respect, I think that is why he wants to talk to you.'

I gave an inward groan. If Laurentius was already questioning everything, Marcus might have to offer him accommodation yet. And who knows what trouble that might cause for him – and for me, as his particular confidant, no doubt. Oh, why did he let his little son show off to visitors?

Aloud I said, 'Then I must call and see him, that is clear, and try to reassure him that the apartment is well placed, and well appointed.' It might be an advantage, now I thought of it, that he had not already taken possession of the place – full of my wet clothes as it presumably still was. And the money bags? I wondered suddenly. I enquired of Fauvus, but he shook his head.

'Another problem, master. They sent a boy to find you, when the message came – and they traced you as far as Properus's flat. I was still waiting for Properus to come, but the messenger assured me that this took priority, and was effectively a summons from His Excellence. So I sent him back, to tell them where I was, and say that I would bring you to the fort as soon as possible. I traced you to the docks. By that time they'd sent Gwengor after me, so it wasn't hard to find you, after that.'

I shook my head. 'But this is inconvenient, by all the gods. I have not finished what I hoped to do. I wanted to look in at the funeral guild, not only to discover if the body there was genuinely Semprius or not, but also to ask them where it had been found. But now it seems that won't be possible, though there is some urgency. They are cremating the body later on tonight and after that the records won't be kept. Which reminds me – if it is Semprius, I promised Florea I'd send a pair of slaves to keep watch on Josephus so she could attend the pyre!'

Fauvus nodded gravely. 'We'd received that message, and I have arranged that for you, master. Since Laurentius is not staying at the flat tonight, there'll be no problem with having slaves to spare. But first I will see you safely to the garrison. I took a chair, as you instructed me, and it is waiting at the corner, as you see. So, if there is nothing further to keep you here . . .?'

'Nothing that need detain me, at the moment,' I replied,

'Though there's something going on in this warehouse, although I don't know what. Importing something technically illegal, I expect.' Nothing too flagrant, I thought privately, since they were hoping to get Josephus to invest. But something, certainly. The maidservant had tried to stop me coming back this way at all, then Brokko rushed me past. At first I'd thought that there were simply rats. But rats don't whimper! I shook my head. 'As a duumvir, I should investigate. But, for the moment, this Roman visitor must take priority. Show me to the litter.'

And he did. It was to be hoped that Marcus would reimburse the carriers, I thought, as I sat back against the cushions – it had been an unexpectedly expensive day, and I had not received the money that I was counting on.

FIFTEEN

I need not have been concerned. 'The litter is already paid for, citizen,' one of the bearers told me as they set me down before the fortress gate, 'Your slave has seen to it. His Excellence Marcus Septimus gave him the wherewithal, he said.'

Evidently that had impressed them (or perhaps it was simply my attire) because they didn't try to charge me a second time – which they almost certainly would otherwise have done! I thanked them with a smile – though if they were hoping for a tip, they were disappointed. My poor purse was empty, by this time, except for that little phial in its leather pouch.

But I watched the litter thoughtfully as it picked up another citizen and trotted off again. Marcus was famously careful with his cash. Yet he'd paid for me to have a chair, when I could fairly easily have walked. He must be very keen indeed to have me here. And keen to have me soon. I turned towards the guard post at the gate.

I had not been at the garrison since the old commander left, and I was interested to see what changes there might be. From here, of course, there was no difference at all. The same surrounding walls, the same guard tower and rows of barrack roofs just visible within.

The only major alteration was in how I was received. Today I was greeted with courtesy by the man on sentry watch, and an escort orderly was promptly found for me. (I'd half-expected that, since I was not only togate, complete with fancy stripe, but announced by Fauvus – who had panted up at last, and who just had time to form the words before he was required to wait outside – as 'Duumvir Libertus'.) But once inside the walls I was on familiar ground, conducted along the customary road, through the usual arch and into the same guard tower I had visited before.

The dimly lit guardroom on the lower floor into which

I was ushered was also exactly as I remembered it. The same hard wooden bench for visitors beneath the window-space (there was even someone else already waiting there); the same bunch of off-duty junior officers warming their chilled fingers by the fire; and one of their fellows who had not yet been relieved, busily at work – at one of the same tables, on one of the same uncomfortable stools – scribbling a requisition order on a piece of bark paper. So far, so precisely as it was last time I came!

There was, however, one startling difference – so significant that I had to look twice to make sure that my eyes were not deceiving me. But there was no mistake – the person occupying the bench for visitors was none other than my patron, Marcus Septimus.

'Master!' I let out an involuntary cry. I could not repress it – I was so shocked to see him sitting there, waiting like any common citizen.

His Excellence has privileges due to rank, so on any previous visit (as I had cause to know) he had always been conducted immediately upstairs – on the occasions when he'd not been taken straight to the praetorium and entertained privately in the commander's residence. Certainly he had never been left down here to wait, without so much as an orderly to attend on him. (Presumably his own attendant had been intercepted at the gates, as Fauvus was – though of course my newest slave had orders not to wait, since I had other tasks for him to do.)

My exclamation had alerted my patron to my presence in the room. That wide-striped toga might look incongruous in a humble waiting room, but Marcus had not lost his sense of dignity. He held out a ringed hand for me to kiss.

I hurried over to kneel politely at his feet. The flagstones were uneven, hard and cold, and I am old enough to creak in every joint, but – though the garrison (or its new commandant) was not according Marcus appropriate respect – he was still my patron. He was no doubt already fuming, anyway, but he would have been more seriously angered (and with me!) if I had not offered the obeisance due. Besides, it had just occurred to me that it might be on my account that he was sitting here at all – if, for example, he'd chosen to remain till I arrived.

'Excellence!' I murmured, pressing my lips against the signet ring. 'I am sorry if I've kept you waiting.'

A shake of the head assured me this was not the case. 'Not you. But I am sincerely glad that you are here. That servant found you? I was not sure he would.'

'Fauvus is intelligent, Excellence,' I said, glad to have the opportunity to praise something which my patron had supplied for me. 'I am most impressed with him. He managed to trace me to a warehouse in the docks. And when he told me I'd been summoned by Laurentius – and that you had added your command – of course I came at once. And with the litter it did not take me long. Thank you for your generosity in providing it.' I raised my head, waiting for him to invite me to stand up, and ease my knees.

He did so with a nod. 'Very well! Get up! No ceremony here! Don't dirty those fine clothes. After all, you are a duumvir – that gives you status now!' He managed a thin smile. 'Though I, it seems, have forfeited my own. Courtesy of my confounded relative, no doubt. I suppose I should not be surprised. He's a Praetorian, or he used to be, and rank and tradition are of no account to them – look at their treatment of the last three Emper—'

Marcus was so roused that he was making no attempt to modify his words – and in front of listeners who were members of the Emperor's garrison! The matter was dangerous enough for me to interrupt him in mid-word.

'Excellence!' I glanced nervously about. The soldiers had all stopped what they were doing, suddenly, and were motionless as stone, though most of them were looking pointedly away. It was clear that they had been aware of every word. 'Laurentius is here already?' I said, to change the subject as I clambered to my feet – though of course I knew the answer, since he had summoned me.

'Upstairs, meeting with the commander as we speak.' Marcus jerked his head towards the ceiling as he spoke. He had obviously perceived that I was warning him and he did not rebuke me for impertinence – though his next words were just as indiscreet. 'You knew that he's decided to stay here in the mansio tonight? As the guest of the garrison, I think we must assume. Laurentius would never spend a quadrans unnecessarily.' He gestured tetchily towards the vacant portion of the bench. 'I imagine you, too, have been ordered to sit down here and wait?'

I was about to take the proffered seat – feeling that I was adding to the general disrespect by intruding on his bench, but unable to refuse since he'd invited me – when I was spared the necessity of doing anything by a sudden clattering of footsteps on the stair. Everybody turned to see who it might be.

It was a burly centurion in full armour who came clanking in to us, carrying his helmet underneath his arm. 'Greetings, Excellence. And you too, duumvir.' He sketched us both a small ironic bow. 'The Legate, Commander of the garrison and the Emperor's Courier will receive you now. So, if you would care to follow me?' He gestured expansively with his unencumbered arm.

Marcus gave him a look which would have withered wheat. I understood a little of what my patron felt – obviously this new commander chose to insist upon his honorary rank and have full centurions to wait on him and carry messages. (The old one would have been content to use an orderly and was always known as simply 'the commander' – though the chances were he outranked this newcomer.) Meanwhile the fulsome terms in which Laurentius was described showed how highly he was regarded here. Indeed, he'd been expressly included as issuing the summons to the commander's room (it could hardly be called an invitation!). No wonder that my patron was affronted and annoyed.

However, there was nothing to be done and we stomped upstairs behind the officer and waited while he knocked imperiously on the door.

A voice from inside answered, 'Come!' and we found ourselves entering the commander's room. The difference here was striking. It had been a place of near-austerity: a handsome desk, a wooden stool, a couple of folding ones for visitors, a statue in a niche – and very little else. Now it was difficult to recognize as the same place at all. The former desk had gone, replaced by a bigger, far more ugly one, while the stool behind it had become a high-backed seat, made of some exotic wood and ivory. In every corner there were chests and cabinets, and someone had spent a long time making holes in all the walls, to support the nails which held a dazzling array of what I guessed were military 'souvenirs' – dented helmets, buckled shields and broken swords – all of an unfamiliar foreign style.

The folding stools had also disappeared, and their place was taken by a little wooden bench, not dissimilar to the one downstairs, and opposite, a pair of exotic cushioned seats. On these were sitting the commander and the spy.

I had never seen either of these two men before – though it was clear which was the Legate, by his uniform. He was a youngish man, thickset with short fair hair, and a face so square and angular it might have been carved in granite and never chiselled smooth. His limbs, however, were bronzed and muscular under the highly-polished armour which he wore.

The other one must be Laurentius, then. Dark hair, dark clothes and small, dark, piggy eyes. That comparison to pigs was not an idle one. For an ex-soldier he had run surprisingly to fat, and his long face with its protruding jaw, splayed nose and flabby lips reminded me irresistibly of one of those sow's heads which the Romans like to serve up at their feasts. His fat pink hands were somehow porcine too, and though he was dressed simply in a dark-coloured travelling-tunic (not the wide-striped toga to which his birth entitled him) his chubby fingers were heavily adorned with golden rings, which glittered in the light of at least a dozen flames. (In contrast to the old commander's modest taper on the desk, there now seemed to be a burning oil-lamp on every flat surface in the room.)

The centurion had finished the long official formula – 'In the name of Septimius Severus, Emperor of Rome and Supreme Commander . . .' And on and on and on (obviously he was required to recite it fully each time he came in) – and had at last announced our names. The blond commander got slowly to his feet.

'Marcus Aurelius Septimus, we meet again,' he said. The words were civil but the manner brusque, and the confident loud voice a little hoarse, as if he had been shouting orders all day long – as probably he had. 'And this must be Libertus, of whom I've heard so much.' He dismissed the waiting centurion with a nod and signalled us to sit down on the bench. He did not offer Marcus his own more comfortable seat, which proper deference might have required, though he did not seem entirely comfortable with this disrespect, himself – so I wondered if this arrangement was his own idea, or whether the Praetorian had suggested it.

Laurentius, even more rudely, had not got up at all. Instead he waved a languid, pudgy hand at us. 'Cousin, I am glad to see you. And your protégé.' (He did not sound remotely pleased to me!) 'Greetings from your family in the capital.' He seemed to feel my disapproving gaze. 'Forgive me, cousin, if I do not rise. You and I are kinsmen after all, and I am very tired. A miserable journey to this miserable place. I am surprised you choose to live here, Marcus, it is so damp and cold. Though if Severus sends one, of course, there is no choice.' He waved a hand toward the bench, and Marcus sat on it.

Meekly and without a word! I realized suddenly how much power this visitor might wield, and how acutely anxious my patron really was – no doubt in part because of the studied and too-casual way in which Laurentius had chosen to use the Emperor's cognomen alone, implying an intimate acquaintanceship.

Laurentius had noted our reactions too. He smiled, but there was no warmth in it. I had seen such smiles on the faces of centurions when they were asking questions of someone they were expecting shortly to arrest. 'You already know, perhaps, why I have come?'

SIXTEEN

I felt the back hairs on my neck rise up but Marcus, beside me, seemed to stiffen into stone and in the end it fell to me to speak – since the ex-Praetorian was clearly awaiting a reply. 'A mission from the Emperor, from what you say?'

For the first time Laurentius looked exclusively at me – as if I might have just crawled out from a rotting midden heap. Indeed, I think he might have viewed a cockroach with more warmth. Evidently the narrow, concessional, purple stripe of low-ranking provincial councillors were nothing to those accustomed to the Imperial court. 'Exactly, citizen.' His tone was one of exasperated patience. He turned back to his kinsman. 'The Emperor has been receiving messages from this colonia, saying that there have been treasonable acts committed here, for which the writer is prepared to offer evidence. As a magistrate and senior member of the curia you would no doubt have preferred to deal with this yourself?'

Marcus said, 'Treason!' in a voice that shook with shock. He was about to speak again – to deny it, almost certainly – but his cousin raised a hand.

'As you clearly recognize, a serious offence – and members of the public have been aware of it, if you have not.' He smiled that strange unpleasant smile again. 'But it appears that nothing has been done and the Emperor has asked me to investigate. I am to be accorded the freedom to detain and question anyone I wish. That is why I have requested you to come here this afternoon.'

My heart had already skipped a beat or two, but now it seemed to have completely stopped. Had we been the first to be 'detained'? Had someone written denouncing Marcus to the Emperor? It was possible – on the grounds of 'consorting with supporters of Clodius's claim' – and if so I was implicated too. Common people had been executed for less – and even for citizens, the penalties were harsh.

Were we about to be thrown into the cell underneath the tower, to be brought out and questioned as suspected criminals? That cell was another place that I had seen before – a dark, damp, stinking ice-hole where I'd been locked for hours – and it was not an experience I was anxious to repeat. And as for Marcus, with his pampered life, I doubted he would survive the afternoon. Perhaps, as Roman citizens, we could yet escape that fate, though suspected traitors are often not accorded the privileges of rank.

I hoped we would, at least, be favoured enough to be allowed to send a message to our homes, explaining what had happened and telling our families we were at any rate alive. Gwellia would be beside herself with worry if I did not return tonight – although detention was not much better than falling prey to wolves.

So it was a huge relief to hear the blond-haired Legate say, with an obvious intention to placate, 'We felt that you, Excellence, as senior magistrate – and as a relative of Laurentius Aurelius Manlius himself – should be the one to announce this to the curia.'

Beside me I heard Marcus breathing softly out, a long slow sigh of released anxiety. 'It would be my honour, naturally.'

Laurentius Aurelius Manlius gave another of his smiles. He was aware of the alarm he'd caused, I thought, and was enjoying it. And he was simply glowing in the dignity of having been accorded equal status with my patron, by the Legate calling him by all three Latin names. He bowed his piggy head in grave acknowledgement. 'Though you will understand, cousin, I will have to question you?'

Even the commander seemed to feel this was unfortunately phrased. 'To ensure that the enquiries seem even-handed, Excellence,' he murmured in a reassuring tone. 'It will be known in the colonia that Laurentius is a relative of yours, and since he's on Imperial business here, he cannot be seen to favour you by excluding you completely from his enquiries.'

The ex-Praetorian treated this interjection with contempt. 'Though of course it may be that you have information, too. These things can hardly happen in a town without the senior magistrates having at least some knowledge of the facts?

Anything else suggests a lack of proper vigilance. Which brings me to the question of where I should be based.'

'I have offered him the facilities of the fort throughout his stay,' the commandant interposed, clearly anxious to show that he had tried to please. 'But though he has consented to stay at the mansio tonight, tomorrow he prefers to move into the town.'

'I presume that this apartment that you are offering is situated fairly centrally, at least? In which case I am prepared to use it while I'm here.' Laurentius spoke as though he were conferring a favour by borrowing the place, rather than the other way about. 'It will be fully equipped and staffed already I suppose?'

I answered that it was. I was about to add that my patron had provided everything when a shake of the head from Marcus warned me I should not. He was right to do so, as the ex-Praetorian made clear.

'In that case, please ensure the slaves are moved. A man in my position cannot be too cautious. Even here, the Legate has offered to provide me with a man to protect me while asleep and take a taste of everything I eat and drink in case of poisoning.'

I was about to make a protest, 'But surely there's no threat—'

Laurentius silenced me. 'My informant warned me to beware, especially of servants and that is what I'll do. I have a personal attendant travelling with my baggage mule and he should be with me within a day or two. Until then I will use the Legate's guard. You may move your slaves to somewhere else, and my own can tend me when he comes.'

Marcus looked outraged at all this, as obviously the Legate had observed, because he glanced at me and put in – very tentatively for a man of military rank, 'Would it not be helpful, citizen, to have one slave familiar with the place, at least to show you around and help you get installed?'

Laurentius shook his head impatiently – rude to the point of insult, as the Legate realized.

He murmured, 'Laurentius's informant has warned him of danger to his life, and he is naturally cautious. But it would be wise, I think, to have at least one extra slave, at least at first, to do the household tasks. Your own will be entirely occupied with guarding you.'

Laurentius glowered. 'You may be right.' He turned to Marcus, rather than to me. 'You may leave one servant long enough to help me settle in and explain to my attendant where things are to be found – oil, water and that sort of thing – but he is not to touch my food or drink and I want him gone by dusk. I have no wish to be murdered in my sleep. I hope that's clear enough. In the meantime, cousin, I believe that's all – except that you might perhaps alert the aediles that I would like to see them all tomorrow afternoon, together with the two duumviri, and any other officials connected with town trade.'

I glanced at Marcus. It was me, then, that he hoped to question first – or among the very first at any rate. But my patron would not meet my eyes. He was suppressing rage.

'That should be possible, of course. With the exception of the official argentarius. He had an unfortunate accident a day or two ago, and I fear that he has died.'

His kinsman leaned back in his cushioned seat. 'Is that so, cousin? That – as you say – is most unfortunate. Not to say suggestive and very interesting. What kind of *accident,* may I enquire?'

He put such mocking stress upon the word that I looked at him surprised. Did he know otherwise? Had his informant known the truth and warned him that something was amiss? Or – the idea struck me suddenly – had the letter writer been Josephus himself, who had foreseen a danger? Was that what he was trying to tell me at the baths? I wondered if I dared to ask Laurentius, but decided it would be unwise.

The commander had already rushed in to amplify. 'Fell and hit his head at the public baths, I hear – and died a few days later of his injury. No question of foul play. Nobody pushed him, or anything like that. If anything, he might have had a touch too much to drink. There is no dispute about the facts – there were lots of witnesses. One of the councillors was there when it occurred.'

I was about to say that I'd been there myself, but a moment's reflection convinced me that I should hold my tongue. Marcus was having a similar train of thought, it seemed.

'I can . . .' He glanced at me. 'That is . . . I will see that the aediles are informed. Tomorrow, after the noonday trumpet sounds? You'll want to interview them individually, of course. We cannot deprive the town of all its market police at once. And, in Libertus, you already have one duumvir.'

Laurentius gave me another of his looks. 'Then I will see him first of all.'

That sounded threatening, but I proffered – in a vain attempt to be accommodating, 'We could start a little earlier, if you prefer – there is no formal meeting of the curia that day, though there are naturally hearings in the courts.'

'Midday is time enough,' my visitor replied. 'It will give me the opportunity to get installed and then perhaps to mingle with the populace, and see if there is anything of interest to be gleaned.'

It was no laughing matter, but I could not restrain a smile. The idea of this patrician 'mingling' unobserved was so unlikely it was risible. I do not know if things are different in Rome – after all it is the biggest city in the world – but news travels fast in this colonia. Word of Laurentius's arrival at the fort would by now have reached every gossip in the town. If he set foot in the market unannounced – no doubt wearing his flamboyant, wide-striped toga by that time! – he was likely to be peered at from every corner, arch and colonnade, to say nothing of the urchins who would dog his every step, openly goggling at this Roman visitor.

'Something amuses you, citizen?' he said, and I instantly wished that I had suppressed the smile.

'Only that I am glad to find that, after all, you won't require my staff tonight,' I improvised. 'Not expecting that you'd be here so soon, I promised the services of two of them elsewhere.' I had been about to explain where they were going, but I once again could see that was unwise. It was dawning on me how the presence of an acknowledged Imperial spy turns the simplest things to secrets, and disinclines a man to speak of anything at all, in case he accidently implicates himself.

So I was glad when Laurentius waved a hand and said, 'You may lend your slaves to anyone you choose, for the whole duration of my stay – though I can't at present tell you how long that's going to be. That will depend on my enquiries. Now, as I mentioned earlier, I am worn with travelling. I should be glad to rest. Until tomorrow, then.' This time he did rise stiffly to his feet, and I saw with some surprise that he was not very tall – barely more than the five feet and seven thumb-widths, by Roman reckoning, which is the minimum height for a recruit. Much the same height as his cousin, Marcus, then. I had somehow expected a praetorian to be much more than that – although of course, they are chosen for their ancestry, rather than their imposing physical attributes. And certainly Laurentius must, at one time, have been muscular enough – though the arm that was raised in mock-military farewell was now distinctly plump.

The Legate had rapped a dagger on the desk and the centurion – who must have been waiting outside like the merest page – came hurrying in at once. 'Our visitors are leaving,' the commander said, before the fellow had time to start his recitation again. 'See that they are escorted to the gates.'

The centurion responded with a smart salute (which made the ex-Praetorian's look sloppy by comparison) and ushered us unceremoniously down the stairs again.

The off-duty officers had by now dispersed, so it was the actuarius – who had finished writing by that time and was in the act of blowing sand across his bark-paper to dry off the ink – who was commissioned to see us to the gate. It was a task which he performed with courtesy.

But having an officer as escort could not assuage my patron's fury at the absence of respect which had just been accorded him. 'If I come safely out of this,' he muttered in my ear, 'I swear by all the gods, I shall write a letter of complaint – to the Emperor himself. Laurentius is acting on his authority and I have been treated like a person of no account at all.'

I nodded. I had too, of course, but I was used to it.

SEVENTEEN

At the gate I was astonished, and delighted, to find young Minimus awaiting me – now dried out and wrapped in another borrowed cloak. With all the various worries of the day I had almost forgotten that I'd left him at the apartment earlier.

'Master!' His grin was almost wider than his face. 'They told me I should come and find you here.' His face grew sombre and he added, in an altered tone, 'That other fellow, Fauvus . . .' He broke off as my patron came across to speak to me.

'My slave has kept a litter nearby to wait for me,' Marcus said, as though Minimus weren't there. 'I'm going into the forum to find the aediles, and then I suppose I must arrange for this announcement to be made tomorrow. Requiring people to attend at once, whenever and wherever Laurentius calls for them.'

'From the steps of the basilica?' I muttered – feeling the need to say something, however obvious.

A brusque, impatient nod. 'Naturally. We'll treat it as an official proclamation. I doubt our visitor would be satisfied with less.' His face was dark with fury at the thought, but he had the grace to ask, 'Shall I send the litter back for you?'

I shook my head, a little fearful of offending him. 'Thank you, Excellence, but it is not far to my apartment, I am content to walk. I would be reluctant to delay you, anyway – should you wish to go elsewhere – and besides I have business to attend to on the way.'

Marcus grunted, 'Until tomorrow then. It's clear Laurentius will not want me to escort him to your flat. Come and see me when he has questioned you – I shall want to know exactly what he said.'

'Of course,' I murmured – thinking, though not mentioning aloud, that the promise depended on my being free to leave and not locked up inside a cell.

'Somewhere private. At the baths, perhaps?' He did not
mean to be ironic, I could see, though at first I had suspected
that. 'It will have to be in town, but I don't want Laurentius
learning that after you left him, you immediately visited my
flat. He will probably have paid informers watching where
you go. Bad enough that he'll almost certainly want to
interview my household in the end, without giving him a
reason for doing it at once. That was exactly what I wanted
to avoid by offering him yours! But I can control what slaves
attend me at the bathhouse, and I can arrange to have the
deaf-and-dumb one there for you again. If we get there early
in the afternoon – as you saw before – there won't be many
customers about.'

'As you require, Excellence, of course,' I murmured, although
I was anything but anxious to go back to the baths. 'Though I
cannot answer for how long my meeting with Laurentius will
last. But naturally I'll come as soon as possible.'

'Very well!' he grunted, and was in the chair and gone.

I sighed. 'That's my tomorrow spoken for!' I said to
Minimus, 'Now, you were trying to tell me something about
Fauvus, I believe?'

The boy was looking sulky. 'Only that he said he couldn't
come himself, he has gone somewhere else, to see about some
money which had not arrived. I was to tell you that. He said
you'd understand.'

I approved this with a smile. 'He has gone back to Properus's
flat to wait. That was intelligent!'

Minimus said nothing and did not return the smile. In fact
he looked more sulky than before. I realized he was jealous
of the newer slave and fearful of being superseded in my
confidence.

'He's merely resuming what I'd ordered him to do,' I said,
to reassure. 'That's where he was when Marcus's summons
interrupted him. So we'll leave him to it, and you and I will
go and look in at the funeral guild for slaves.'

Minimus glanced sharply at me. 'About Josephus's old
manservant, I suppose? They told me at your flat that he was
dead, but I'd forgotten about him. But didn't I hear that they
were taking care of things?'

I nodded. 'I promised the remaining slave I'd find out what I could. A body was picked up by the army cart, I understand – it was only my discussion with the watch which prevented it from being thrown into the public pit – but I would like to make quite sure that it was him, and discover exactly where it was found and when.'

I had been walking briskly towards the forum as I spoke, with Minimus trotting obediently at my heels. He looked up at me. 'If he was picked up by the death cart, will the slave guild know the details?'

'I am hoping so. When a dead body is presumed to be a slave, and if they're asked to leave it at the guild, the army tends to leave such information as it can, so that the owner can reclaim his property. That is why I'm anxious to call on them today. The corpse is due to be cremated later on, and once that's safely done, it isn't likely to linger specially in their memory.'

'I suppose they deal with dozens of dead slaves every moon,' Minimus murmured. He was visibly upset – doubtless remembering my own slave, Maximus, who had been murdered not very long ago. (I, of course, had arranged that funeral myself, but the two had come to me together – a gift from Marcus, who had bought them as a pair – and they'd been so close they used to finish each other's sentences.) The loss had grieved me very much, but Minimus had never quite got over it.

To rouse him, I said slyly, 'You have been to the slave's guild several times, I think, so you could lead the way.'

That did it. 'I know a quicker route!' More cheerful now that he thought himself of use, he set off at once down a side street to the right, at a pace that left me panting red-faced after him.

We were very soon in the area just inside the eastern wall, where the land is boggy because the river floods and where those who can afford it do not choose to live. Here the wide streets and pavements of the central town give way to narrow shadowed streets and narrower alleyways, while warrens of neglected buildings and decrepit sheds take the place of neat apartment blocks. The whole area smelt of midden heaps and damp.

'Here!' Minimus led me round a corner to a wider thoroughfare – and there indeed was the hanging sign featuring
the painted symbol of the guild we'd come to seek. 'Will you
go straight in, master, or should I announce you first?'

I had been lifting my best toga's hems up as much as
possible along the way, but I was suddenly aware of how
dirty they'd become. I should have found a friendly doorway
and removed it earlier, and given it to Minimus to carry while
we walked, but I had not thought of it. I made a vain effort
to brush away the mud.

'We'll go in together,' I declared, after a moment, aban-
doning my failed attempts. 'Announce me if you like, but I
have had dealings with this establishment before.' Suddenly,
though, I was less than confident. If I were to identify the
corpse as Semprius, I hoped I could be certain of being shown
that scar – I wasn't sure that I would recognize his face.

I followed Minimus into the anteroom for visitors – unfur-
nished except for a table and a wooden stool. The public face
of the establishment – a freeman from the way his shoulder
had been scarred by the removal of a brand – was using chalk
to write something, in tiny letters, in a vacant square on a
piece of wooden board which was nailed to the wall and
marked in dozens of little sections like a grid.

He heard us enter and whirled around at once and I realized this
was not a man I'd met before. This one was aging, tall and skinny
as a javelin (probably a former amanuensis slave who'd been
released by his owner as of little further use) but – alerted by my
toga and Minimus's loud announcement of my name and rank – he
was anxious to be as helpful as he could.

'Great Mercury! I hope there is no problem, councillor?'

I shook my head. 'A private enquiry. Hoping to identify the
money-changer's slave. On behalf of the household, that is
all.'

'Ah, the corpse that we're cremating later on! The one that
we are treating as' – he consulted something written on a list
– 'Semprius! Of course. I was just entering the name on our
plan of the columbarium, so we know which niche is his. He
will be the second on our pyre tonight. So how can I assist
you, citizen?'

'I understand there was a robbery, so – if it is him – we're anxious to know where he was found, in case that leads us to the thief and the retrieval of the stolen property.' (I did not add 'and to his murderer'. The law regarded Semprius as 'property' himself, and whoever killed him would be liable to recompense the loss.)

The long, lean face assumed a doubtful look. 'It appears to have been the work of bandits, citizen – I doubt that you will ever track them down. But as to where he was discovered, I can help you there. I spoke to the officer who brought him in – fortunately the watch had been warned to look for him, and realized that he might be a paid-up member of the guild.'

He paused to be sure I'd understood. I nodded. 'Brought him in from where? I hear he was discovered on an ancient lane – not a place the army death cart generally goes. They usually confine their work to military roads.'

'Indeed. But their informant said it was bandit handiwork, and they are always under orders to investigate such things. The track was very steep apparently and once or twice they nearly overset the cart. But they persevered and in the end they found the body, lying by a pond – which is where the gooseboy told them it would be. He was afraid it would bring a curse down on his flock.'

Beside me, I heard Minimus draw in a startled breath. His thoughts had evidently echoed mine. A pond? Beside a lonely, steep and narrow track? 'Not the ancient track which leads south-east of here?' I said.

He looked at me, surprised. 'That's the one. Leads to a few farms and roundhouses, I think – and finally comes out on a little lane that links back to the military road. You know it?'

I should do, since it is the track I take myself almost every morning and evening of the year! 'I live in one of those roundhouses,' I said. 'Which gives me an added interest in the case – the notion that there have been murderous attacks near there is very worrying. We do not often hear of bandits on that lane.' I frowned. 'But what on earth was Semprius doing there?'

He made a deprecating face. 'Going on some errand to His Excellency, Marcus Septimus, perhaps – I understand his country house is out that way? Or perhaps he was dumped there after he was robbed – the army noticed hoof prints round about so it is possible the bandits had one horse, at least.'

I smiled grimly. The army are rarely so observant, in my experience. In fact they are not generally much concerned with slaves – or with any death-cart corpses, for that matter – but they would have more than usual interest if they suspected that bandits were involved.

He took this as an indication that I was satisfied and had concluded what I wished to learn. 'Will you be at the crema-tion, duumvir?'

I shook my head – to Minimus's evident relief. 'We shall be leaving Glevum long before that time – especially now we know that there are dangers on the road.' My movements were no business of his, of course, but – after my questioning – I felt compelled to add, 'I've made arrangements to allow the maidservant to go, since she is likely to be the only private mourner at the pyre. She was grateful for your help in taking charge of things.'

He smiled – a strange, cadaverous sort of smile. 'And she was very helpful in her turn. Provided us with a clean tunic for the corpse and even with a cloak. Would you like to see him, councillor. To pay your last respects? We've done our best with him, though it wasn't easy – as you may suppose. If you'd like to come this way?'

Poor Semprius, I thought. Obviously he had been badly beaten while he lived – protecting his master's property perhaps. 'Perhaps for just a moment . . .' I began, though this was exactly what I'd planned for all along.

At my side I could feel my servant stiffening – like anyone raised in a Roman household, he has a fear of ghosts. I gave him a reassuring wink. 'However,' I added, quickly, 'I cannot stay for long. I have other urgent business to attend to in the town. Minimus, you can wait outside for me.'

I was rewarded with a grin of pure relief, and my servant padded out into the street. I followed the thin guildsman through the curtained aperture that gave onto the larger space beyond. This was a place I'd never been before. My previous business had all been conducted at the desk.

We went through what was clearly a storage area – full of the basic requirements for a funeral. There were heaps of tallow candles, boxes of the less costly funeral herbs, amphorae of cheap wine and inexpensive oil (for sacrifice) and even several empty 'biers' – plain wooden stretchers, like doors with carrying handles at each end. Enough to ensure that members of the guild would have at least the minimum for a decent funeral and cremation on the guild's communal pyre.

Beyond this, through another curtain, was the 'waiting area' for the corpses which – for some reason – were not stored at home. There were three, at the moment, squashed into the room, though they'd been treated with what dignity was possible. They had been washed and dressed and readied for the bier – each laid out on a separate table with a lighted taper at its feet and head, though the smell of herbs and candles was not quite enough to mask the smell of death, even on a chilly winter day like this. In the summer it must be unbearable.

It was obvious which one was Semprius, from the feet alone. The other two were clearly females, one of middle age and the other very young – though it was evident what accident had caused their deaths. Both bore signs of dreadful scalding, and I turned away, trying not to imagine the toppling, boiling pot.

Semprius appeared to be swaddled in a cloak, its hood raised and pulled forward to half-obscure the face. Or rather, as I swiftly realized, to obscure the place where the face should be. For though the shape was suggested by a ball of linen rags, the head itself was missing. I let out a groan.

'That's what you meant by bandits!' I exclaimed. 'Druid rebels!' They were famous for beheading their victims, stripping them and dangling the naked forms from nearby trees (as a terrible warning to other travellers) while the heads were borne off to the sacred groves as triumphant offerings to the ancient gods. Though their targets were more often purely Roman ones: soldiers ambushed on patrol; tax-inspectors and other officials of the state; or simply wealthy citizens who'd been unwise enough to travel on unfrequented roads with insufficient guard. Attacks on humble slaves like Semprius were very rare – unless the victim had surprised them in some way, and they wished to silence him.

The guildsman cut across my thoughts. 'Exactly, citizen. I said that I doubted you could track them down. But – forgive my impudence – where Druids are concerned it is not wise to pursue enquiries. See what they've done to him! Though, as I say, we've done our best. If that old slave woman can be required to keep her distance from the pyre until the fire burns down, I hope she'll never know. I fear it would distress her terribly. Bad enough that we had to ask her for a set of clothes for him.' He paused, then added in a different tone, 'I should not perhaps, have brought you here at all – it isn't usual. But all our other staff are elsewhere dealing with a corpse, and I should be outside at the desk in case of customers. So – since you're a duumvir – if you would like to be with him alone . . .?'

'Thank you.' I smiled. 'A moment will suffice.' I bent towards the corpse and – when my guide had gone – gently lifted the tunic from the legs. But what I murmured next was not a prayer at all. 'I'll find whoever did this, Semprius,' I said. 'Though I don't believe that Druids had much to do with it!'

EIGHTEEN

Minimus was pathetically relieved to see me come out onto the street – I sometimes forget how very young he is, and how very Roman in his upbringing. Even now he was worried lest I might have attracted some infernal curse from having been so close to corpses of the newly dead. 'Their spirits may still be lingering nearby and who knows what ill-luck they'll cause if you've disturbed their rest? Do you wish me to go and buy a prayer disc from the temple steps for you, and have the temple slaves attach it at the shrine?'

I shook my head. 'I rinsed my hands and face in pure water before I left the premises. I'm sure that is enough. The funeral guild know what rituals are required. Besides I have no money, till Fauvus comes with it – unless, of course, he is already there.'

But when we got back to the flat, there was disturbing news. Fauvus was waiting, but without my money bags.

'I went to Properus's apartment, master,' he explained, as my new household helped divest me of my cloak and mud-stained toga. 'As you instructed, I went directly back, after I had left you at the fort. But there was no one there.'

Minimus gave me a look which said 'I-told-you-so', but I glared at him till he went off to fetch a stool for me.

'Not even the servant?' I found that I was frowning at Fauvus by this time. I was not sure I trusted that unctuous Scito at all (the very name means 'the clever, cunning one'). 'It would be like him to refuse to answer, to discourage visitors, especially if his master was not home.'

It crossed my mind to wonder if he was cheating Properus, in fact. But I did not voice the thought – there were too many listening ears about – while my new servants swarmed around my stool. They had taken off my sandals, wiped my wet feet clean, produced a brand-new pair of house slippers for me,

and sponged my expensive toga to respectability, almost before
I'd had a moment to draw breath. Even Laurentius could not
have faulted them for their efficiency – supposing that he
deigned to accept their services. When they had finished, I
waved them all away – except for Fauvus.

'You're quite certain Scito wasn't there?'

'Perfectly certain, master. Like you, I was at first suspicious
of some trickery, but that big woman from the upstairs attic
rooms came down while I was hammering on the door. She
must have recognized me from above, because she'd come to
tell me that it wasn't any use. "He's out, gone. In a hurry, too.
I saw him leaving here a little while ago – charging downstairs
like a startled horse, while I was coming up".'

It was such a lively imitation of the woman, that despite
my worries I actually laughed.

Fauvus was encouraged to go on. '"Knocked my bunch of
turnips from my hand, he did, and it took me minutes to collect
them up again. And when I shouted after him, he did not even
stop – just hollered back that I could go to Dis!" Apologies,
master, but that is what she said.'

His sudden change of character was so acute, that I had to
hide my smile and was grateful to sip at the goblet of spiced
mead, which had been laid out on a table for me as soon as
I arrived. I looked about for Minimus, who normally prepared
this drink for me, but he was standing sulking by the further
wall. He had taken my dismissal of him rather hard. I raised
my goblet to him in a mute salute and was glad to see him
smile, before I said to Fauvus, 'Did that woman tell you where
Scito might have gone?'

Fauvus shook his head. 'She said she didn't know, before
she waddled off. I did check with the people in the businesses
nearby, but all of them were busy with their noisy trades and
hadn't even noticed that he'd left. But then I found an urchin
on the street who pointed out that the windows of the flat were
shuttered from within, and that convinced me that he had really
gone. They certainly weren't shuttered when I was there before.'

I breathed in sharply and almost choked upon the mead.
'Shuttered? At this hour? So they're not intending to return
today!'

Fauvus sketched a bow. 'My first thought, master, and I was about to come and tell you so – but something happened then which changed my mind. That woman came toddling down the stairs again, with a sullen child trailing after her, and took me on one side. They had been watching from her window-space, she said and – having seen that I was still outside and asking questions of the tradesmen round about – they'd come to seek me out. Her son had just told her some interesting news, which I might like to know – if I promised not to report her to the authorities.'

'Report her? For what?'

'For sending her children out to beg – or even steal, I rather think. The boy seemed very anxious that I should not talk to him direct, just stood by and nodded as she told the tale. It seems that he'd been purposely left out on the street – "looking out for errands or a horse to hold" is the official version – when they came back from market and his mother went inside. Scito, as we know, chose that moment to come charging out. And he did find an errand for the son, which apparently was most unusual.'

'An errand?' I took a sip of mead.

'To go into the marketplace to see if Properus had called in at the money booth today. He was to run back with the answer, and deliver it to Scito later on, when he returned.'

I nodded. 'I see. But was there any sign of Properus? We know he wasn't at the booth a little earlier – we looked for him ourselves.'

Fauvus shook his head. 'He's not been there all day. The boy was still waiting to pass the answer on – which is why they were looking out and saw me in the street. And, incidentally, that message is correct. The booth was closed all day. I checked again on my own way back here. Though it is interesting that Scito did not appear to know.'

'Though one would expect him to, of course!' I sat back so heavily I almost spilt my mead. 'And it must have been a last resort to look – he told us himself that the booth was closed today. You're right, it's very odd. And something else has just occurred to me. You remember that Scito told us when we called, that his master had gone to pay respects to Josephus?

But Properus hadn't been there either – although he'd arranged to come and Florea had been expecting him.' I shook my head. 'So where do you think he's gone?'

For the first time I felt a tremor of concern. He could not be missing, surely? That would put a totally new complexion on affairs. Should I be looking for a pattern here? First Josephus, then Semprius, and now Properus as well?

Fauvus shrugged. 'I presume that Scito had some idea in mind and has gone to look for him. Though the woman thinks he won't be gone for long.' Fauvus gave his rare and sombre smile. 'Why would her son be asked to bring a message, otherwise? I mentioned the shutters and she simply laughed at me. "If you had all that money on the premises – oh, don't look so surprised, it's hardly a secret when it came here under guard! – wouldn't you secure the window-spaces if you were going to leave, even for a moment? They've been doing that for days. Especially when that urchin boy is always hanging round." As near as I remember, that is what she said.'

His rendition was amusing, but it was accurate. I was quite sure of that. Good slaves can memorize a message word for word – indeed they're trained to it, so that they can accurately carry them. And one word in particular had interested me. 'An urchin – the same boy as we saw ourselves, you think?'

'I presume so, master. It occurred to me. I tried to describe him, and she seized on it – though, of course, these street boys all look much the same. "Skinny as a whistle, with protruding ears? That's the one," she said. "Of course, it is not a wonder that he hangs about – that Properus was always very kind to him. I've seen him slip him money more than once. Foolish, because it just encourages the lad. And he needn't look for gratitude, the boy has shifty eyes. Wouldn't surprise me if he could climb a wall, like one of those mousing cats the Romans like to keep – and, if you ask me, he was sizing up the chance. Why else would he notice that the shutters were in place? He's so small that he'd have to lean back purposely to see so high! It's not like us, we're looking down on them".' He reverted to his own voice, with comical effect. 'A simple thing, but it had not occurred to me.'

It had not occurred to me either. 'I doubt the woman's right.

That urchin could not have stolen very much – he's nowhere to hide booty in those rags of his, and if he suddenly had lots of cash to spend somebody would notice and march him to the watch. More likely she is jealous, on her son's account. She doesn't mention Properus giving alms to him!' I grinned. 'Though Scito no doubt paid him for his work today?'

'I rather think the promise was to pay when the answer was received – which is why they were watching out for his return. Though she made it clear that she was hoping for a tip from me.'

'You gave her one, I hope?'

He shook his head. 'I had nothing left until I came back here, and Marcus gave me the money for the chair. So I told her that you were a duumvir and – if she had any sense – she should be content for now with knowing that you would not prosecute her son for begging in the street. I hope I acted wisely, master? I did say if the information proved of use to you, you might return and give her something on another day. I did not want her spreading discontent. And if anything has befallen Properus, you might be glad of her cooperation later on?'

I was beginning to think highly of this slave's intelligence. I should miss him when Laurentius had gone home – despite the dark looks that Minimus was giving us. 'You have done very well. And you are right, I am concerned for Properus – and anybody else who was close to Josephus. That is why I have another task for you. I promised Florea that I would send those slaves tonight. I know that you've selected them, but – more than that – I'd like you to go with them yourself and keep a watch on Florea at the pyre.'

'And our Roman visitor?' I had forgotten that Fauvus had not heard the news.

'He does not want the slaves that Marcus chose for him – pretends that he's been warned that some of you are dangerous, though I can't imagine that's the truth. I suspect he simply wishes to insult his Excellence – he has already done so, in several ways, in fact. He now intends to spend this evening at the garrison. He seems to have made an ally of the new commandant. So he won't be here until the morning, at the earliest. So when those slaves go to keep vigil for Florea tonight, you go with them and take him the key – tell the fort that you're the one who'll help him settle in. He may send for you tomorrow. Though only the gods know what I'm to do with all the rest of you. If all else fails, they could attend on Josephus, I suppose, until Marcus can arrange to have you sold again.'

Fauvus did his little bow again, but I saw the look of disappointment cross his face – and was equally aware that Minimus was grinning with relief. He tried to suppress it as I turned to him.

'And Minimus, I have a task for you. It is getting late. Go to the workshop and tell Junio to come, and bring the mule. We'll have to use the panniers to take our wet clothes home, and hope to bring the money back another time.'

The little redhead nodded and rushed off eagerly.

'And now,' I said to Fauvus, 'bring all the slaves in here. I'd better tell them what they can expect. It's possible that his Excellence may take on some of you – yourself and the door-keeper among them, I expect. Though, I confess, I shall miss your services. You have not served me long, but you have served me very well.'

To my surprise, he coloured instantly. 'And I shall never have a better master,' he declared. 'I had hoped I could escort you home – but naturally, master, I am at your command.'

'Then fetch the slaves to me!' Embarrassment had made me sound severe.

He leapt to obey me and no more was said. I made my announcement, to general dismay, but slaves must do as their masters tell them to, and they accepted they would shortly be resold. By the time that Junio and Minimus arrived, I was cloaked and ready, with the wet clothes – and both my togas – neatly and separately bundled for the mule.

NINETEEN

I did not take the litter, I was glad to walk, talking to Junio as we trudged home together along the ancient muddy track. Minimus trotted happily ahead, with Arlina – safely out of earshot, which was just as well.

'The tanner's wife from next door came in twice this afternoon – the first time to tell me that Laurentius was a spy, and the second to tell me that he wanted to see you!' Junio looked wryly at me. 'I thought that spies were supposed to act in secrecy.'

'Not this one, it appears! He could not make it clearer if he had slogans written on the forum walls. And if she has heard it, it will be all around the town – she is the biggest gossip this side of Londinium!'

'But it was clear that she was genuinely worried, too.'

'I imagine there is a lot of anxiety about,' I said. 'Everyone will have something that he wants to hide – if it is only having celebrated the fall of one or other of the recent Emperors, or having spoken too freely in a tavern recently. I confess that I'm concerned myself. If Marcus falls, he'll take me with him, that is obvious. That's why I'd like to stop by if I can, and have a look at the place where Semprius was found. I fear that if Laurentius has his way I may not get another chance – though don't tell your mother so. Time enough for her to worry if the worst occurs.'

Junio gave me an anxious glance, but only said, 'Of course. And naturally we'll stop and search the place. Though it's unlikely you'll find anything at this late stage. We can't even be sure exactly when Semprius was killed.'

'Properus saw him the morning that Josephus died. He told me so himself.'

'So it must be after that. But it's been raining ever since.'

'But you never know. There might be something which was overlooked – the army won't have lingered to look around, especially if they thought that Druid rebels were involved. They'd be concerned with collecting the corpse as fast as possible and making sure that it was not a rebel trap, designed to ambush them!'

Junio gasped, 'You're certain that it's not?' I raised my eyebrows at him, and he gave a sheepish grin. 'In that case, shall I stay and help?'

I shook my head. 'You'd better catch Minimus and tell him where I've gone. I don't want to upset him any more. He seemed very jealous of my new slaves, earlier – especially of Fauvus, who after a single day has managed to make himself seem indispensible – that I was anxious to give him an important job to do.'

My son grinned back at me. 'That's why you decided not to ride the mule? I had rather wondered, since we haven't got the money bags, and the panniers aren't heavy with just your clothes in them.'

'And that—' I broke off and we both leapt back sharply to let a horseman past – a hooded fellow in a short slave's cloak, going far too fast for such a narrow lane. As he passed us he did not slow at all – quite the contrary, he seemed to urge his horse. It forced us off the track at either side, and the rider did not even glance at me, but turned to scowl at Junio as he thundered by.

My son raised an eyebrow at me. 'Rude! I wonder who that was? Looked like a courier slave from the message pouch that was slung across his chest.'

'That wasn't merely rude, it was outright dangerous. If I knew whose slave it was, I'd tell his master so. It would earn the man a flogging but – for once – I think it is deserved. He almost ran us down! Though he doubtless prides himself on horsemanship. I wonder where he's going, at such a speed?'

Junio shrugged. 'A messenger for Marcus, possibly? There's not much this way but your patron's villa, after all.'

'Then it's a wasted journey! Marcus was intending to spend the night in town. Though it's possible it is a message for his wife! In which case, let's pray it doesn't bring unpleasant news. Laurentius will make trouble for the family if he can – despite the fact that he's a relative.'

'You think that was his servant? It could be that you're right. Certainly I didn't recognize the face. And he must have had directions, he seemed sure where he was going. Let's just hope he hasn't startled Arlina, or we'll have her bolting off into the woods, dislodging panniers, and it will take an age to find her and reassemble things. I'd better go and see what's happening. Meantime, here's the pond, if you still want to go. Or are you too concerned about that messenger?'

'I'll call on the lady Julia later on, perhaps,' I said. 'I'd like to hear her views about Laurentius, anyway. But since we're here I'll go and look around. I promised Semprius's spirit I would find his murderer, and – as I say – this may be the only opportunity.'

Junio nodded. 'Then I'll find Minimus and then come back for you.' He set off down the track.

I turned towards the pool. From here the banks were always screened from view – even at this leafless time of year – by a curtain of thick branches and scrubby undergrowth. (In summer, one might pass the pond entirely and not realize it was there.) But today the whole hollow was covered in a shroud of winter mist, which had not lifted from low-lying areas all day. However, I had been this way before and soon found the little trampled path down to the water's edge. It was treacherous and slippery after all the rain and I picked my way down it very cautiously – though I could not resist looking out for hoof prints in the mud.

It was ridiculous of course. There had been mention of horse tracks, but there was nothing visible now except a confusion of human footprints and a groove – now half-obscured – which might have been where something had been pulled. Almost certainly the corpse, I told myself – the army death patrol was not renowned for its delicate treatment of dead slaves.

But something about it, instinct told me, was not right. Why was it half-obscured? I stopped, feeling a prickle of cold fear run down my back, and looked again. My impression was correct. The groove was crisscrossed by another, far more recent, set of tracks, that seemed to have been made by a pair of badly hobnailed soles.

Not the army then! Soldiers kept their hobnails in excellent repair. And not the gooseboy who had found the body first – he was unlikely to return in any case, for fear of ghosts, and besides it was unlikely he had proper shoes at all, much less expensive hobnailed ones. Poorer people generally wear the so-called 'rawhide boots', literally a piece of raw hide tied around each foot and left to tan and adapt itself in wear. But there were no signs of such bag-like shoeprints here, nor any of the tracks made by the distinctive webbed feet of his flock. So who else had been this way? Semprius's murderer again perhaps? I caught my breath – tasting the musty tang of fog – and paused. Was it foolish to go on? I'd presumed that this was a private murder – but there might indeed be rebels lingering nearby.

There could hardly be much to learn after all these hours in any case, I thought, especially after the army death patrol had done their worst. Soldiers are not noted for the lightness of their tread. Their cart was wide and heavy, it could not have come down here – but they would have sent a two-man squad, at minimum, to come and fetch the corpse (probably more, to guard their flanks, in case of ambush). Obviously they'd found the body and dragged it after them, paying no attention to where they put their feet – so any useful evidence was probably destroyed.

I sighed and was about to tiptoe back towards the lane – taking pains to make as little sound as possible – when I was halted by the sound of a sudden movement close nearby. Human noises – almost like a splash, the crack of branches, followed by a curse. I froze. Was this the owner of the sandals? Some farmer coming to fetch water for his animals, perhaps? I shook my head.

Once the story of the corpse was out, country people would avoid this place as much as possible, for fear of bringing trouble to their herds – especially when there had been recent rain to fill the water butts. A rebel tribesman, then? Or – it unexpectedly occurred to me – was it perhaps the missing medicus? I was prepared to think that he was behind this whole affair. He must be hiding somewhere – could this be the place?

Well, there was only one way to find out. Cautiously – extremely cautiously – I crept on down the path until I reached a corner where I was half-concealed but could still crane forward and steal a wary look.

I edged my head out from my hiding place and almost cried aloud.

There was a cloaked and hooded figure further down the bank, bending over a group of scrubby bushes in the mist. It was so grey and formless it looked almost like a wraith. I am not a great believer in the ghosts of murdered men coming back to haunt the place where they were killed, but it was enough to make me gasp. In fact I was alarmed enough to take a backward step. Idiot! As I did so I heard a twig snap underneath my feet.

At once the figure straightened up and whirled to look at me. Clearly human – and probably a man, although the hood still hid the face. A moment later I was convinced of that, and of the fact that my attempts to hide had failed. The cloaked man dropped the bundle he was carrying, snatched up a stout staff that he had laid nearby, and lunged towards me with a snarl. And with what was clearly murderous intent!

TWENTY

It was too late for me to duck away, and in any case my aging legs had turned to stone. I raised a pair of helpless hands to shield my face and let out a loud despairing cry, 'Junio! Minimus! Help me! Junio!'

Pointless, of course, my son was out of earshot down the path! But my shout did save me – in an unexpected fashion. The man stopped charging at me, dropped the staff, leaned his head backwards in a bewildered way, then walked towards me, pushing back his hood.

'Councillor Libertus!' I recognized the voice before I registered the face. It was Properus – his handsome face now lighting in a delighted smile. 'Citizen!' He hurried over, seized me by the elbows and pumped both my arms in cordial Roman style. 'For a moment there, you frightened me. It's lucky that I recognized the name of Junio. I feared you were a rebel and about to pounce on me! I was about to hit you with my walking staff!' He let go of my arms and clapped both hands across his heart, as if to still its thumping beat. His voice was breathless, too. 'I might have killed you. Thank all the gods I realized who it was, in time! But this is a surprise. What are you doing here?'

For a moment I was so relieved that I could only gawp. It was Properus, indeed, but not the dapper, confident Properus I had seen before. Though he was smiling, his face looked strained, his blue eyes tired, and his clothing was dishevelled too. The cloak had flown open in his forward rush, revealing a short, stained and crumpled tunic underneath – most unlike his normal neat attire. He seemed more relieved than I was, if that were possible.

I could hardly have been more surprised myself. 'Properus,' I countered. 'I am glad to find you here. We were fearing for your safety.'

'Mine?' He sounded mystified.

'I called on you today to collect my money bags. Your slave invited us to wait, but you did not appear, and in the end he was clearly worried too. He set out to look for you. But I might ask you the same question. What are you doing here?'

He gave me that flickering look again, and shook his head. 'The same thing as you are, councillor, no doubt. Wondering if this is the place where Semprius was killed. I was coming back to Glevum on the military road, but I met the army on a route march exercise. I would have had to stand aside for ages and wait to let them pass, so I asked a passer-by and he directed me down here, but warned me that a body had been found – lest I was superstitious, I suppose. But when he told me it seemed to be a slave – I thought of Semprius, of course. I felt that I must come, if only to purify the place.'

'You had the wherewithal?'

He gestured to the bundle. 'Fortunately I was carrying the herbs and salt that I'd intended to take to Josephus's flat. I wasn't sure, in fact, that the corpse had been removed – my informant didn't know that, I presume – and, if it was Semprius, I was prepared to take it back for burial. But I see that it has gone. Have I to thank you for arranging that?'

I shook my head. 'The army death cart took it earlier today. A gooseboy found him and alerted them. And it was Semprius all right – I went to see the corpse. He's been stripped and robbed – and badly damaged too. They seem to think that rebels were to blame.'

Properus looked thoughtful. 'He had my master's seal-ring too, I think – he had it earlier – though no doubt the robbers will have taken that.' He sighed. 'I don't know what the guild will say, when they find out it's gone. It will probably delay my licence even more. But I sound very selfish, with poor Semprius dead. I was fond of the old man – and he of me, I think.' He turned to me, his handsome face grown grave. 'Was it really Druid raiders, do you think? I understand that's what the army says, but I cannot imagine why rebels would want to kill a harmless aged slave.' He made a rueful face. 'Or for that matter, why anyone should send false messages to me.'

I stared at him. 'And did they?'

He nodded. 'Indeed so, councillor – taking me out of town

for half a day to meet a member of our guild who was not there. That's why I wasn't at my apartment when you called.' He ran an embarrassed hand across his face. 'I was to meet him on the Aqua Sulis road, at the first civilian inn, and he would endorse my application to the guild – but though I waited hours he did not arrive, and I've come to the conclusion that the messenger was false. You're famously skilled at solving mysteries. What is your opinion, citizen?'

He looked so hurt and baffled that I warmed to him. 'I imagine he was hoping for some kind of a reward? As you, no doubt, suspected for yourself? Why else would he have asked you to meet him out of town?'

He spread his hands in a gesture of despair. 'You are as astute as my poor master said you were. I was indeed expecting something of the kind – and I blush to say that I was briefly tempted to agree. I even carried a quantity of gold, sufficient for a bribe' – he gestured vaguely to the bundle on the ground, again – 'but then it occurred to me that this might be a test, and by agreeing I might forfeit my opportunity. But it was all in vain, there was no one there at all.' He frowned. 'Someone clearly wanted to have me out of town – today of all days, when I should have called on Josephus to pay respects. But I can't imagine who. Or why. Unless it was to stop me mingling with members of the guild. They will have called upon my master, by this time, I am sure.'

'Somebody jealous of your success, perhaps? Or there was something which they wanted you to miss? Possibly the arrival of this visitor from Rome.'

'He has come then, has he? I heard that he was due. I know that Josephus was terribly impressed. An ex-Praetorian visiting the town! It is a pity that he did not live to see him come – though people are saying that the man must be a spy.'

'He makes no secret of it,' I agreed. I told the young man briefly about our meeting at the fort. 'Extremely disagreeable and seeking to find fault. I don't think your master would have cared for him at all. And I have been obliged to offer him my flat while he is here, though I don't imagine I shall be thanked for it. And there is more than mere ingratitude to me. He has refused the servants that Marcus Septimus arranged – is threatening to send

them all away, and replace them with a single attendant of his
own. I'm only to leave Fauvus – the best of them – to help him
settle in, then he's to leave as soon as possible. It seems there
have been omens – or warnings of some kind – and he comes
to Glevum half-fearing for his life.'

Properus was staring at me, with a frown. 'So what will
you do with your new servants now?'

'I shall send them to stand vigil at your master's bier, I
suppose – there is no time to sell them before the funeral,
Marcus does not want them, and I've no room for them at
home.'

'My dear Libertus, what a dreadful thing!' He almost placed
a sympathetic hand upon my arm, but he recognized the impro-
priety himself. 'I am sorry, citizen, I am taking liberties. But
I cannot envy you your visitor.' He gave a rueful smile. 'It is
an inconvenience for me as well, I own. I was going to offer
to bring your money bags to your apartment, tomorrow before
noon – in person, to make amends for the delay – but if this
man is there perhaps I'd better not. I do not want to interrupt
those interviews.'

'He'll want to see you, at some time in any case,' I said.
'Along with all the other civic licensees – though what they
can tell him about treason I don't know. So don't look so
reluctant and dismayed. I know you are not fully licensed yet,
but he'll want you all the same – in the absence of Josephus,
I'm sure. But he is promising to come a little before noon. If
you brought the bags round early he would not be there, and
my slaves could take possession of them till I came, myself.
Or you could take them to the workshop, and give them to
my son . . .'

'Father?' It was Junio himself, forcing his way through the
bushes further down and hurrying along the narrow bank to
join us at the pond. 'Minimus thought he heard you call for
help . . . Ah!' he broke off in surprise, as Properus turned to
face him and he realized who it was.

'It is as well he shouted when he did!' Properus declared.
'We have been frightening one another half to death! I almost
felled him with my staff – but fortunately we recognized each
other just in time.'

'Properus had heard about the body here, and thought it might be Semprius,' I explained. 'He didn't realize that the corpse was gone, but he brought some herbs and salt, in any case, to purify the place.'

'I have already sprinkled water where I think he lay,' Properus hastened over to his pack. 'I'll spread a pinch of each of these as well.' He burrowed in the parcel, lifting out a garment of dark-coloured cloth. 'My mourning clothes,' he said. 'I took them off while I was travelling – I thought to show respect – and at that inn. It's not salubrious – I was terrified that I'd be robbed while I was there, especially if I wore expensive clothes. And now look at the state my under tunic's in! And all for nothing in particular.' He frowned at me. 'You don't suppose I need to put the dark robe on again, to do the ritual?'

I shook my head, and he went burrowing again. I turned to Junio, mouthing that I'd tell him the full story later on, and bent to search the scrubby grass beside the lake.

He nodded to indicate that he had understood. 'Father, was there anything to see?'

'If there was, the army has tramped all over it.' I straightened up and explained about the missing seal-ring. 'That's what I'm looking for. But I presume that Semprius must have had it in his pouch. He would hardly have worn it – for one thing that would be presumptuous, and for another he would never keep it on his hand. He was thin and Josephus was plump. Certainly he wasn't wearing it on the bier, when I went to see him at the funeral guild. And I can't see it here.'

Properus looked round at me. 'I hope you took precautions against bringing home a curse? Would you like a little of this salt?' He scattered a pinch of the substance as he spoke, then clambered to his feet, rubbing his hands as if to move the dust.

'Thank you,' I said. 'The guild took care of that. But the gooseboy will be grateful that you've purified this place. Let's hope you've done enough. You can't be sure exactly where the body was.'

He gave me a strange look. 'I think we can be certain, councillor. For one thing you can see the groove where he was dragged away, and for another' – he pointed – 'there is the little matter of the blood.'

'Blood!' I had not seen it, but of course there had to be. Junio was already kneeling, peering at the place – a little hollow space beneath a bush.

'He's quite right, Father,' he exclaimed, lifting the long, darkened leaves of grass, so I could see them for myself. 'Not as much as one might have expected, probably, but it is possible that it has seeped into the ground. It's very damp down here.' He rose, and rubbed the damp earth from his knees and hems, and I realized that Properus and I both bore the self-same stains.

I must be getting old, I told myself. I was no longer noticing the things I should. 'Of course, Properus has already spread water on the place,' I said, sounding weary even to myself. That, no doubt, accounted for the splash. 'Besides, I am sure that Semprius wasn't knifed to death. There are no wounds on the body, I checked for that of course. More likely he was strangled, or struck sharply on the head, but the killers – even if no rebels were involved – clearly wanted to make it look like Druid work. If they did their hacking afterwards, there would not be much blood.'

'Meaning that they cut his head off after he was dead?' Properus put in. 'I hope it happened in that order then, for Semprius's sake. That poor old fellow would not have hurt a flea.' He broke off suddenly. 'I assume that is what happened? Since you spoke of Druids?' He waited for my nod, and then said suddenly, 'I wonder what the robbers did with it – his head, I mean. Took it somewhere to a sacred grove, to hang up as a trophy for the gods, no doubt?'

'Or if they were not Druids, threw it in the pond,' I said, and saw him flinch. 'But whatever they have done with it, it clearly isn't here and there is nothing more that we can do tonight. While you've been doing the purifying rites, I have been looking round and I can see no signs at all that would tell us where the killer – or the killers – went. And if we do not hurry, it will be getting dark.' I turned to Properus. 'And you are unaccompanied and on foot? It might be safer to walk back with us and retrace your steps to meet the major road.

The route march will have cleared by now of course. And the junction with the connecting track is right outside my home.'

Properus smiled. 'Is it, indeed? I did not know. And you are very kind. But—'

Junio interrupted. 'We saw a donkey tethered in among the trees, a short way down the track. Minimus was anxious for the animal, in case it was stolen and abandoned and would not be fed, but I assume it's yours?'

'Mine in the sense that I hired it for the day.'

'Of course,' I said. 'I should have realized that you had done something of the kind. It's a very long way to that civilian inn – too far for you to comfortably walk out there and hope to get back this afternoon in time to call and pay respects to Josephus.'

His smile had broadened. 'You're quite right. And I'm too lazy to go that far on foot. Though I was going to carry the body back to town, if it proved to be Semprius. I could hardly have done that, without an animal. Hard enough, unaided, to get it to the track and lifted up onto the donkey's back – though I thought I'd manage it. Semprius wasn't heavy. He was very thin and slight! But, all the same, the day is drawing on and I would be safer on the military road. I'll go back and join it. And I would be grateful for your company, if you are going that way. I understand that there might be wolves and bears about at night.'

'Or even rebel bands,' I muttered as we scrambled up the path. 'Though – like you – I doubt they were responsible for Semprius's death.' And, I added, inwardly, I still have no idea who was. It had crossed my mind to think of Properus himself, but that wasn't possible. Semprius was killed sometime since the day Josephus died, and – until this morning, when the corpse was already with the guild – Properus had been in Glevum all that time, and there were impartial witnesses to that.

I was still considering all this, when we met up with Minimus, the donkey and the mule, and our little party walked together to my gate.

TWENTY-ONE

Outside my enclosure we paused to say farewells, while Minimus unpacked the panniers and tended to the mule. Junio went next door to his own house and family, but I delayed while Properus positioned his donkey by a tree so that he could mount it and ride away – when we were almost scattered by the galloping return of the horseman we had seen before.

This time, however, he looked back as he passed, then checked the horse and wheeled it expertly around before bringing it abruptly to a stop, a dozen paces down the lane from us. As he slithered smoothly to the ground, the hood of his great cape fell backwards and revealed his face, and I saw to my amazement that it was none other than the handsome slave I'd seen at Properus's flat.

I was astonished at his expertise – few slaves can ride like that, even those specifically employed as couriers – but I was in no mood for compliments.

'Scito!' I said, sharply. 'You should take more care! You almost caused a serious accident out there in the woods, to both my son and me. If we hadn't jumped aside you would have run us down. And I'm saying so in your master's hearing, because I think he ought to know.'

The slave ignored this and went straight to Properus. I realized he was seriously distressed, as he dropped to one knee and murmured in an agitated way, 'Master! I have been riding up and down, searching for you everywhere. I did not know what to do!'

He was so clearly frantic that Properus held out a soothing hand to him. 'There is no problem, Scito. I was delayed, that's all – that message this morning proved to be a false alarm – and then I diverted from the track on the way home, because I'd heard that a slave's body had been found. Shockingly, it was Semprius, I'm afraid – this councillor had verified the

fact.' He assisted his – still shaken – slave to rise. 'He's a
lucky man, in fact – when he came to the site, I thought he
was a threat, and very nearly felled him with my staff.
Fortunately, I stopped myself in time! Don't look so worried,
Scito, he took no offence, in fact he helped me search while
I purified the place. But there was nothing to be learned.'

Scito turned and looked malevolently at me, but then I saw
a dawning comprehension in his eyes. It seemed he had not
recognized me, in my humble garb, as the smart decurion he'd
encountered earlier. He gave me a curt nod and turned back
to Properus. 'But it's getting urgent, master. The day is almost
gone and it will be too late to act. I was looking out for
you, but you see how it has been' – he made a hopeless
gesture with his hands – 'I had to do something, so I rode
out here hoping to find you somewhere on the r—'

'Urgent?' Properus spoke sharply, suddenly. 'That message
that you're carrying? Let me see!' He stretched out a demanding
hand.

Scito glanced doubtfully at me, but he obeyed. He took the
pouch from where he had it slung across his chest, opened
the drawstring, and produced a small but handsome writing-
block. The ribbon tie had been secured with a seal.

Properus seized it, tore free the ribbon, and glanced at the
message scratched into the wax. 'Great Jupiter!' He closed it
with a snap. 'Forgive me, citizen. It is imperative I hurry back
to town. There have been developments.'

'Regarding your future as argentarius?'

'Exactly, citizen. I am summoned to meet important
members of the guild – they have been seeking me all day,
apparently – and if I do not hurry I will be too late. I fear I
may already be so – that false message has neatly seen to
that.' He gave me a little bow. 'You are perspicacious, citizen.
You suggested that the motive was something of the kind.'

I murmured some acknowledgement.

He smiled and turned back to his slave again. 'You have
done well, Scito. It was intelligent of you to have hired a
horse – the circumstances clearly merit the expense. And you
did especially well to find me. Did one of the soldiers tell
you that I had come this way?' He did not pause for a reply.

'However you contrived it, I am very glad you're here. I took the precaution of carrying this staff – as you can see – in case of meeting wolves or other animals, but now you can take it and guard me on the road. You'll manage it on horseback more easily than I, and it's still possible we may have need of it – judging by what happened to that poor old slave. Though, as the duumvir suggested, we'll take the main road home.'

Scito nodded slowly, looking much relieved. He assisted his master to his mount, then leapt up easily onto his own, and I stood and watched them as they moved away – an ill-assorted pair – deep in discussion as they trotted down the lane. I was still watching when my wife came out to me.

'Husband,' she said, briskly. 'I am glad to see you home. There have been such dreadful rumours. I was concerned for you. And then that horseman riding up and down as if Cerebos himself was snapping at his heels!'

'Rumours?' I said, feigning innocence – although I could guess, of course. The discovery of Semprius's corpse was clearly common knowledge now. Nevertheless I allowed myself to be propelled indoors, where Gwellia waved the waiting slaves away and came to help me with my cloak, herself – an indication of how worried she had been.

'There are tales of headless bodies discovered in the woods,' she told me, moving a pot of stew to the trivet on the fire, and pulling my stool forward so I could sit beside the blaze. 'The women were talking of it at the spring, today, when Tenuis and I went to gather rushes for the bed. People say the rebels must be active here again. Then someone came rushing from a visit to the town with a story that she heard from the sentry on watch, that Marcus's cousin – to whom you've lent our flat! – is not a simple visitor at all, but an Imperial spy! And he's here to deal with reports of treason in the town, and wants to question all the members of the curia!' She began to ladle warm stew into a bowl. 'Is any of it true?'

'I'm afraid it is.' I sat down by the fire, and gave her a gently edited account of the major happenings of the day. I even alluded to my visit to Comux and his friends – saying that I'd asked them about Josephus – though claiming interest only in how he came to fall, and what he might have hoped to say to me that day.

Gwellia rounded on me, much to my surprise. 'I wonder at your judgement, husband!' she exclaimed. 'Wandering into a questionable warehouse, on your own – without a slave! And taking time to go and see the corpse of that old Semprius as well, when you know we are expecting an important visitor. And one who is alleged to be the Emperor's private spy!'

'I'm not surprised that story's reached the gossips,' I remarked, glad to change the subject. 'He makes no secret of the fact, or what he's come about. So I'll have to leave early in the morning, to be sure of getting to the flat before he comes to take up residence.'

'And what about the money Properus wants to bring?'

'I'll have to get that to Junio, I suppose – back where it began – though at least we didn't leave it unguarded overnight.' I broke off as Gwellia handed me my meal. 'It's only a pity Josephus is dead. I might have thought of giving him a portion to invest – he used to charge commission, but one did get interest! And he was very shrewd.'

I said this in case there were rumours about his new invest-ment plans, but if they existed, Gwellia had not heard. 'Do you think you ought to wear your formal toga again tomorrow, husband?' she enquired. 'If you have to meet with this Laurentius for a second time? It might persuade him to treat you with a little more respect.' She took up the spoon and began to serve herself. 'Not that he pays much attention to curial rank, from what you say.'

'All the same,' I answered, 'it would be a good idea. There are other people who might be impressed.' Such as the town watch, I thought, if I were accused. Aloud I said, 'It's already packaged up and fairly clean. Those new servants cleaned the hems for me today. I will take it as it is and put it on when I arrive. Make sure I'm waking early.'

She certainly did that. When she roused me it was not yet dawn, and the roundhouse was still dark and chilly as I pushed the covers back, though Gwellia already had a taper lit, and had poked the embers into life and stoked the fire. A smell of baking oatcakes filled the air. My favourite morning snack! I sat up reluctantly and rubbed my eyes.

'At your service, master!' Minimus was waiting by the bed with my overtunic and sandals, prepared to help me dress, and Kurso, the little kitchen slave, was also standing by with a bowl of fresh cold water in which to rinse my face. There was nothing for it, but to rise. And go to face Laurentius, and whatever threat he posed!

I groaned and swung my bare legs to the floor. The slaves sprang into action instantly, and a short time later I was washed and clothed and sitting by the fire while Gwellia withdrew the baking tray, shaking the remaining embers from the lid before tipping the fresh oatcakes onto a wooden plate.

My fragrant meal, washed down with a cup of water from the spring, revived my spirits enough for me to say, 'Minimus, you can come with me, with the mule. It isn't light yet, so you'd better fetch a birch-bark torch to light our way – I know we made a batch of them some moons ago, and I think there are a few left out in the dyeing hut. And Kurso, you can call on Junio, at first light, to tell him not to wait for us today. I'll bring the money to the workshop when it comes, so I will see him then.'

Kurso was grinning hugely at me. 'Master, there should be no need for that. He knows you're leaving early and he plans to come with you. His slave was here to say so a little while ago – they were up with the children and they saw the lights.'

I nodded. Junio and Cilla had two small children now, the youngest small enough to still be cutting teeth, so it was no surprise to learn that they were stirring at this hour. 'I shall be glad to have his company,' I said.

I was doubly glad, when he met us at the gate a short time afterwards, because not only had he brought a second lighted torch, but his was a superior Roman lime-and-sulphur one which was not affected by the drizzle (unlike our homemade version, which sputtered out, leaving only a wisp of smelly smoke, long before the sun was fully up).

There was not much daylight, even then. The sun was wholly hidden by the clouds and – apart from the persistent misty rain – the wind was very chill. I hunched myself further into my hooded cloak, but – though it kept me dry – it could not protect me from curiosity. When we reached the town gates I was hailed at once by the sentry on guard.

'Greetings! Duumvir Libertus, isn't it? Not a pleasant day. Pity it isn't officially ill-omened, so you could have stayed at home. Though I hear today's a bad one anyway, for all the curia.'

I muttered something in reply, and hurried on. The story of Laurentius's summons was clearly all around the town – it had been announced in the forum yesterday, of course – and there were whispering huddles on every street corner. I was anxious to reach the sanctuary of my flat as soon as possible. So, pausing only to take my precious parcel from the mule, I left Junio to hurry to the workshop, and Minimus to go and lodge the animal, while I went upstairs to my apartment to put the toga on. There were a few top-floor residents to greet me as I passed – on their way to market stalls or preparing to hawk some product round the streets – but the daytime idlers had not yet amassed, and it took me very little time to reach my door.

But when I did so – expecting to be greeted by my giant new doorkeeper – I was surprised, again. This time there was no answer whatever to my knock.

I rapped again, more loudly, wondering if – by some mischance, the slaves had failed to wake. Still there was no response. I was beginning to consider if I should try the door, when I heard the sound of footsteps on the stairs, and turned to see Fauvus hurrying up them from the street.

'Master!' he panted. 'Forgive me that I was not here to welcome you. You've heard the news, of course? Laurentius has changed his mind again, and has decided to move in here at once. I received a message earlier to move all your servants out, at once, so I took them over to Josephus's apartment, with instructions to assist in the lamentation at the bier and follow his body to the pyre. We've taken everything that was supplied for us. I hope that was in order?'

'Thank you, Fauvus. You have done very well.'

He gave me his slow, self-deprecating smile. 'The message said that we were all to go, and I should stay there, too, until he sent for me. But I am your servant and my duty is to you.

I knew that you would come and expect to find me here. Besides, I doubted you'd have warning of his change of plan – there was hardly time to send a message to your house – so I hurried back, hoping to find you before he should arrive.'

I nodded. This servant was a model of what a slave should be, full of initiative and helpfulness. I was going to miss him when Laurentius was gone: he'd made himself so useful in the last few hours I was already wondering if I could contrive to make him permanent – despite what Minimus might feel.

What I said aloud, however, was: 'All the same, I can't conveniently walk away at once. Properus is promising to bring me my money bags, and I foolishly told him he would find me here. Though we did agree that he should come as early as he could.' I sighed. 'I'll have to stay here till the money comes – though I don't know what Laurentius is going to say to that. I was planning to take it over to my son, so we could carry it in the mule-panniers tonight.'

Fauvus smiled. 'In that case, master, I have good news for you. I have just seen Properus and his servant in the street. I thought they had been visiting the early market stalls – which is doubtless the impression they intend. They have a hired handcart with them, and an urchin pulling it – though the load is covered with a woollen rug. If there is money, rather than produce, underneath, as I now suspect, then at this hour it is a good disguise.'

I could see his reasoning. 'That slave said yesterday that lots of angry citizens had come up to the flat demanding what was due. Obviously they are delivering it now.'

'And they're not far away, so they should not be long with yours. There's every chance they'll get here before Laurentius does. I couldn't lock the flat, Laurentius has the key.'

He stepped past me and opened up the door.

'Thank you, Fauvus,' I said, gratefully, though I glanced quickly round the apartment as I spoke. But nothing had been stolen, as far as I could see. 'I'll be prepared to move out instantly. Just come and help me put my toga on, and when the money comes you can go and hire a carrying-chair for me. There'll be no problem in affording it, by then, and the bags are too heavy to carry on my own.'

I took my precious toga from its bag, raised my arms – like the pampered councillor I was becoming – and permitted him to wind the garment onto me. He was skilled and swift, and when he had finished the folds felt more secure than any other toga I had ever worn.

'You had better stay here until Laurentius comes – though, on second thoughts, didn't he tell you that he might send to Josephus's for you? He might wish you to escort him here. In which case, join the others at the bier, and I will join you there as soon as possible. When I have my money I'll be able to make sure Florea can send out for a meal for all of you, and herself as well – I doubt she'll have sufficient in her house. And I'll work out where you're all going to sleep tonight.' It might have to be on my workshop floor, I thought.

'Should we take some sort of offering?' Fauvus said.

'Oh, and I've got a phial of something here, which should go on the pyre.' I took the little bottle from its hiding place – taking great care not to disturb the toga tucks (though I need not have been concerned: they had been arranged to leave access to my purse). 'I'll bring it when I come. But first, I want to call in at the medicus again, to see if I can find out what it is – though I don't greatly trust his expertise. I didn't have time to do it yesterday, but – if Laurentius lets me go – there should be no problem in doing it today.'

Fauvus smiled. 'I'll take it for you, master. It would save you the walk.' He saw my doubtful look. 'I'll ask him to write and seal his findings if you would prefer.'

'I'm sure you're to be trusted,' I told him with a smile. 'I'll leave it here, and you can take it if there's time.' I put it on a handsome onyx table by the wall – one of the items my patron had provided yesterday. 'But find a litter first, and have it standing by. I know it's an expense. But if Laurentius is summoning all the councillors to visit here today, chairs are likely to be in short supply. And I will need one for carrying the cash. I can always take the phial to the medicus myself.' I sat down on one of the two new, exquisite stools.

He bowed politely. 'At your service, master.' And he went out, leaving me alone.

Or so I genuinely thought.

TWENTY-TWO

Fauvus seemed to be taking an unconscionable time fetching the litter and after a few minutes I grew tired of sitting there. I was impatient, too, for Properus to come, so that I could vacate the flat completely before Laurentius came. No matter that the change of plan was his, I was extremely anxious about displeasing him. The last thing I wanted was to have him find me here.

I found myself actually pacing up and down, though willing myself to keep away from the balcony, where I could be seen from the crowded street below and thus become a public spectacle. So I was very pleased to hear the echoing sound of footsteps running up the stairs followed by a tapping at the door.

In the absence of attendants I answered it myself, but it was neither of the men that I was waiting for. It was only little Minimus, reporting that he'd arranged to leave the mule with the hiring stables just outside the gate.

'They've actually got room for her inside today, because several of their animals are out on long-term hire. So Arlina won't be stuck out in their muddy field. And when I asked them what the cost would be, they said that it was free for councillors.' He gave me a cheeky grin. 'Though they hoped you would remember who'd been helpful now and then, next time you wanted to hire transport anywhere.'

I was in no mood for banter. 'Never mind all that,' I told him gracelessly. 'We need to be ready to vacate this place as soon as possible. Everything of mine has already been removed – including my new servants, as you can no doubt see. I even took my damp clothes home with me last night.'

Minimus frowned. 'What about my tunic, master? Has that gone as well? I left it yesterday, together with my cloak, because they had got wet. I exchanged with one of the other slaves – your patron ordered it. I thought I was going to change it back today, but has the new slave now taken it as his?'

I looked at him, ashamed to realize he was right. Minimus was wearing something we'd not given him. We've never dressed our servants in any shade of puce – largely because Gwellia spins and weaves most cloth herself and the mordant for puce dye is an expensive one. But I had been so concerned with other things I hadn't noticed this till now, although he must have worn his borrowed garment overnight.

'I don't know what's become of your damp clothes,' I told him gruffly. 'The household all left here before I came. You'd better go and check. While you are about it, look in every room. I don't want to leave things here for Laurentius to find.' Especially not wet slaves' uniforms, I thought.

Minimus nodded and scurried off to search. I heard him, in the inner corridor, opening and shutting doors to the slave quarters and the storage rooms – apparently with no success, because he did not pause.

It was quite a large apartment (naturally, since it was designed to meet the size requirements for election to the curia) and – equally naturally – it was laid out to please wealthy Roman tastes. So apart from the small cell in the entrance corridor, intended as a waiting area for doorkeepers and slaves, and the large exedra where I was waiting now, there were several further rooms within, lying off a central passageway.

The left side had no windows and was relatively cramped, with a little study (which I used for meeting supplicants, but which could double as a sleeping room for guests) a copious storage room and a rather airless sleeping cell for slaves, (though that had not been a problem for me until yesterday). On the right was the attractive owner's suite – adjoining but separate bedrooms for the man and wife, with shuttered window-spaces overlooking the communal courtyard at the back, with its water fountain and convenient latrine. Those were the rooms that had been readied for Laurentius's use.

Though it was fairly pointless looking there, I thought. I had inspected those rooms only yesterday and not only were they stripped of everything of ours, they had been most energetically scrubbed and cleaned. But I'd instructed my young slave to make a thorough search and I heard his obedient footsteps move in that direction – and abruptly stop.

'Master!' If I had not known that it was Minimus, I would scarcely have recognized the voice. It was high with some emotion – suspiciously like shock. 'Master, I think you'd better come.'

I hastened to investigate. All sorts of dreadful possibilities were flashing through my mind. The flat had, after all, been unsecured. Had Marcus's new, expensive furniture been stolen – or destroyed? Had someone thrown ordure through the window-space? (Such things were not unknown – and people might go to surprising lengths when Imperial spies were due to stay!) Or, despite the frantic cleaning of the day before, was it possible that a rat – or something similar – had crawled in there and died? Any of these would be a dreadful augury, of course, and Laurentius would be justified in blaming me.

I hurried to join Minimus at my bedroom door.

It was not a rat, of course. If only it had been half so innocent! There was the ex-Praetorian himself, and he was clearly dead. Nor could this conceivably have been an accident. The ligature which killed him was still around his neck – the cord belt of his own dark travelling tunic, by the look of it.

He had been ugly yesterday – he was more ugly now, with his pig-like face mottled, his pale-blue eyeballs bloodshot and bulging from their lids and his throat scratched where his frantic fingers had clawed to free the cord. The bed and bedclothes were in hopeless disarray, as if he had been thrust struggling and lurching onto it – but otherwise the sleeping room was unnaturally neat.

His patrician toga was folded on the stool, as if in readiness for him to put on; a little travelling *lararium* had been set up in the niche beside the door, complete with tiny statues of his household deities; and (bizarrely for a bedroom in a private residence) there were signs that he'd been drinking – and not alone. On a chest beside the window was a fine glass barrel-jug, still half-full of wine, and two used goblets standing next to it, though there was no sign of any amphora from which the wine had come. Nor, of course, of whoever his companion might have been.

I do not often panic, but I did so now. For a long moment I was too terrified to move – the death of an Imperial

representative obviously spelt trouble of the most appalling
kind. The courts, even if one were not handed over to appear
in Rome, dared not be lenient. The punishment was likely to
be exile at best, deprivation of fire and water throughout the
Empire – on pain of death for anyone providing it. Or something
far, far worse. Furthermore, it was certain that some guilty party
would be produced and charged, even if on the slimmest evidence
– anything else was likely to bring down the Emperor's wrath
upon the town concerned.

And the authorities would not have far to look. The garrison
commander had witnessed for himself the veiled threats
towards my patron (and myself) made by the murdered man,
and that – together with the fact that the crime had happened
on my property – was already halfway to confirming that I'd
had a hand in it.

Unless I could prove otherwise. Conclusively and as fast as
possible. Preferably by producing a better candidate.

I took a deep breath and walked towards the corpse.
Minimus, who was busy rubbing spit behind his ears in a
hopeless effort to ward off both ill-luck and ghosts, looked at
me in frank astonishment. But I ignored the omens and bent
forward to lift one lifeless hand. Already cold, but not remotely
stiff – Marcus's unpleasant relative was only newly dead.

I drew in a breath between my gritted teeth. This was
more troubling than if he had been dead for hours. I could
have provided several witnesses – including the sentry at the
gate – to say that I had not been in the town until a short time
earlier. But obviously this must have happened very recently
– Laurentius had clearly been alive when he set off from the
garrison, and that could not have been till after the morning
muster call. Which made it far harder to prove my innocence,
and much more likely that I'd end my days starving to death
on some far-off barren rock. All for a crime that I did not
commit.

But think! Since I had not killed him, who else could have
done?

My first thought was that his servant must have turned on
him. Presumably that worthy had arrived, since Laurentius had
spoken of waiting for him to appear before he moved into the

flat – and no doubt he'd found his master in impatient mode. I could imagine the Praetorian being so continuously difficult to please – and so cruel and capricious in his choice of punishment – that it might drive any man to desperate things. In fact, if there was a slave about, he was already guilty according to the law. There was no sign of him attempting to protect his master from attack – as he should have done, or died in the attempt – nor even that anyone had rushed out to the street to raise the alarm.

But I was frowning as I straightened up. My convenient theory was, at best, improbable. Not so much because the punishments for hericide were so severe – this slave was liable to be condemned to death for failing in his duty, as it was! – but because Laurentius was a Roman patrician, through and through. There must have been another person here. He would never have consented to drink in company with a man of humble rank, let alone a person of no rank at all. And a slave was not officially even that – not a person, but a chattel, a sort of household tool.

A professional poison taster, then? Hired to protect him while he was in the town? Such people did exist. Our visitor was clearly a suspicious man (with reason, it appeared!) and the garrison commander could no doubt have found him someone desperate enough to agree – for a pittance – to accept the risk! I shook my head, again. A man with any sense requires his pregustator to drink out of his cup, not merely taste his wine – poison is too easily spread upon the rim. An ex-Praetorian, of all people, would be alert to that. But who else would be invited into his private sleeping room? And where, in any case, was the Roman's slave?

That question, at least, was answered – almost instantly.

'Master?' Minimus had slipped out behind me – still fearing ghosts, no doubt, and terrified by my interference with the corpse – and reappeared now round the door from the adjoining room. 'There's a dead man in here, as well.'

There was. It was the slave, of course, as one could see at once from the elaborate uniform – and he'd been despatched with less efficiency. He was a big man, muscular although no longer young (possibly a veteran, as one might expect from the travelling attendant of an Imperial spy) and he had clearly struggled as he died. It looked as if he had been sitting on a stool, facing the connecting door – ready to be summoned – as any slave would do, and had been unexpectedly set on from behind.

His arms were tied behind his back, and something had been pulled tight around his neck – a red line showed clearly where it had tried to throttle him – but evidently his struggles had prevented that, and he had fallen sideways on the floor. There – judging by the bloodstains congealing round him now, and the curious carved hilt which still stuck out of his back – the dagger that killed him had been plunged with force between his shoulder blades, ruining both his handsome tunic and the brand new woven rug.

Curiously, it looked as if he had been drinking, too. That made me pause and think. Servants do not generally drink on duty, anyway, unless by special dispensation from their masters, and rarely do they share their owner's wine. Yet it looked as if exactly that had happened here. A coarse pottery wine cup (which I recognized as mine) lay upturned, cracked but otherwise unharmed, with liquid drops still clinging to the sides.

Though it seemed the contents had not been willingly consumed. The slave's head had been forced backwards while he lived and – from the still-forming bruises round his nose, the foam around the lips and the dribbled vomit running down the chin – it appeared that someone had blocked his nostrils up and, when he gasped for breath, had forced the liquid into his protesting mouth.

I looked around, but again there was no amphora, or any other wine container in this room – I checked inside the little cupboard by the wall, but there was nothing there at all.

And, wherever it had come from, the drink had not been mine! I had put some little delicacies, like Roman cheese and figs, in the storeroom as a courtesy to my guest – and a pail of fresh well water, naturally – but at Marcus's suggestion I had left no wine. I rarely drank it and was no judge of quality, so he'd refused to let me purchase any for my visitor, saying that his cousin would have 'sophisticated tastes', and promising to take him to the vintners later on. So this was nothing I'd provided – though I might find that hard to prove. But was it the same liquid as in the jug next door?

I put an exploratory finger into the drops left in the cup. There was a trace of sediment, which looked – and smelt – like wine, though there was an overtone of something I could not identify. I was about to taste it, when my slave tugged at my arm.

'Master, it may be poisoned.'

I paused. The boy was right to be hesitant, of course, but – as I pointed out to him – neither of these victims had been killed by poisoning.

'Yet it seems the killer was anxious to make the servant drink.'

I nodded. 'And the master was clearly lured into doing so, before he died. But why?' I touched the drop of liquid to my tongue, ready for burning sensations – or even worse – but there was nothing of the kind. In fact – though there was a slightly bitter aftertaste and a trace of the lees that Marcus was so contemptuous of – it was not dissimilar to some imported wines, that I'd been forced to drink at one or two official banquets recently.

'You see?' I said to Minimus, and downed the remainder of the lees to prove my point, and in some spirit of experiment. It had occurred to me it might include a sleeping draught. However, there was no discernable effect.

I should have known better. Not even the strongest poppy juice could possibly produce any real result in so short a time. It must have been a short time, too – no longer than an hour. Fauvus had barely managed to take my slaves across the town and get back here again before I met him outside in the street. And Laurentius had not been here when he left.

Or so he said. For the first time since I met my model servant, I began to doubt. The timing of events seemed too fortuitous. How – without a spy within the household – could a murderer possibly have known when my apartment was going to be devoid of slaves? Or even that it was going to be devoid of them, at all? And, more importantly perhaps, how could anyone have identified precisely that brief, overlapping period when my slaves were gone, but Laurentius and his servant had arrived – and so were conveniently alone?

Someone must have told the killer when it was safe to strike – and who but Fauvus could have done so? He alone had received the notification that Laurentius was coming earlier than planned. Indeed, I only had his word that the request to move my slaves had ever come at all. Furthermore, thanks to my instructions of the day before, Fauvus – alone – had the freedom to move unescorted and unquestioned round the town.

So he was the only person who could have passed on the news that Laurentius was in my flat and with a single guard! Supposing that he was not himself the murderer! Until now I had not thought of that! But a warrior, from Dacia – where Pescennius Niger had such strong support? And one who was known to have possessions of his own – including possibly a stoppered jug?

Once that had occurred to me, a lot of things made sense.

'Master?' Minimus cut across my thoughts. 'Shouldn't we try to purify the place in case of ghosts? And send a message to the garrison?'

We should do exactly that, of course. The latter thing at least. This was no matter merely for the watch. But I did not want a squad of guards arriving at my flat before I'd had the time to work out – if possible – what had happened here. At the moment, I had no proof of anything.

'Of course we must,' I answered, trying to think fast. 'But not at once, perhaps. First I think that we should let my patron know. Laurentius was a member of his family after all.'

Minimus looked much relieved. 'It would be right for him to close the eyes, at least, put a coin in his mouth to pay the ferryman, and call his name in case the spirit lurks. I'd feel a good deal happier if that was done.'

I had quite different reasons for wanting Marcus here, but I nodded. 'His Excellence spent the night at his apartment, I believe, so if you hurry you should find him there. He was expecting to meet with me this afternoon. Tell him that Libertus needs him, urgently, and it concerns his relative. You need not tell him what has happened here – this is serious, and at his flat there are too many listening ears. Just say that something has occurred which he should know about at once. Can you remember that?'

Minimus nodded. He could hardly wait to repeat my message back to me – word for word, as he'd been trained to do – so that he could hurry off and deliver it. I could understand his eagerness. He did not care for corpses, especially murdered ones.

I watched him go, and had turned back to examine Laurentius's dead slave before it occurred to me that I had – in all likelihood – just contrived to make things worse. It was certain that Marcus would take his own, patrician time. Meanwhile, if Properus arrived, as he was due to do, he would find me entirely alone with these two murdered men. That would obviously look bad. Minimus could vouch for me, of course – it was he who'd found the men – but he would not be here until Marcus was, and even then his testimony would be of little help. And I'd like to save him the necessity of giving it. Slaves were expected to lie to save their masters, so he'd be routinely tortured if he was called upon.

Though the same went for Fauvus, I thought confusedly – unless he was in the pay of the authorities. Which seemed improbable. Was I mad to suspect him of having killed my visitor? Could he have been acting in my defence perhaps? Laurentius had made no secret of his contempt for me, or of wanting to interrogate me first. On a question of 'treason' too, for which the penalty is death, even for the most high-born of citizens.

Or for Dacian warriors with a grudge!

I shook my head. I'd wanted to think the best of Fauvus because I'd formed a high opinion of his intelligence, and that fact was interfering with my reasoning. He was the only person who knew exactly when Laurentius would be undefended here. But . . . I checked myself again. Four murders in as many days – surely that could not be a mere coincidence? And though Fauvus might be responsible for these two deaths today, he could hardly have murdered either Josephus or his slave. He was not even in the town when they were killed.

Or could I really be certain even about that? Granted that he'd been purchased at the slave market just the day before – I had Marcus's own testimony for the truth of that – but anyone can put a servant up for sale. Our local dealer is not notably discreet and had no doubt boasted of his wealthy customer. Suppose that Fauvus's previous owner was not dead at all, but was a local man, who had discovered that my patron wanted slaves to serve Laurentius and deliberately ensured that his own clever servant was among the merchandise? A traitor, who had reason to fear the presence of the spy, and so arranged that Fauvus should be attending him?

Once I considered it, that made a lot of sense. Fauvus had made a point of telling me that he did not know the town, but he'd found his way about it with considerable skill. Including finding me at the warehouse of Comux and his friends. I'd put that down to his intelligence, but perhaps his cleverness was of a different kind. Suppose that he already knew the place? Had lived there, possibly? Hadn't he told me that his previous owner was an importer? And Boudoucus had spoken of their household having recently disposed of all their slaves!

That would certainly give Fauvus a link to Josephus!

Which sparked another thought. The description of the elusive medicus – olive-skinned, well spoken, slightly foreign-sounding and intelligent – all that fitted Fauvus perfectly. It had not occurred to me before that 'the doctor' might simply be an educated slave, but of course that would be more than possible. Many private doctors were effectively just that, although they were officially 'employed' rather than being in servitude. Furthermore, I suddenly recalled, one of the 'imported luxuries' his owner traded in, had been exotic herbs, so Fauvus was likely to be familiar with their curative effects – and, presumably, their less attractive ones. Why had I not made the connection earlier?

So what was in that phial I had been carrying? There was no chance now to ask that question of the medicus. Perhaps I should have made the same enquiry of my new slave! And was it the same liquid as in the jug and drinking vessels here? Interesting that he'd been so anxious to take it from the flat!

I went back into the exedra and picked up the little phial, and took it back to where Laurentius lay. Not even looking at the figure on the bed, I dipped a finger into each of the two goblets on the tray. That distinctive bitter, gritty, aftertaste again. I fumbled the stopper from the little flask I'd got from Florea, and sampled that. The flavour was the same.

I squatted on my haunches. That seemed, past question, to link these deaths with Josephus. But if this was not poison – as it obviously was not – whatever could it be? The 'medicus' had claimed it was a potent sleeping draught, but I did not seem to have taken harm from it. Emboldened – and a little thirsty, now – I took a mouthful from the jug as well. Clearly the same mixture, but what part could it have played? And even if Fauvus had provided it, what motive could he possibly have for those earlier two deaths?

I shook my head again, smiling at my own stupidity. If Fauvus was working with his master, as I must now assume – then, according to my theory, one or both were guilty of treason of some kind. Support for Pescennius, perhaps? I remembered that cargo in the warehouse which Comux and his partners were at such pains to hide from me. What was it they were trying to export? Or import, possibly? It seemed to be alive. Snakes? Rebels? Some unknown animals with toxic bites to poison enemies? So many things were possible.

But suppose, whatever they were plotting, Josephus learnt of it, and – hopeful of reward – had notified the treason to the Emperor in Rome? Had he made the error of letting that be known, attempting to warn off the conspirators? Florea had spoken of her master sending 'lots of messages' in the days before he died. And many messages (like the one that I'd just sent to Marcus) were carried verbally. Of course! That would explain why Semprius had to die – if he were carrying a word-for-word reply to Josephus. Offering to bribe him into secrecy, perhaps? (It would have to be a verbal message, I theorized – there was no reason otherwise to kill the aged slave, who would (or could) not read a written one.) But suppose the sender then found out, too late, that an Imperial spy was on his way and realized that his words incriminated him . . .?

A pattern was emerging which suddenly made sense – both of events and when they had occurred. But how could I prove any part of this?

I was still frowning over this when there was a noise outside. Someone had come, uninvited, right into the flat and was making the wooden floorboards creak in the reception room.

TWENTY-THREE

'**M**aster?' A silky, cultured voice was calling me. Fauvus! I felt the hairs on the back of my neck stand up. It seemed important that he did not find me here. If he was capable of throttling an ex-Praetorian and stabbing a healthy military guard, I thought, what might he do to an aging man like me? Oh, why had I been so anxious to send Minimus away? For the first time I understood the Roman principle that a citizen must have trusted slaves around him at all times.

If only Marcus or Properus would come! I should be safe enough once someone else arrived. But though Properus was expected there was no sign of him, and I could not realistically expect my patron for some time. Marcus, like any Roman of high rank, always leaves visitors to wait before receiving them – longer if they are merely slaves, like Minimus. Then it would take Marcus some little time to dress – and his apartment was several streets away.

So what was I to do? Perhaps – I reasoned desperately – if I met Fauvus out in the reception room and didn't mention what had happened here, I could persuade him to betray himself by demonstrating that he already knew about the deaths.

'I'm coming,' I answered, trying to sound as casual as possible, but aware that my voice was wavering. Panic seemed to have taken the power from my limbs but somehow I stumbled to my feet and out to the passage, meaning to shut the doors upon Laurentius and his slave – at least until my patron should arrive. But Fauvus had been too quick for me. He was already behind me at the bedroom door.

'Master!' he said again. 'I could not find a vacant litter, I'm afraid . . .' He broke off, looking past me at the crumpled corpse. His face composed into a mask of shock. 'What has been happening?'

A man of many talents, I thought bitterly. I had learned

yesterday, when he was telling me the story of that woman on the stairs, how cleverly he could change his voice and act a part. As he was doing now.

'Master, is that who I think it is?' Not only did his tone of voice convey surprise, he was skilfully suggesting that he'd never seen Laurentius in his life before, and therefore this must be my handiwork. Or had that been his intention all along? Not to kill me, but to see that I received the blame for this?

I decided that bluntness was my best defence. 'Laurentius has been murdered,' I replied, and added in a futile effort to dissociate myself, 'an informer will always have secret enemies, I suppose, and Laurentius fairly boasted that he was working as a spy. And this is the result. Someone in the town has killed him, and recently at that.'

I looked at Fauvus as I made that last remark, hoping it might startle him – if not into incriminating words, at least into showing by his face that I was near the truth. I was disappointed.

'Unfortunate for you that it should happen here. No wonder, master, that you're looking flushed. But did he not have his servant to protect him? I thought that we were told he was to bring one here.'

That 'we' was an especially clever touch, I thought. 'He did. The servant's dead as well.' I gestured to the adjoining room, and Fauvus stepped away to glance in there as well.

'Stabbed *and* poisoned?' He emphasized the 'and', thus managing both to appear increasingly astonished by events, and to imply that – in a single glance – he'd taken in all the important details of the scene. He was silent for a moment, then: 'Should someone be informed? The garrison, perhaps? I can see that you are far too shaken to go out yourself, but I am at your service, naturally, should you want a messenger.'

I was tempted. It was clearly wise to notify the guard. And Fauvus could not safely accuse me to the garrison – as my slave he would certainly be tortured to ensure he spoke the truth, whether he spoke against me or in my defence. But if he left these premises I did not trust him not to simply disappear, and then I'd never prove that he was liable. (One must produce the man accused to the authorities, in person, or there is no case.)

I shook a stubborn head. 'I've sent for Marcus. He should be on his way. This man was, after all, his relative. He will decide what it is best to do. In the meantime, let us shut this door and go back out to the reception room. There is nothing to be gained by staying here.'

In fact, I wanted to go back into the sleeping rooms and have a closer look, in case there was anything else of interest to be gleaned, but I did not want Fauvus to accompany me. Too easy for him to discretely tamper with the evidence – remove anything incriminating him, or introduce some spurious clue suggesting me!

Fauvus looked reluctant and – I thought – concerned. Perhaps there really was something in the room I'd missed. I was just considering how to deal with this, when he said suddenly, 'As you command, of course. But you're looking very dazed. Perhaps you should come outside and sit down. Though I fear you won't have privacy for long. I encountered Properus outside in the street. He is about to call here – indeed he's at the door. I suggested he should wait there while I announced that he was here. He has that money with him, I believe. Do you wish me to go and tell him he should go away? Or ask him to call again this afternoon? There can be no urgency about his visit now. And, as I say, you're obviously shocked.'

Anyone was entitled to be shocked, I thought, if he became convinced that the servant he had trusted was a murderer. And one with enough intelligence – and experience of war – to vary his methods of attack! We'd had a smothering, a strangling, a beheading and a stabbing up to now – who knows what other methods this ex-warrior might be able to deploy? I looked at him slyly, but he was gazing back at me, with a very strange expression on his face. I began to worry, suddenly, not about what Properus might think when he arrived, but whether I was likely to live to see him come at all.

'On the contrary, let Properus come in! I would be glad to have my money bags.' I began to move towards the exedra as I spoke, though my legs had turned to the consistency of cheese. Then an idea struck me and I added – secretly pleased with my own cleverness – 'Perhaps you and he could go together and alert the garrison.'

He looked surprised. I forced unwilling lips into a smile.

'On second thoughts, Fauvus, I realize you are right. If it is discovered that Laurentius has been killed, just after he moved into my flat, and I've not reported it – that might be misconstrued. My patron was treated very badly yesterday – an outright affront to his official dignitas – and the commander witnessed that. We cannot have it suggested that I did this, on Marcus's behalf, as some . . .' I broke off as there was a knocking on the door.

Fauvus had fetched the stool from somewhere and was guiding me to it. 'Ah, that will be Properus – impatient, I expect. Are you quite certain I should let him in? Or that you wish to involve him in all this, by sending him as joint messenger with me? Might it be not better to keep this in the household, as it were? At least until your patron has arrived.'

I shook my head. 'They will take the message better from a freeman than a slave. And two of you will be accorded more respect than one. I could have sent you with a letter,' I added cleverly, 'but my writing equipment has been moved – with all my other things.'

'The ex-Praetorian must have some, master. He'll need them for sending messages to Rome. And his luggage parcel's here – he's clearly got his lararium and toga out of it. The rest is probably in that chest beside the bed. Would you care for me to look?'

I did not want to write a letter, even if I could, and I did not want Fauvus going back into that room. I frowned in what I hoped was a disapproving way. 'Bad enough that the man is in my flat and dead, without making myself liable to be accused of theft. A spoken message will be good enough – especially if there are two of you to carry it.'

'Then naturally, master, I will do as you command. I'll fetch Properus and you can give us instructions what to say. He will already be wondering at the delay, no doubt. He asked me to apologize because he was so late, when you'd stressed that it was urgent that he came betimes today. I'm sure that he'll be happy to act as courier. Though I'm glad to know your patron's on his way. I should be loath to leave you in the flat alone for very long. You're looking flushed and troubled. The shock's affected you.' And off he hurried to attend the door.

I breathed out audibly. I'd circumvented him. He had been very anxious to send Properus away, but I'd avoided that. If I had not the intelligent idea of sending them both as messengers, I would have condemned myself to staying here alone with Fauvus. That was a troubling thought. For an aging citizen, I am reasonably fit – apart from creaking knees – but I am no longer nimble and I do get out of breath. I was no match for a Dacian warrior, damaged arm or no.

I was still complimenting myself on my wiliness when Properus came in. His handsome, reassuring presence seemed to fill the flat, and I felt an instant welling of relief. He was wearing the dark mourning robes I'd glimpsed the day before, but – since he was obviously making business calls – he'd not rubbed ashes in his face and hair. The effect was fortunate, from my point of view – he was the picture of respectability and grief. The sort of messenger that any sentry at the fortress should treat with courtesy – even though clearly not a citizen.

'The freeman, Graeculus Properus, master.' Fauvus's announcement, in the formal style, echoed my very thoughts. 'He craves an audience.'

I rose to offer the visitor my hand, rather expecting that he'd bow over it. That would be usual, since I was the owner of the flat and he was merely on commercial business here, but instead he seized my elbow as he'd done the day before, and gave my arm a cordial Roman greeting-shake.

'It's good of you to see me, councillor. I know you're expecting an important visitor.' He glanced around the flat, lowering his voice as if unwilling to be overheard. 'But I have your money, on a handcart close outside. Scito is taking care of it, of course – I would not have felt it safe to leave it otherwise. I planned to bring it here. But I think you mentioned yesterday that it might be easier to take it to your workshop and give it to your son? Would you prefer we did that – if this Roman visitor is due?'

I shook my head, suddenly impatient, although until this

morning the money bags had been my chief concern. 'It does not matter now. It's probably simpler just to bring them in.'

Properus looked anxiously at me. 'Is there some sort of problem, citizen? You do not look yourself.' He frowned. 'And what do you mean – it does not matter now? I thought you said your visitor was likely to object to you and your possessions being in the flat. Or has he now decided not to come here after all?'

I glanced at Fauvus. 'Bring another seat here for our visitor,' I said – and as my doubtful servant hurried to obey, I sank down on my own stool and turned to Properus. 'Laurentius is in no position to object to anything. The fact is, there has been . . .' My courage failed me and I trailed lamely off.

'An accident?'

'Let us call it an unfortunate event. Unfortunate, since he and his attendant guard are dead. I found them when I came here earlier with my slave.'

Properus frowned as if he were confused. 'You came here with Fauvus? But I thought, when I first saw him in the street, he told me that you hadn't yet arrived? He was taking the whole household somewhere else, he said, before you came to town. Curious – but I assumed that it was true.'

'Not that slave,' I said, quickly, to explain. I was talking too much, and failing to make my meaning clear. 'I had a whole household full of slaves who stayed here overnight. Fauvus was one of them, but this morning he took them to attend your former master's bier. I meant my young slave Minimus, whom I brought from home with me.' Properus gazed around again – looking more puzzled than before – until I added, 'I've sent him out to fetch my patron, so he isn't here just now.'

'Ah! I must not delay you then. If Marcus Aurelius Septimus is due!' He stressed the rank and the Imperial name, rather as if he thought that, in casually summoning my patron to come here, I had been guilty of impertinence.

Which – on reflection – possibly I had, but I attempted to sound brisk and confident. 'He will have to know. And he will want to make arrangements for a fitting funeral – Laurentius was a member of his patrician clan. In the meantime Fauvus thinks we should inform the guard.'

Properus looked grave. 'I'm sure that would be wise. This is no mere civil matter after all, since the dead man was both an ex-Praetorian and expressly here on business from the Emperor.'

Put like that it sounded more serious than ever. 'When they find who did it, the punishment is bound to be severe.' I signalled with my brows towards the Dacian, who was standing behind him with the stool, but my visitor showed no sign of having understood. Nor did he make the least attempt to sit.

Instead he turned towards my slave and said, 'Your master feels that we should take a message to the garrison at once. Help me to bring the money up, and then we can do as the citizen requires.' His tone to Fauvus was peremptory – like any Roman speaking to a slave – but he turned to smile at me. 'I should not be happy leaving it outside in the street, even with Scito to keep a watch on it. If we empty the hand-cart, he can deal with that and then come back to me, in case we need his services again. For instance – from what you told me yesterday – we ought to let them know at the basilica, not to repeat that announcement from the steps requiring all members of the curia to come here later on.'

'Supposing that it's not too late already,' I remarked. 'Most councillors will by this time have made arrangements to be here.'

He bowed acknowledgement. 'So you will be occupied with them – telling them that they are not required. And I'm sure that there will be many other things to do. I'll put Scito entirely at your disposal, citizen.'

I tried to thank him for his generosity, but by the time that I had gathered my disjointed thoughts he and Fauvus had already left the room. I could hear them clattering down the staircase to the street. It dawned on me, suddenly, that I was shivering. This business had affected me more than I'd supposed. Of course, the discovery of a murdered praetorian in one's bed would leave anyone trembling with shock. Indeed, if it were not already occupied, I might have thought of lying down myself. And I was thirsty – a thing I've noticed, often, after drinking wine.

However, there was no time to think of that. Almost before

I realized they had gone Fauvus and Properus were panting in again, each carrying two weighty money bags. At a sign from Properus they dropped them on the floor – Fauvus with a grunt of evident relief. If I had not suspected him to be a murderer, I would have sympathized – I had occasion to remember how heavy they had seemed and he, of course, had one half-useless arm.

'I believe that these are what you wanted, citizen?' Properus gave a courteous little bow. 'Please check the tags so I can keep my records straight. The guild, you understand?'

I bent to have a closer look, but there was scarcely need. These were the bags we'd taken to the booths – sealed with the tags that Josephus had used, and marked with my own identifying signs.

I nodded. 'That seems to be in order.'

'Then if you'd sign that they have been received?' He held out a piece of bark-paper to me.

I shook my head. 'I have no signet ring or seal about me now. Nor do I have the receipt you gave to me. Everything's been moved away, so the Praetorian could come. If you have a tablet, I could make a mark, perhaps – scratch my name, or something of the kind? Saying I'd received my property, of course.'

The handsome face was clouded, but it cleared at once. 'A splendid notion. I have one here, in fact.' He reached into the recesses of his robe, and pulled out a small wax tablet in a handsome folding case. 'I always carry one, for making calculations on. But it can easily be cleared.' He took it to the brazier, which was still alight, and held it there until the wax was soft. Then he took the stylus from its little storage groove within the case, and used it to smooth the surface clear. 'There, citizen. You may write your own receipt, and add your name to it.'

My hand was shaky, but I managed it. 'I, Libertus, citizen and councillor, hereby acknowledge the return of four money bags which I left for safe-keeping at the booth. I have examined them and find them sealed as they were left.'

I was about to sign it, but he interrupted me. 'Do you wish to count the money before you write your name?'

I shook my head. 'I'm satisfied,' I said. 'Josephus was famous for his tags. Nobody could tamper with them, and not have the change observed.' I wrote my name, with several flourishes, and folded the little writing case. It was a handsome thing, very like the one I'd seen him open yesterday, bearing the urgent message from the money-changers' guild. 'Do all argentarii possess these?' I enquired. 'I seem to remember Josephus having one as well.'

Properus was moving the money bags onto the dining couch, behind the table, where they were out of sight, but he whirled round at this. He seemed affronted. 'I know that I am only a trainee, but my master gave me this himself, as a little token of his certainty that I should get my licence and succeed him at his post.'

'Then may you have many profitable years of using it.'

The annoyance vanished as quickly as it came. 'Thank you, citizen. And now, with your permission, I will leave you here, and your slave and I will take that message to the garrison and the basilica.' He peered anxiously at me. 'You are sure I should not have sent you Scito while we're gone? Unfortunately he's now gone to store the handcart, but he will soon return.'

I shook my head. 'I will await my patron,' I replied, and watched as he and Fauvus went out and closed the door.

TWENTY-FOUR

My immediate thought, despite what I had said to Fauvus earlier, was to return to the murder scene and hunt through Laurentius's possessions. It was possible that he was carrying papers – supposing that Fauvus had not disposed of them – which might give me a clue as to which of Comux's partners would have cause to want him dead. The idea of luggage had not occurred to me till Fauvus mentioned it – though clearly nobody could travel empty-handed all the way from Rome.

I stood up from the stool to go and look, but strangely – since I was anxious to make my search before anyone returned – I seemed to be afflicted by a dreadful lethargy. My fingers felt as if they were twice their normal size, and my movements were hampered by a sudden giddiness and a tendency to blurring of the eyes. It must be the shock, I thought. Panic can do extraordinary things. It was all I could do to concentrate on shuffling down the hall – and even then I had to steady myself against the walls.

Fortunately the master bedroom was the nearer one, and I reached it without incident. As I looked in at Laurentius and his tidy, folded clothes, I realized that – to look into the chest – I would have to move the tray, which still held the jug and the two empty drinking cups. The cups were those that Marcus had supplied. The jug, however, was a distinctive one – I was fairly certain that I'd not seen that before.

However, that was another problem. I did not want it to delay me now.

The lid of the chest seemed very heavy, suddenly, or perhaps it was simply that my hands refused to work because I was afraid of what I'd find. I need not have been. Fauvus was correct – the Praetorian had indeed stowed his luggage there. It was not extensive. Two clean tunics and a dining synthesis, a loincloth, two fresh wax tablets and a little box, containing stylus, seal block, plus sealing wax, and a little candle rack with which to soften it. The writing materials Fauvus had been confident I'd find!

There was a bunch of letters, too, but they were tied with cord and my clumsy fingers could not loose the knot (though I carefully placed the bundle on the floor, with some idea of looking at them later on). That left a fine horn comb, some scented hair pomade, a pumice stone for filing corns, a purse containing a few small silver coins, three withered apples and a loaf of army bread.

That was all. No sign of the Imperial warrant which one might expect, nor any container which might have carried wine. So that had been supplied by the murderer, it seemed.

That was a puzzle. I could see how Fauvus could contrive to bring in an amphora, or something of the kind, but how had he managed to take it out again? I'd met him this morning right outside on the street, when presumably he had just left the flat, and he was not carrying anything at all. Unless he simply had brought the liquid in the jug? Part of the possessions he'd carried in that sack of his? There was provision for a stopper on the jug, so that was possible. But if it wasn't poison . . .?

Probably that was why it now occurred to me – for the first time – that it might have been the contents of the jug which had caused my current racing heart, and limping thoughts. After all, if this were the same mixture as I'd carried in the phial, wasn't it supposed to be some kind of sleeping draught? Yet I wasn't sleepy – none of the eye-drooping that comes from poppy juice – rather I had an urgent drive for action. Mixed with a total lethargy of limbs.

I went over to the jug and picked it up, staring at it rather foolishly, as if it could answer my questions in some way. As I did so, though, I had another thought (only one, my mind was working extraordinarily slowly, it appeared!). There was still a lot of liquid in the jug – in fact it was very nearly halfway full. I could not think why, but that seemed relevant.

Still acting in a kind of semi-dream – (I would never have done this, if I were properly awake, for fear of compromising the evidence) – I took up one of the handsome empty cups and began to pour the mixture into it. Only began, though; I had to stop, because it would have more than filled the cup. Taking great care not to spill the liquid (a necessary precaution, since it seemed to swell and sway) I poured it back again – and realized, as I did so, what was remarkable.

The jug was one of those designed for intimate affairs, and held enough for two – usually a host and his most honoured guest – one full goblet and a refill each. That was not, itself, unusual; there was a current fashion for such things, many of them much smaller ones than this. The point was this jug would hold about four cups in all. I did the mathematics very carefully.

Two goblets had been produced from my store cupboard and filled, so that would be correct. Three cupfuls if one included the servant's mug next-door – yet fully half a jug of liquid still remained. And there was no other container to be found. There was only one conclusion to be drawn – one person had not actually drunk the wine at all, and his share had been carefully poured back into the jug. I was triumphant at my clever reasoning.

But why bother, in that case, to pour it back at all? And why leave two used goblets to be found, rather than suggesting that Laurentius had been drinking on his own, which would have seemed much less remarkable? To suggest that I'd been drinking with him, possibly? I was trying to make fuddled sense of this, and wondering whether I should search the storage room myself, in case an amphora might be hidden there, when I heard voices in the other room.

'Councillor Libertus?' The disdainfully raised voice which was calling out my name was not that of Fauvus, nor of Properus, and assuredly not my patron or my little household slave. But I knew it from somewhere, I was sure of that, although at present I could not think where.

I was still trying to collect my thoughts and decide if I should answer – in the circumstances and in my befuddled state – when the same voice spoke again. 'You're quite sure that he is here? He has not taken flight? After all, nobody was answering the door.'

It was Properus who answered, to my profound relief. 'His patron is expected, so Libertus would not leave. He must be somewhere in the flat.'

'Supposing that he's not been murdered in his turn, while you were gone!' The first voice sounded half-amused at the idea.

Properus, conversely, seemed alarmed. 'Let's pray it's nothing of the kind. I'll go and look for him.'

'No need to search,' I shouted, hurrying towards them as quickly as I could – a little more co-ordinated now, but not as spritely as I would have liked. 'Just ensure that Fauvus does not leave. I was—' I broke off in surprise as I came into the room. Properus was accompanied, not by a member of the garrison or even the town watch, as I had expected, but by Rufus, my old enemy – the high-born aedile who so resented my election to the curia and in particular my role as duumvir. He was accompanied by a diminutive slave. Of Fauvus there was no sign at all.

Properus saw me looking for him, motioned the page toward the servants' waiting niche, and gave me another of his warm, gleaming smiles. 'Pardon me for overriding your commands, councillor, but this is clearly an emergency. Your servant and I parted company in town. My doing, I confess. I thought it would be quicker if we did. I went to the forum – to countermand instructions for the curia to come here – while he went on to notify the fort.'

I found that I was frowning. That decision was intelligent of course – but I had wanted them together, if only to make sure that Fauvus did not run away before I had time to denounce him to the authorities. Very likely he'd go straight back to his former master now and be smuggled down the river in the first departing boat. Though I could hardly blame Properus for that – I'd not alerted him to my suspicions, apart from a feeble attempt to do so with my brows!

I nodded. 'Then it is to be hoped he comes here quickly with the guard.' If not, I'd send them after him, I thought. And tell them where to look. In Boudoucus's warehouse! I turned to Rufus. 'You've heard what happened here?'

Rufus answered with a brief, disdainful nod.

'I have been considering events,' I told him, loftily. 'I believe I can tell you who was responsible.'

Properus and the aedile exchanged a startled look. Rufus said, 'You do?'

I nodded my still strangely buzzing head. 'Though to prove it I need to call on some freemen traders from the docks: Comux, Boudoucus and Brokko. Could we arrange to have them brought?' I smiled at Properus. 'That is, if . . . if . . .' I found the name, and said triumphantly, 'if Scito . . . has returned?' All the same, I realized that my voice was rather loud, and I had to concentrate to make my words make sense. 'You promised that I could use him for such tasks, I think?'

Properus was looking quizzical. 'Comux, Boudoucus and Brokko?' he said to Rufus, with an enquiring look.

'I seem to know the names. They occasionally ship items for the garrison, I think – through some ship in which they have an interest.' The aedile shook his head. 'I can't imagine what they have to do with this. Does anything suggest itself to you?'

Properus shrugged expressive shoulders. 'I've never heard of them.'

'You might have done, in passing.' I was eager to involve him fully in my reasoning. 'They were at the baths with Josephus the afternoon he fell. Or you might have met them afterwards, when they came to visit him. Comux in particular came several times, I think. And Brokko admits to being there when that so-called medicus arrived.'

'The "so-called" medicus?' Properus sounded shocked. He seized me by the arm and propelled me to the stool, adding as I sat down heavily, 'What are you suggesting, councillor?'

I waved a hand at him. It moved at my command but did not feel like my own. 'I don't think it was a proper medicus at all.' I smiled triumphantly. 'What do you think of that?'

Rufus said sourly, 'Is this relevant?'

Properus looked doubtfully at him. 'It might be, aedile, I can't be sure. I did not see this medicus myself. I could not call on Josephus the day he fell. I was on duty in the market-place. I heard that he'd fallen but was resting, and I thought no more of it. The next day was nefas, so I did not expect him at the market anyway, and I went to the money-changing booth as usual. Florea sent a message that he had not improved, but I was not able to visit him myself until the close of business – by which time he was dead. I did not see any traders in his flat at any time.'

'And this medicus?' Rufus barked at him, impatiently.

'I never met the man. I simply heard that a physician had been called, and had appeared to help – for a little while at least. It was a visit I was ready to applaud. But it appears your fellow councillor may know something more.'

'I do,' I told him. 'When that supposed new slave of mine gets back (supposing that he does in fact bring members of the guard) and if Comux and his friends are fetched – I shall be ready to make a formal declaration, I believe. I hope my patron will be here by then, as well, and he can witness it. You too, Rufus. I'm very glad you've come.' I was aware that now I was sounding rather drunk.

Rufus looked at me as if I might be crazed. 'You are sure you want to do that, citizen? Surely you would not wish His Excellence involved?'

I noted that he had deprived me of my rank. 'Aedile,' I retorted – emphasising his – 'I am a duumvir, and I have made a curial request to have three tradesmen brought to me for questioning. This is not a matter for argument, I think.' (That, at least, was what I meant to say although my words were blurring even to myself.)

My two visitors exchanged uncertain looks. Then Rufus said, 'I think he has been drinking, but he is within his rights. We'd better fetch these men and hear what they have to say. I'll send my page for them.'

Properus shrugged his shoulders. 'Whatever you say, aedile, of course – though I can't imagine tradesmen will be of any use. But if you think that it's essential, we could use my slave. He should be waiting at the entrance to the street. I sent him on a message, but he should be back by now.' He walked across and peered out of the window-space. 'Indeed he is, I can see him standing there. That's most convenient. We can send him with a message that he should escort these tradesmen here, and not deprive you of your page.' He smiled at Rufus. 'Although you might care to take command, in your capacity as aedile. These tradesmen might obey the summons better, if it came from you. They are common traders, and have – or would have – no respect for me or for little pages,' he added with a smile.

'I assume you'll want to tell your man that you are putting him at my command?' Rufus said, addressing Properus above my head as though I were myself a slave of no account.

Properus waved the words aside with a dismissive hand. 'Oh, Scito is well trained, and will accept your word for it. Tell him I'm staying with the duumvir meanwhile. Our councillor is clearly affected by the shock, and should not be alone. And it would be more fitting if I attend on him – rather than a man of your exalted rank.'

The flattery was blatant, but it had exactly the effect desired. Rufus was visibly preening as he left the room. Properus watched him go, and then came back to me, squatting beside me like the merest slave.

'Councillor,' he urged me, conveying warmth and understanding in his tone, 'you may not care for Rufus – indeed I sense that you do not – but you can confide in me. If you've discovered something pointing to the murderer, tell me what it is. I will support you, if it is in my power.' He stretched out a friendly hand to touch my arm, and almost seemed ready to defy the Roman code and put his own around my shoulders, when there was a noise outside the door and he leapt away and rose sharply to his feet.

A moment later he was bowing to the floor as Fauvus reappeared – very much to my astonishment – announcing the arrival, not merely of a guard but of 'His honour the Legate, Commander of the garrison'.

I struggled to my feet to greet the visitor, but before I'd fully risen from my stool, the commander himself was already sweeping in, followed by a pair of burly-looking guards, both fully armed and armoured – and with their helmets on – making it clear their visit was no social one!

TWENTY-FIVE

The Legate had not struck me as forceful yesterday, despite his trappings of authority – he'd seemed to be entirely at Laurentius's command. But today he looked magnificent. The burnish of his armour was only matched – and crowned – by the sculptured ripples of his blond, wavy hair framing a face as emotionless as stone. Every inch the hardened commander of a garrison.

He nodded at me by way of greeting and shrugged off his cape – not even deigning to turn his head, as his two attendants neatly whipped the cloak from his shoulders and handed it to Fauvus. (Who, in the role of model servant, folded it deftly and took it away to the doorman's anteroom, to be presided over by Rufus's young page.)

The Legate had meanwhile taken possession of my stool – without waiting for my greeting or any invitation to sit down. Nor was he apologetic in the least. On the contrary, he seemed imperious – an impression strengthened by the presence of his men, who took up station on either side of him, as though he were about to hold a court. (Perhaps I should not have blamed Laurentius for our discourteous treatment, after all!)

I found myself embarrassingly unsteady on my feet. Fauvus clearly noticed, and fetched the other stool, but before he had placed it for me the Legate snapped, 'Councillor Libertus. At your disposal, naturally. But I hope that my summons here is justified. I am a very busy man, and shall be most displeased if this turns out to be some foolish errand, which might have been resolved by messenger. Your servant informs me that there is what he calls "a regrettable emergency" with regard to Laurentius Aurelius Manlius and his guard. Is that correct?'

I murmured that it was, but before I could elucidate he held up a haughty hand to silence me.

'Meaning that you've disobliged him in some way so he no longer wishes to remain here in your flat?'

I was about to answer – but a glance made it clear that I was not to interrupt.

'It's most unfortunate! He should have taken notice of the warnings he received,' the commander went on, with an impatient sigh. 'I suppose we'll have to accommodate him at the fort, as we did yesterday – at his insistence, though it was not ideal. However, as I am here now I will try to arbitrate. So how have you displeased him? Be careful what you say. Since he's an Imperial agent this is very serious. If your offence is grave I may be forced to mention it – and you – in my next despatch to Rome.'

Fauvus placed the stool behind me, and I was glad of it. Perhaps it was the mixture I had unwisely sipped, or perhaps it was simply that the implications of the Legate's speech were so alarming, but – whatever the reason – I found that I was very anxious to sit down. I did so – telling myself that as councillor and host I was entitled to – and waved the slave impatiently away. I was still unsteady, but alert enough to ask (now that I had permission to say anything at all), 'Warnings, Legate?' I was aware of sounding strident. 'Warnings about what?'

'Warnings, councillor, that there was danger here. What would you suppose?'

'But who could possibly have suspected that?' I was finding it difficult to balance on my perch, but his words astonished me. Who could conceivably have seen the threat before I did myself? There'd been no reason to have doubts about Fauvus, till today. Unless . . . again . . . it had been Josephus who wrote those warnings. Of course! I tried to moisten my unwilling lips. 'This came from the argentarius, I assume?' It came out as 'the assumarius I aggent', so I amended it. 'I presume it was letters from Josephus that brought Laurentius here?'

Properus, who had been pointedly excluded by the Legate from all this, and had been standing meekly with Rufus by the wall, stepped forward suddenly and seemed about to speak. He was prevented by the soldiers, who – at a signal from the Legate and in perfect unison – moved to restrain him and propel him back again, by seizing either arm and using sufficient force to make him wince.

He stood there rubbing both his injured limbs and glowering sullenly. The commander frowned at him. 'Townsman, it is time you knew your station,' he declared. 'I am speaking to the duumvir. If there is something that you wish to add, wait till you're addressed. You understand?'

Properus glanced at Rufus, as though for some support, but the aedile was looking carefully elsewhere, so he simply nodded.

The Legate turned to me. 'Meanwhile, duumvir – I should answer you. I will not prevaricate. It was indeed the messages that Josephus sent, which alarmed our noble Caesar enough to send a spy. Though Laurentius would have preferred that to remain a secret, I believe.' He pinned me with a glance as sharp as a javelin. 'I am surprised he told you.' The granite eyebrows rose. 'Or did he change his mind and question you at once? If you simply deduced this, I can see he'd be displeased – though I understand you're clever at such things, duumvir?'

I shook my head. I did not feel clever at anything, today. 'I did not have the chance to talk to him at all. When I arrived he was already dead.'

'Dead?' If my sole intention had been to shock I could not have judged it more effectively. I had not meant to blurt it out like that, but the effect on the commandant was quite remarkable. He fairly leapt up from his stool, looking at me as though he could not trust his ears. 'Did you say dead?' His voice had lost its smooth patrician loftiness and he was speaking as any common soldier might. 'Great Mercury! We'll have reprisals from the Emperor! How, dead? A fall? A seizure? Pray Jove it wasn't something that he ate with us!'

I myself had risen, a little shakily. 'It rather looks as though he has been strangled,' I explained – adding, with some dim, foolish notion that he might be reassured, since the garrison's kitchens could clearly not be blamed. 'With his own belt, it seems.'

My words appeared to make the Legate doubt my sanity. 'Strangled? An ex-Praetorian? That isn't possible. True he hasn't been in proper training for a year, but any soldier who was not weak from wounds could defend himself against a mere civilian with a cord! And he was protected by a body-guard!' He gazed around. 'Where is he, anyway?' He rose and motioned to his guards, as if to order them to be prepared to search. 'He will be questioned. I'd like to speak to him.'

I stood up, rather shakily, myself and took a long, deep

breath. The time had clearly come. 'Legate, I fear that won't be possible. The slave is dead as well. Though he at least attempted to defend himself – there's evidence that someone tried to strangle him.' I realized that the soldiers were all staring at me now. 'It seems he fought off his assailant, though his hands were tied, but then was stabbed instead,' I finished, lamely.

There was nothing lame about the Legate's response. 'And all this in your apartment, duumvir?' The words were dripping with unspoken threat.

'In my apartment, but not when I was here.' I was babbling. 'They were dead when I arrived. Though I believe I can convince you who is responsible.' I glanced around to see where Fauvus was, but he'd taken my dismissal as a cue to wait outside, so I added – with what dignity I could, 'I am awaiting the appearance of three tradesmen witnesses, whose testimony should confirm what I suspect. They should not be long. I've already sent for them.' At least, that's what I attempted to pronounce.

The Legate was running both hands through his sculpted hair, leaving it in startling disarray. He was clearly imagining what the Emperor would say. 'So this is the reason that you sent for me?'

I was about to acknowledge that it was, but before I could do so Properus intervened. He flung himself upon his knees at the commander's feet. 'Permission to address you, Legate, now? I promise you that it is relevant.'

Even then, the commandant looked at Rufus and at me, as if to check for our consent. I gave my permission with a little smile. I was beginning to feel smugly confident. 'Perhaps he will confirm what really happened here. Of course he can only tell you the latter part of it.'

'Properus only came at all today at the duumvir's request,' Rufus put in.

The Legate looked at me.

'Money,' I agreed. 'That's what it was about. He opted to come here today and sort it out – since he didn't manage to do it yesterday.' I was finding it very difficult to tell the tale at all. 'I did not actually see him when he first arrived, but I know he was able to . . .' I could not find the word 'corroborate', so I waved my hands instead. 'When he had finished, he was free to leave, of course.' I glanced at Properus, who had risen to his feet and was looking at me with a strange expression on his face. 'But instead he chose to come back here and offer me his help.'

'He said he'd found the corpses,' Properus confirmed. 'He sent me and his servant into town, to pass the message on together, so he said.'

I nodded stupidly. 'I did not wish to have him run away.' Or to be here unprotected with a murderer, I thought, but I could not find the energy to frame the utterance. Time enough for that when my witnesses arrived.

The Legate who had been listening to all this with gravity, then turned to Properus. 'In that case, townsman, have you any more to say?' He sat down regally on his former stool, and gestured that I should sit beside him on my own.

I did so thankfully, convinced that Properus would confirm my words. So I was rather startled to see him, as he rose, scowl at me as though I'd been the cause of his distress.

'Legate I regret these deaths with all my heart,' he said. 'I feared that something of the kind might come to pass, ever since I heard Laurentius was coming here in response to my late master's letters.'

'You did?' The Legate's brow was furrowed in a frown. 'You were not the one who sent those warning messages?'

Properus gave him a deferential smile. 'The ones that warned him that there was danger here? It wasn't me, I fear. I only wish that he had heeded them. Though perhaps the warnings were mere general ones?'

A wary look. 'Not at all. I saw the latest message – he showed it to me last night when he came. And that was quite specific – there might be danger from the household in this flat, and he would be safer with a servant he could trust. And, though he was sceptical, he did take heed of that.'

'Though it did not save him, in the end.' Properus looked grave. 'And you've no idea who the informant was? It can't have been my master, he was already dead.'

'He had received another letter in Londinium, I believe,' the Legate said, 'Warning him against coming here at all.'

'Then the letters must have been from somebody who knew

that he was coming, before the rest of us,' Rufus put in, adding – with a knowing look at me – 'and who more likely than a relative? Or the trusted confidant of one?'

The commander turned to me. 'Councillor, do you have anything to say? I understand – from what you said before – you believe these murders here today are related in some way to Josephus, and his letters to the Emperor?'

I nodded. 'And, furthermore, to his untimely death!' There! I had mentioned that, and I had not intended to – at least not until Comux and his partners came.

The Legate seized upon my words at once. 'But, by all the gods, that was an accident? Or are you going to tell me now that it was nothing of the kind?'

'The duumvir does not believe so, it appears,' Rufus said. His tone was mocking, and it nettled me.

'Oh, he fell and hit his head. There is no doubt of that. But I don't believe he died of injuries. Any more that I believe his slave was set upon by rebel thieves,' I retorted, stung. I'd spoken over-loudly, but I'd framed the words.

'And you no doubt have a counter theory, as to that, as well?' Rufus was overtly nasty, now.

'It must have been to silence those who knew the truth.'

'Truth?' The Legate's tone of anger startled me. 'If you know something of this affair which I do not, Duumvir Libertus, you'd be wise to speak.'

'Laurentius said there had been "treason" locally . . .' I struggled to summon my scattered thoughts and said – or tried to say – 'But . . . failing evidence, and the testimony of those tradesmen who are on their way, at the moment this is all surmise. I cannot tell you what treason there has been. But if you'll summon my servant in for me, I'll tell you what I think I have deduced. Though, with your permission, Legate, I'll delay a formal accusation until my witnesses arrive.' I realized the words were tumbling out, not exactly in the order that I'd planned, and everyone was staring at me in perplexity. I added, carefully slow and sounding piteous, 'Forgive me if I'm not being very clear. All this has been a dreadful shock to me.'

Properus shot a look at Rufus, who returned it with a nod. And that was when I got the greatest shock of all.

TWENTY-SIX

Rufus stepped forward with an icy smile. 'Legate, do not listen to the duumvir. I am the one to make an accusation. This well-known and highly regarded townsman' – he gestured towards Properus, who acknowledged the gesture with a bow – 'knows what I'm about to say and will attest the truth of it.' He coughed and went on, in a declamatory way, clutching the toga folds around his chest as though addressing a magistrate in court. 'I, Rufus Appius Claudius aedile of this colonia, formally accuse this man, Libertus – a Celtic ex-slave, as his name suggests, despite his current role as councillor – of murdering a visitor to our town, the ex-Praetorian Laurentius Aurelius Manlius, knowing him to be the valued agent of his Divinity, the Emperor.' He paused, just long enough to take a breath. 'And further, of arranging the murder of his slave. All this when these people were formally his guests. To this I swear before yourself, this company, and all the gods. Seize him soldiers.'

I gaped at him – and so did the commander. The soldiers did not move.

'Well,' Rufus demanded, 'what are you waiting for?'

The two guards looked uneasily towards their officer, as if awaiting a command. He gave it with a reluctant nod, and I found myself with a soldier at either side hoisting me roughly to my unsteady feet.

The Legate leaned back importantly and crossed his arms. 'Duumvir, you will wish to deny the claim against you, I've no doubt. Indeed you have a counteraccusation, I believe?'

I nodded. Fear had turned my wits to army gruel, my mouth was dry and I seemed to be seeing two of everything. By concentrating hard I managed to reply, 'I did not kill Laurentius, or his slave. Though I can see that things look bad for me.'

'Bad!' It was now Properus who spoke. 'Legate, I regret to have to say this of the man, because I know that my late master valued him. But everything about this matter indicates his guilt. This is his apartment—'

'Which he insisted on offering to the ex-Praetorian,' Rufus interrupted with a sneer, 'immediately this stay in Glevum was proposed. Why should the duumvir do that? Laurentius was no relative of his. Unless there was some private motive for suggesting it?'

The commander ran a hand through those sculptured curls again. 'Aedile, that same question had occurred to me. One would have expected Laurentius to stay with members of his family – or, if that proved impossible, to seek accommodation with me at the garrison.' He frowned at me. 'What have you to say? Why did you ask Laurentius here?'

I hesitated. I could hardly reply that Marcus had as good as told me to – that might lead to questions which would draw attention to the incriminating chatter of his son – so I muttered weakly, 'I wanted to oblige my patron, that is all.'

That was an error. The Legate pounced at once. 'So he's involved in this? I suppose, as the aedile suggests, I should have surmised as much. No one in Glevum but Marcus Septimus had ever heard of Laurentius before he came – and it was clear, from the moment the two cousins met again, that there was hostility.'

I shook my head – then wished I hadn't. I was seeing sparks. 'His Excellence knows nothing about this.'

'But you do?' the officer snapped back.

I realized that I'd walked into another trap. 'That isn't what I meant . . .' I burbled, just as Fauvus came in, under guard. He looked bewildered – even more so when he saw me in the firm grasp of a soldier, too. But like any slave he held his tongue, of course – he knew better than to speak till he was spoken to.

I waved a hand towards him, aware that I was suffering from a growing thirst. 'Legate, I am accused, unjustly, and physically detained, but I am a citizen and councillor. Could I have a drink, at least? There is water in the storeroom. Perhaps that would help me form my words more easily.'

The soldier holding Fauvus looked at the commandant, who seemed to consider for a moment then solemnly replied, 'Very well. Escort the slave to fetch a drink. Ensure it's really water which is brought. I don't wish his master to have the opportunity to avoid the courts by being given hemlock or something of the kind, in an attempt to save his dignity.'

The guard saluted and propelled my slave, in no gentle manner, into the inner corridor and the storeroom where the pail was kept.

Rufus took a step towards the commandant. 'Come Legate, we are wasting time. What more proof do you require? Libertus takes fright the moment that he learns that an Imperial spy is coming here. He lures the man here to his death. Clearly he had planned this murder from the start. This is his apartment – he had servants here, which he took pains to send away this morning, I believe.'

The injustice of this should have penetrated even my befuddled brain, but suddenly I felt invincible, remote and wonderfully content in spite of everything. I could scarcely restrain a smile as I said, 'Only because Laurentius himself requested it! We had a message from him shortly after dawn – sent from the garrison.'

The Legate frowned. 'He did send a message – I was with him at the time – saying that he wished to come this morning after all. I offered to send a courier here myself, but he preferred to entrust it to an urchin at the gates, saying that the boy would attract less notice in the street. He wanted his arrival to be unobserved – because of those warnings, I suppose. But hadn't you agreed to leave a servant here to greet him when he came?'

'That was specifically countermanded.' I tried to be lofty but stumbled on the words.

The Legate's granite brow was furrowed deeper now. 'Not that I am aware of, citizen. I heard him give the message, and there was no mention of any change, except the time.'

More evidence of Fauvus's clever treachery! I sighed. 'I was afraid of something of the kind.'

'Then why did you send away your slaves, if not to ensure that there was no one here?'

'Because Fauvus assured me that it had been required. Here he is – ask him,' I added as he came into the room. 'Of course there was no witness but myself, but he would be well advised

to confirm my words.' The guard passed me the beaker and
I took a grateful sip – a small one, as there was very little
water in the cup. But my throat felt so swollen I could hardly
swallow the mouthful that I had.

I had no sooner done that, than I regretted it – whatever
was in that wine jug might be in the water pail – but I did
feel a little better for the soothing cool sensation in my mouth.
(Better enough to recognize that, with the soldier there, Fauvus
would have had no opportunity to drug the cup. But he must
realize that I had drunk some of the mixture he'd prepared
– even I was aware that I was not acting like myself. Perhaps
that was why he'd given me as little water as he dared.)

Meanwhile the Legate was asking Fauvus about the message
from the fort, and the slave confirmed exactly my account.
(Of course, he would – I realized – since what had really
happened was that I had just vouched for him, and reinforced
his perfect reason for having cleared the flat of staff.)

But Rufus was impatient. 'Of course the slave confirms his
master's words. It is his duty – what else would you expect?
We'll see if he still says so under questioning! But that need
not detain us, the truth is manifest. Legate, you have the
evidence of what you heard yourself. Laurentius did not ask
for the slaves to be removed, yet Libertus ordered it. Leaving
the apartment conveniently free of witnesses – at a time when
only he could possibly have known.'

'I didn't know until I met my slave today,' I protested,
though I seemed to be suspended several inches from the
floor in some mysterious way, and was finding it increasingly
difficult to think. 'I was not expecting Laurentius until this
afternoon. Besides he was a soldier, one of the elite. I am
an aging man. I could not—'

Rufus interrupted. 'Of course the duumvir's not capable
of killing two trained men himself, but he has a slave who
could – especially if between them, they drugged their victims
first – as I understand to be the case.'

'But master . . . Legate . . . that cannot . . .' Fauvus protested
– and received a stinging blow, so hard it might have felled
him if the soldier was not holding him.

That water had helped me a little, but not much. 'But why

should I want Laurentius dead?' Like Fauvus, I found I could not restrain my tongue, though the outburst earned me a painful squeeze on my right arm.

'To oblige your patron? Those were your words, I think?' The commander had reverted to his stony face and tone. 'A pity then, you did not leave the matter in his hands. If this was a question of family discipline, he might have pleaded that, as the senior member of the clan, he was provoked to anger by a public show of disrespect from a more junior one.'

'Meaning that, as senior, he had power of life or death?' I had some confused idea that I had heard of this, but that it was largely in abeyance nowadays, except where disobedient – or immoral – wives and daughters were concerned.

The Legate treated this suggestion with contempt. 'Naturally not. Laurentius had a father of his own and was not under your patron's *potestas*. But the courts might have some sympathy for loss of *dignitas*. His cousin's rudeness was unfortunate – and deliberate. I hesitated to remark on it myself – Laurentius had the Imperial favour, after all – but he did not hide his view that Marcus was too full of self-regard, and should learn that an agent of a ruling Emperor had more status than a favourite of an executed one.'

Rufus shook his head. 'This was not a matter of dignity, I think. This was something far more serious. And not involving His Excellence at all, as far as I'm aware. Purely the avarice of the duumvir.' I drew a startled breath, on which I nearly choked, but the aedile ignored me and went on, 'You know, I assume, Commander, what the "treason" was that Laurentius was sent here to investigate?'

The Legate looked at him with sudden interest. 'You know about it too? Laurentius was anxious not to have it generally known, in case the evidence might be destroyed, or the perpetrator flee with his ill-gotten gains, before he could be arrested and sent to Rome for trial. So who told you, and when?'

Rufus bowed. 'It was brought to my attention yesterday,' he said. 'One of the herb sellers in the market came to me, asking where an official money changer could be found, because he thought he'd been given a false denarius and there was no argentarius on duty at the booth. I asked him where

he'd got the coin, and when he traced his sales, he told me
that it must have been given in purchase of some funeral herbs
for Libertus the duumvir, and tendered by his slave.'

'A false denarius?' I had struggled to follow, but I'd seized
on that. The idea seemed hilariously slight and I found that I
was grinning like a fool.

The Legate's stare was frigid. 'The aedile's correct. That is
indeed the nature of the treason here – and it is no small
matter, duumvir. Imitation of the Emperor's coin is fraudulent
at best. According to the strict interpretation of the law, falsi-
fication of his image is desecration of his divinity and an insult
to his majesty. Men have died for less. Furthermore, the
Emperor Severus has recently decreed that anyone issuing
false coin – with or without his image – is traitorous, and
should be punished, accordingly, with death. Intended to
prevent the spread of money issued by Pescennius Niger, I
suspect – but when he heard that it was happening here—'

And then I remembered. 'I did have such a coin. Properus
gave it to me at the booth. He told me it was worthless and
I'd forgotten it. I must have found it in the bottom of my
purse and given it in error to my servant to buy herbs. It was
not intentional . . .' I tailed off. It was too difficult to bother
to explain. Anyway, lack of intention was no excuse in law.
(It was one of the lessons I had learned as a junior
magistrate.)

Properus nodded. 'Commander, that is true. I recall the
incident. Libertus had come to look for Josephus, he said –
though I later learned they'd been together at the baths, when
my former master hit his head, so he must have known about
the injury. He asked specifically about the faulty currency,
which should have alerted my suspicions, I suppose, but – in
all innocence – I gave him one which I had noticed earlier
and withdrawn, warning him about its worthlessness. Of
course, he pretended that he'd never seen one in his life – and
he convinced me too.'

'But you, yourself, could identify these coins?' The Legate's
tone suggested disbelief.

Properus responded with surprising dignity. 'Of course,
Legate. I am waiting to be licensed as an argentarius. When

Rufus brought that coin to my attention earlier today, I recognized it as a forgery at once – one of a type which had been circulating here in Glevum recently. If I had a copy, I could show you now. There's a rather crude blurring of the images and a slight discrepancy in weight – though well enough constructed to deceive a casual glance.'

'Not your glance, however?'

'You are kind to say as much. In fact, I was the first to notice them at all. And brought them to the attention of poor Josephus, since he had failing eyes. It worried him, I think, that he had not perceived them for himself. All of which the duumvir could certainly confirm – though he may deny it, for reasons of his own.'

'I do not deny it,' I murmured, squirming as the Legate turned to me. It was hard to frame the answer, though I was aware of every syllable. It all seemed far away. I still seemed to be floating in the air. And now I was seeing two of everything. I lapped the remainder of the water in the cup.

'Then perhaps he will also confess the awkward truth that the death of Josephus – which he now declares himself was not an accident – did not take place when this "medicus" was there, whom he pretends to blame.' Properus was maundering on again. 'Indeed my master was declared to be asleep, until Libertus visited the premises – when the death was conveniently "discovered",' – he gave the word ironic emphasis – 'by none other than the duumvir himself. I had this from the maidservant, the next time that I called, though – interestingly – there was no suspicion of it being murder then.'

'The man had been smothered by his pillow while asleep,' I muttered. 'And I do indeed suspect the so-called medicus, who – I now believe – was nothing of the kind, but an educated slave.' I gave a smile, contented with myself.

'And why would he kill an injured, aging man?'

'To protect his master,' my wits were working a little better now, but – despite the water – my thirst seemed even worse. 'Josephus had sent a letter to the court, complaining to the Emperor about the forgeries.'

Of course, of course! No doubt Comux and his friends had either passed the false coins off around the town, or had actually shipped them in – possibly disguised as payment for the troops, since there was no Imperial mint near here.

I forced my brain to focus. 'Obviously the killer's master was involved in issuing the coins, and the intention was to silence the argentarius before Laurentius came. And the same thing could be said about the ancient slave – who, according to the maidservant, was carrying messages – no doubt highly incriminating ones . . .' It came out as 'imimmicrating' and I stumbled to a halt.

'All of which applies entirely to the duumvir himself!' Properus pointed out. His face was sorrowful. 'Indeed I met him at the very place where Semprius was killed. I went to purify the spot, and find my master's seal – in which I fear I failed. The duumvir was there. He claimed that he was looking for any evidence which might lead him to the murderer. I should have seen that was suspicious at the time – everyone else had taken it to be a Druid raid. I am forced to claim, with Rufus, that this man is culpable and I will attest that in the courts. Arrest him, in the name of Severus.'

This was not a court of law – not yet – but a three-fold accusation cannot be ignored, just as a witness at a trial is always asked the self-same question thrice. It seemed unreal to be standing here, dressed in my toga, in my own apartment too – with a dead praetorian lying on my bed – being accused of murder, fraud and treason (any of which might have me done to death) while underneath my window normal life went on. I was aware of the familiar smells and sounds – hot grease, manure, cooking, and humanity – drifting from the street: the shouts and oaths and hammering of builders opposite, the rattle of a cart, the cries of vendors selling milk and cakes. Simple things that an exile never knows. Suddenly Glevum felt very dear to me.

'Properus,' I was now fighting a wild desire to weep, 'I understand your reasoning. In your place I would probably have argued just the same. But I promise you, by my ancestral gods, I am not the guilty one.' There was something, wasn't there, I had to add? I found it, finally: 'And I believe that I can prove it, Legate, if you can permit me time to question Comux and his friends, when they arrive. And then we shall see what my servant has to say.' I had to laugh at my own pomposity – I sounded like a diner who has taken too much wine.

'There is no point in waiting, Legate,' Rufus said. 'Libertus can argue most persuasively – when he is sober anyway. But surely all these factors – the flat, the time, the opportunity, his passing off the coin – can allow no doubt. And now we hear that he was also present at the death of Josephus – which he admits was murder – which I had never heard about till now. That alone would be enough to call for his arrest.'

'I have him prisoner, as you will observe,' the Legate said, clearly relieved to have a culprit found. 'And he will remain so until I send to Caesar Clodius, our Provincial Governor, and determine how and where he should be tried. It may be that Clodius will want him sent to Rome, or he may choose to try the case himself – it would suit his cause to have prevented treachery.' He turned to me. 'Meantime, Libertus, you will stay here in this flat – I will post a man to watch you at all times. You are permitted to speak to visitors, under the supervision of the guard, but they may not enter and they will be searched, and only one caller is permitted at a time – until the trial at least.'

'But, Legate, surely you will take him into custody?' Rufus sounded shocked. 'And there is the question of the body here. It is not respectful—'

The Legate interrupted. 'The accused is, after all, a councillor and – whatever he has done – that earns the privileges of his rank. He is not violent nor, in my view, dangerous. There is no need to throw him in the cells. This calls for house arrest, until he comes to trial. You may release him, guard.'

The soldier did so and I almost fell.

'Indeed,' the commandant went on, to the guard, 'you may go back and report this to the fort. Tell them that I require another three men here – one to remain on guard outside the door, and the other two as escort for myself. I'll leave your fellow as the warder here.'

Warder! I thought, as the soldier made a smart salute and hastened to obey. It was a dreadful word. It seemed to echo round the room.

The Legate was looking expectantly at me, and I realized dimly he was waiting for a response. I was only just sensible enough to stammer one. 'But my patron . . .' I managed, 'I am expecting him. He will not submit to searches.' I was close to those un-Roman tears again – though, surprisingly I was not feeling sad. Nor even really frightened, though I knew I should have been. 'And my tradesmen witnesses? How, without them, can I—'

The Legate heaved a sign. 'Libertus, it is fortunate you are a citizen and councillor. Since the only proof of treason involves a single coin, a skilful advocate may see you cleared entirely of that charge, so – with luck – you may only face the question of the deaths. That may mean no more than exile, in the end. Pray that the Emperor does not nominate the rock to which you're sent, and you may yet survive. But do not try my patience. You will have your chance to make a counter-allegation at your trial. You will do as I instruct. You may purchase food and drink, but nothing that is not agreed and sampled by your guard. And there's an end of it. Though I suppose some effort must be made to move the corpse. Or corpses – since there is the servant too.'

Properus looked at Rufus. Rufus looked at me. 'Before we make arrangements for all that, I propose we should make certain that it *was* a single coin – and that Libertus does not have many more he hopes to circulate. Properus informs me that there are bags of money here, lodged with Josephus just before he died (which in itself might be significant) and returned here this morning at the duumvir's request. Would it not be interesting to examine them?'

'They are on the couch behind the dining table in the tablinium recess,' Properus said with a helpful smile. 'I helped to put them there. Still sealed with my master's personal seal – and that is missing, as I said before, so they cannot have been tampered with and resealed. Indeed I have a signed receipt to that effect, provided this morning by the duumvir himself.' He pulled out the little writing-block again.

The Legate looked at it with care and pursed his lips. 'That seems indisputable,' he said. 'Very well. Guard, see what's in the bags.'

The man who had been holding Fauvus let him go, thrust him towards Rufus – who took firm charge of him – and went across to lift the money bags onto the tabletop. At a signal from the Legate he drew his dagger out, and – ignoring the drawstrap with the seal attached – made a large gash through the leather of the nearest bag. A stream of silver coins came tumbling out – all of them shining, bright and obviously new.

Properus went over and regarded them with a professional eye. 'You hardly need me to confirm this, Legate, I am sure. Worthless forgeries, the whole lot of them. Silver-plated iron copies, judging by the weight. And all of them entirely unused.' He signalled with a nod. The soldier slashed the second bag, and then the third and fourth. The cascading contents were – even from this distance, and to my hazy eyes – quite clearly similar.

My euphoria had abruptly disappeared and I was back in harsh reality. I remembered, with a sinking of the heart, the fabled skills of Dacian silversmiths. And I had a sudden vision of what had really been contained in that sack of 'possessions' which Fauvus so conveniently owned.

Properus picked up a handful of the worthless coins and let them trickle through his fingertips. 'All bearing the – purported – image of the Emperor.' He selected one and read in full the damning message carried by the letters imprinted round the edge. 'Lucius Septimius Severus Augustus Imperator.'

It was a death sentence. My unsteady legs refused to carry me and – now without the guard's restraining hand – I sank in an unhappy heap upon the floor.

TWENTY-SEVEN

Properus was immediately all concern. He came forward to assist me to my stool, saying as he did so, 'The duumvir needs more water – he has had a shock. Obviously this has affected him. Though who can be surprised? He must have supposed he'd get away with it. A man with such a reputation for total probity! If the aedile had not been vigilant, and brought that false denarius to me, no one could ever have suspected Libertus of anything like this!' I caught his eye and saw an expression of disappointment and contempt – no doubt the whole colonia would shortly feel the same.

Rufus appeared to do so, certainly. He gave a mocking laugh. 'In my experience it is always the sanctimonious who are secretly the worst. I never did believe Libertus was as honest as he pretends to be. No one in power is wholly incorruptible, though he's managed to convince the populace. And he argues very well. Indeed, if it were not for the incriminating coins, he might have been found with half a dozen corpses in his flat and still found a way to persuade the mob that he was innocent.'

'But of course I'm innocent!' Panic made me reckless, and I was shouting now – though the words were indistinct. My tongue felt swollen in my mouth with thirst. I was so enraged – by my own incompetence as well as by events – that for half a quadrans I would have lunged at him. Some instinct for survival prevented that, at least, and I appealed to my servant in a helpless, hopeless wail. 'Fauvus, is there nothing you can say? Whatever your loyalties, surely you would not let me die without a single word in my defence?'

Fauvus took advantage of his freedom from the guards to come towards me with his hands outstretched. 'Master,' he murmured.

Rufus hauled him back, 'What value is the testimony of a slave?'

But it was Properus who said, 'Better for him to do as I suggest and bring his master a reviving drink. There must be wine here, surely, even if there's no water in the house. The duumvir was expecting visitors.'

'A whole pail of water,' I said, through swollen lips. 'In the inner storeroom, as Fauvus knows too well.'

Fauvus was already being pushed towards the door, but he stopped at this and turned to look at me. 'Hardly any, master. I brought you what there was. I thought you must have used it to purify the room – the bowl beside it seemed to have been used.'

I shook my buzzing head in real perplexity. 'I didn't.' Though the Legate would think I should have done, of course. Most citizens' first act would probably have been to sprinkle some oblation on the site – water, salt and herbs – at least as a preliminary gesture to dispel bad luck. I had all three items in the house and Minimus had actually suggested it. But I'd been more anxious to work out who the killer was, deciding that cleansing rituals could wait. Perhaps it served me right that I was in such trouble now – one can never be too careful with the gods.

'There must be wine left, surely?' Properus insisted. 'Your servant tells me that your guests were drinking some.'

Rufus laughed. 'Perhaps Libertus drank the rest. It's clear he's taken some.'

I shook my head. 'Not my wine, townsman. I left none in the flat. The killer must have brought it. There was a drug in it. The same that was given to your master Josephus.' I looked towards the table where the little phial had been and remembered that I'd picked it up again. 'I had a phial of it. Left by the false physician at your master's flat,' I was uttering short sentences with elaborate care, although the words came strangely through my swollen lips. 'I must have left it in the other room. I took it there to test the contents of the jug. You'd recognize it, Fauvus?'

He bowed acknowledgement. 'I have seen you with it, master. Earlier today. I offered to take it to the public medicus for you, but you preferred to keep it and to go yourself.'

How cleverly the fellow could twist the truth to tell against me, I thought bitterly. Though he must be certain of his ex-master's powers to rescue him. He was as calm as if he were not likely to be flogged half-dead and then to share my fate.

His next words confirmed it. 'Although, judging by the symptoms which my master now displays, I think I know what it contains, without consulting the medicus at all. I think it is a plant much valued in the east – they call it *datura* – among other things. It has a lot of names. It's said that priests in Delphi induce a trance with it. But it is dangerous. Even a small dose can interfere with movement and thought. A larger one will plunge you into unconsciousness – my previous master had a surgeon client who wanted it for that. My master succeeded in importing some, after much trouble and at very great expense, so that wealthy patients would not feel it when the *cirurgus* needed to remove a limb or cauterize a wound. But the dose is critical. Too little can cause excessive movement, and too much can kill. The surgeon did not find it satisfactory, and never called for it again . . .' He trailed off, suddenly, as if aware that he had said too much.

He had. Enough to make me quite certain of his guilt. No doubt that exotic drug had been fed to Josephus at the baths – under the guise of some refreshment there – that would explain his apparent drunkenness. And probably his fall. And when it did not kill him, Fauvus brought him more, purporting to be a medicus. The Dacian would have been perfect for the role, and Florea had said that he had a foreign look. But again the dosage hadn't been enough, and Josephus had by that time partly slept it off, so Fauvus had looked in again and – while he was asleep – helped him, with a pillow, on his way. But I realized that I could not well accuse him, now – he was my servant – and all this would be taken as admission of my guilt. Unless I could work out who his previous master was.

While my sluggish brain was still working all this through, Rufus was confronting me, with smugly folded arms. 'A potion which induces sleep and helplessness? How convenient that your servant knew of it. And you took it into the bedroom, citizen? (I won't demean the rank of duumvir by any longer applying it to you.) To test the jug, you say? I suggest, Commander, that it was the opposite. This man took the potion in to add it to the jug!'

'You deny that charge as well, Libertus, I assume?' the commander said. He was conforming to the law, but I liked him better for giving me the opportunity.

'I deny it utterly.' I wished my lips would move to my command. 'Fauvus knows what happened here and why. If he chose to, he could tell you everything.'

'And he will do, shortly,' Rufus gave a laugh. 'He must have helped you overcome the men – even if they were half-drugged anyway. So if he hopes to save himself additional suffering, he would do well to confess it straight away.'

Fauvus gave me a look of mild reproach. 'Master, I cannot tell them what I do not know – and I do not know what happened here. But I do know what is impossible.' He turned to the Legate. 'Sir, you are a soldier. Like me you have seen battle. I appeal to you. You have not seen the body of the murdered guard. But if you had, you would understand at once that it is impossible that my master murdered him. Anybody who has seen a living person stabbed will realize that the blood spurts everywhere. The murderer must have it on his clothes.'

Rufus gestured contemptuously at me. 'There are smears of bloodstains on his hems.'

I glanced down at my toga and realized this was true, though only where the garment brushed the floor. It must have happened when I went into the room. In my fuddled state I hadn't noticed it. But it was proof that what Fauvus said was true. There was a lot of blood.

And yet there was no trace of it on him! Was that where the water had mysteriously gone – had he washed himself and changed his tunic too, to another which was hidden in that possessions sack? But how could he do that? Hadn't he taken everything to Josephus's flat? Or was I wrong again, and he had hidden that sack somewhere close at hand? If so, I'd like to have it found. Presumably, it held the true coins from my money sacks.

He was giving me a small, enquiring smile, as though I should be pleased at his response. But I had thought of something. Fauvus had been in the flat with Scito, that was true, but he had gone back later. By his own account, he told me that he'd seen the slave depart. Suppose he had contrived to get back in, somehow, and switch the money bags, or simply the contents? I could see him in my head – breaking the seals and opening the bags – so vividly that for a moment I thought the dream was real. And when he'd refilled them with the false coins from his sack, I saw him close the bags again and reseal them with a ring. I shook my head and the picture disappeared. But, I realized faintly, my fevered mind was conjuring a likely truth. All I had looked for, when giving that receipt, was Josephus's unmistakable seal – and, Fauvus had no doubt taken that from Semprius's corpse, so he could have indeed reapplied it very easily!

But how could I prove any part of this?

The Legate, though, appeared to be convinced by what my servant said. 'You think so, slave?'

'I know so, Commandant. And so would you, if you had seen the corpse. There must be someone who has either stained, or changed, his clothes. No doubt he used the water in the pail to wash his hands. And there is nothing in the flat, you can search it for yourselves.'

'Libertus was not wearing his toga when he came. He never does.' Rufus made the accusation, with a laugh. 'Perhaps you should examine the tunic underneath.' His own toga was immaculately clean, and Properus's full-length mourning clothes – though dark – showed no sign of recent staining anywhere.

I dimly knew this was significant, but I was so hot and thirsty I could hardly think – I would almost have admitted everything to have a cooling drink. Or cold wind on my face. With desperate energy I escaped the guard and rushed towards the open window-space, gulping down air and twitching like a dying fish.

'The man needs water,' the commander said. 'We cannot have said we let him die of thirst. Clearly we can't release his slave to fetch it – he is implicated here – but you have a servant, aedile, I think?'

For answer Rufus clapped his hands and shouted 'Page!'

The boy came running, 'You called me, master?'

'Certainly I did. Fetch the water bucket from the storeroom, over there, go out and fill it at the fountain in the communal court and bring it back again. No questions. Simply do as I require.'

The slave looked startled but he followed his master's pointing finger, and went to find the pail. I tried to croak a protest, knowing what horrors lay beyond that door, but the soldier who'd been in there had the same idea. He stepped through, seized the water bucket and gave it to the boy who – with a swift bow to the assembled company – dashed off in the direction of the street. From the window-space, I watched him scampering, relieved to feel the cool rain on my fevered face and putting out my tongue to catch the precious drops. Not appropriate behaviour for a man of rank, but I was desperate.

'Master?' I heard an anxious voice exclaim, and I looked down to see my little Minimus standing on the pavement and looking up at me. 'Master, are you ill?'

I shook my head – although the gesture was a lie. I felt as ill as I have ever been. The action made my head spin, too, and I was forced to grasp the windowframe with both hands to stop myself from plunging down into the street. 'Marcus?' It was all that I could contrive to say. But Marcus wasn't there.

'Gone before I got here, master.' Minimus had raised his voice so I could hear. 'Gone to the basilica with those visitors of his – something about a contract to be signed. I said it was important, and they've sent for him, but I only gave your message, word for word, and he won't realize . . .' He was still shouting and passers-by – shoppers, street vendors, scurrying slaves – were by this time turning round to stare. He became aware of this, and shook his head. 'I'll come up and tell you!'

I tried to stop him – I did not want him to be taken prisoner too – but I could already hear his footsteps on the stairs. And did my eyes deceive me, once again, or could I just make out – turning the corner at the far end of the street – the figures of three men in Grecian robes, Brokko and Boudoucus, with Comux at their heels? And in the company, not of Scito – as one might expect – but of that urchin child?

TWENTY-EIGHT

M inimus was not permitted to come in. I learned, in that moment, what it meant to be a prisoner in my own apartment, as the remaining guard crossed swiftly to the door, drew his sword, and thrust it across the entrance to the room, keeping my little servant pinned in the passageway.

'Permission to address my master?' Minimus beseeched.

'You may address him, but from there,' the guard replied.

The boy was clearly frightened, though ready to defy the sword and try to come to me – but I shook my head. I already knew what I required to know. Marcus was not here. He would get my message, but with no urgency – and doubtless he would call here later in the day. In the meantime, I was incarcerated here with a pair of murdered men for company. Any hour now, they would begin to smell. Already I was sure that I could catch the whiff of blood.

'Take a message to your mistress, Minimus,' I declaimed, with an absurd notion of theatrical effect. 'Tell her I've been taken into custody, accused – by a fellow member of the curia – of murdering Laurentius and his bodyguard.'

'And Josephus and his messenger, as well,' Rufus added, with a wolfish grin. 'Don't overlook that detail. And most of all, caught in the act of issuing false coin, and thus of treason against the Emperor.'

'But you didn't, master,' Minimus broke in, and I thought for a moment that he would be punished with a blow, but the Legate forbade it with a gesture of his hand.

'You and I know that, Minimus,' I pronounced. 'But it may be very—'

I broke off as we were interrupted by the page, struggling from the stairwell with a heavy pail. It was painful to see him permitted to come past, while Minimus remained exiled in the corridor. I was, however, glad to get the drink which Fauvus now poured out and offered me. It was a brimming cupful this time, though I still found it half-impossible to swallow anything.

I looked up, spluttering, and saw Minimus still there. I sent him on his reluctant way with an extravagant gesture of my arm.

'Should you not, perhaps, have sent him to the undertakers too?' Properus gave me that helpful smile again. 'There are those that deal with visitors, who are not therefore members of any local guild. His Excellence will arrange things for his relative, no doubt, but one could at least arrange disposal of the slave. I could send Scito, he will soon be back and should be waiting for instructions on the stairs, or Rufus here could send his little page. Though, I suppose that might involve immediate expense and that might fall on us, since Laurentius was not carrying much coin.'

Fauvus bent forward and murmured something in my ear. It took me a moment to see the force of it, but I repeated it. 'How do you know that?' I said to Properus, though it was hardly a dignified enquiry. That lethargy had wholly left me now, and my legs and hands were moving of their own accord as though possessed of a mad desire to dance.

The young man looked startled – as well he might – but answered with a smile. 'He must have told me. I am sure he did.'

'I see,' I murmured, and really felt I did. Another prompt from Fauvus. I took another gulp of water to refresh my brain. 'And when, exactly, do you think that might have been?'

Properus glanced at Rufus, as if he hoped to find some inspiration there. But the aedile was frowning. 'The duumvir is right. I did not know you'd had the chance to meet Laurentius. When did you speak to him?'

The Legate pressed his fingertips together and tapped his lips with them. 'It must have been this morning, argentarius,' he said. 'It could not have been while he was at the fort.'

Properus had turned as scarlet as I felt. 'You are correct, of course. I met him on the street. I was out with Scito and the cart and we encountered him – his servant asked the way and I realized who they were. In the excitement, I had forgotten that – or rather, I confess, I did not mention it, in case it raised suspicions about me.' He flashed Rufus an artless, apologetic smile.

'And what, meanwhile, had happened to the escort that I'd sent with him?' The Legate's tone had turned to ice by now, and his granite face was stonier than before.

Properus raised his hands in innocence. 'Ah, they were an escort! I did not realize that. I saw them, of course, further up the street, but one does not pay undue attention to a pair of soldiers in this town. Perhaps he had deliberately moved away from them. You mentioned, Legate, that he hoped to be discreet.'

The Legate was still frowning, but he gave a nod. 'You may be right.'

Properus smiled. 'He said he had a meeting – with his informant, I suppose. Libertus. Though he did not tell me that.'

'I am surprised he told you anything. And why should he enquire the way of you?'

'I cannot answer that – but that is what he did. Legate, you cannot be meaning to suggest I had some hand in this? That I came up here, calmly murdered a man I'd never met, and then for good measure stabbed his servant in the back? For one thing, as Fauvus pointed out, I would be drenched in blood!'

This time I saw his error for myself. 'Then how did you know the wound was in the servant's back?'

Properus was breathing rather quickly now, and the look he gave me was simply venomous. But he maintained his outward calm. 'Duumvir, you told me so yourself, when I first got here and you described the scene.'

I was certain that I hadn't but that was hard to prove, with only Fauvus here to witness it. And I was hardly in a state to be reliable – even to myself. But what was Properus doing, I thought suddenly, in the street outside of my door when Laurentius arrived?

And then (thanks to that water, possibly) I understood! How almost right – and how completely wrong – my reasoning had been! Of course it had been Properus and Scito all along. Properus, 'the hasty one', who could not simply wait until he had his licence and could run the booth and make a comfortable living for himself, but had to try to make an instant fortune by dishonest means.

It was Properus who had drugged his master, just before the visit to the baths – Josephus had declined to lunch elsewhere – which did not kill him, but led to his collapse. And Scito was the educated slave who brought the 'soothing draught' and finally smothered the old man in his unnatural sleep. I'd forgotten that Florea had never met the slave before. Properus's dead father had lived in Hellas, once – as the young man's name proclaimed – and he would have known about the Delphi drug. And as a manufacturer of salves for eyes, no doubt he knew importers who could find ingredients – just as Fauvus's dead master had done.

No wonder Properus had been so anxious to guard his special wine, when he had shared the flat with Josephus! No doubt the location of that apartment gave him the idea for duplicating the new Severus denarius, before it was in general circulation here and imitations easily perceived. Right above the workshops of the silversmiths – one of whom he'd clearly bribed to coat his worthless forgeries. How cleverly he'd chosen to move away from there, though perhaps the ironsmith beneath his new abode had helped to make the dies from the original. And how supreme his cleverness had been, in choosing to identify the first few fakes himself – persuading Josephus that he'd been missing them, and thus removing all suspicion from himself. He must have been convinced there was a fortune to be made.

And then his master spoiled it, by reporting the forgery to Rome. That was a dreadful shock. An agent of the Emperor was despatched, and would not be deflected – though Properus and Scito obviously tried. It must have been one of them who wrote those warning messages. So Josephus must be silenced before Laurentius came – perhaps he had suspicions by this time – and his poor servant, too.

Not that they'd intended to kill the spy, at first. There'd simply been a hurried scheme to run away – Properus changing identities with Semprius, so that he'd never be looked for – and taking the money he'd been storing at this flat, leaving the forged coins in its place. But the gooseboy and I had interrupted that.

And so the forgers had recourse to this – and implicated me!

But I had no proof of this at all. Properus had made a few unfortunate remarks, which – when challenged – he had either brazened out, or just denied. The Legate might be inclined to take my word, not his – but Rufus socially outranked me, and he would be believed.

I could appeal to Marcus, when he came, but that could be dangerous for him, since I was known to be his protégé. And it was unlikely Fauvus would escape a dreadful fate. I had foolishly suspected him, myself. And worse, had made that clear. Or thought I had. Looking back, I could see that Properus had misinterpreted, and concluded that I was accusing him! That's why he had turned the tables, as he had, with his usual cleverness.

I was still thinking slowly, although more clearly now, and was wondering how I could proceed when there was a tapping at the door. I was still by the window, and I glanced outside, half-expecting this to be the escort from the fort. But there was just the urchin boy, leaning on the wall of the wine shop opposite, talking to Scito who had clearly just returned.

I had just time to wonder where Scito might have been, and whether I dared demand that he be brought upstairs, before the door was opened by the 'warder' with the sword, and three astonished tradesmen were revealed beyond. They were already boggling at the naked blade, but the sight of the Legate made them goggle even more.

Boudoucus decided he was spokesman. 'We were sent for, by the duumvir.'

The Legate looked enquiringly at me.

'It's not important,' I said wearily. 'I called them, it is true – to accuse them of involvement in the fraud. Importing forged coins and spreading them through trade. And of having schemed the murder of the Imperial spy, to prevent him from investigating this.' I spoke with bitterness, though I did remember not to mention Fauvus and what I had imagined was his part in it. It would be hard enough to save him, as it was, without equipping Properus with snares to catch him with. I waved a hand at Rufus who was scowling back at me. 'But we now have a different version of the truth, from this townsman and the aedile, and a formal accusation has been made – which I do not accept.'

I was not prepared for the result of this. Comux rushed forward, ducked beneath the sword and flung himself abjectly at my feet. 'Believe me, councillor, we are innocent. We have never been involved in fraud, or any plots to kill. All we did was falsify a shipping manifest, and keep a pair of hunting dogs to breed. I freely confess it and admit that it was wrong – we are ready to pay reparation and a fine, and would pay for the reshipment of the dogs, but no one knows where the ex-commander's gone . . .' He glanced up and saw my face. 'Is something else the matter, councillor?'

I had heard of course, like everybody else, of the interrogation methods the authorities employed – accusing someone of a major crime, with hideous punishments, to induce them to admit to a more minor one. It seemed I had employed this, most effectively, without intending to. I said, with some attempt at dignity, 'Your confession has been noted, in front of witnesses. I shall tell His Excellence what you have said, and no doubt he will assess the fine.'

Comux kissed my feet in gratitude, scrabbled to his own and was about to bow out backwards, when I thought of something else. 'That was the "business opportunity" in which you hoped to interest Josephus? Breeding British hunting dogs, is that correct?'

Comux nodded. 'We needed some investment. They're expensive things to keep. Though if we were successful there were profits to be had. They are hard to get and men will pay a lot for them, not just in Britannia but throughout the empire. And there was already a litter of puppies on its way. He would certainly have earned his money back.'

I thought of the rustling, squeaking creatures in the warehouse gloom. 'Except that the creatures were not yours to breed,' I said. 'We'll see what Marcus says. In the meantime, see they're warm and fed.'

Comux was almost incoherent in his thanks. He blushed and burbled back towards his friends, and I realized that the other people in the room were staring at me in a kind of disbelief.

I turned to the Legate. 'Part of one's duties as a councillor,' I said. 'Investigating infringements of cargo manifests. One matter, at least, is satisfactorily resolved.'

'And I see you also paid that medicus . . .' Brokko was speaking from the hall. 'I'm glad you managed that.'

It was my turn to stare. 'The medicus?'

'Well, I assumed you'd paid him. We saw him just outside. Wearing a different tunic, but I'd know him anywhere.'

'Brokko,' I said quickly, 'come over here to me. Look out of the window. Can you see him now?'

Brokko looked out of the window-space. 'There!' he said pointing. 'What's the mystery? If you set out to pay him, you must know that yourself?'

'Brokko,' I urged him. 'Be careful what you say. Remember you are speaking in front of senior rank, from both the civil and military authorities. Do you confirm that is the medicus that visited the argentarius when he was ill?'

Brokko nodded. 'Seemed to help him too. Had some sort of soothing medicine which made him sleep, and left some more for the maidservant to give him when he woke – though he said that he was resting and was not to be disturbed.' He frowned at me. 'And I will swear to that – as no doubt Florea will. If it is important, citizen.'

'Oh, it is important, Brokko,' I replied. 'You see, that is not a medicus at all. That is Scito, Properus's slave. And Legate, I believe I have the proof I need—'

Properus was past me like a ballista from a sling. 'I should have killed you in the forest, when I had you there alone, or strangled you today – but Scito thought it better to foist the coins on you. And just when we were ready to escape!'

The soldier had recovered from his shock and had lumbered over, brandishing his sword. 'I should arrest him, Legate?' he enquired, and when this was answered with a nod, he advanced on Properus, with a nasty smile. 'Don't try resisting!'

But it was too late. Properus had already made his choice. He reached the window-space. For one agonising moment he teetered on the sill, and then plunged downwards. There were screams from passers-by as he fell and hit the road, but none from Properus.

He did not die at once. Perhaps he was even conscious of people crowding round – including the Legate, Rufus, the soldiers and myself – but he gave no sign of it. Only a faint twitching of the shattered limbs, and bleeding from the ears. And then there was nothing.

I turned to Rufus, who was shocked and white. My throat was dry again and that dreadful buzzing had returned. I fumbled at his sleeve. 'Where's Scito?' I managed, before my legs betrayed me and I, once more, crumpled to the ground.

EPILOGUE

I came to consciousness in an unfamiliar bed – an expensive Roman bed-frame with goat's-hide springs and a feather mattress, by the feel of it – to find Fauvus leaning over me. He seemed to be squeezing water from a sponge onto my face and lips. I tried to move my head, but it was made of aching lead.

'Ah, master you are stirring, finally. His Excellence will be relieved.'

I forced my eyelids open. This was my patron's flat – of course! I should have recognized it. I had been there before. 'What . . .?' I gave up the attempt. I could remember nothing but strange, tormented dreams.

'Your patron had you brought here yesterday when you collapsed, as soon as his other visitors were gone. They had concluded their business anyway and you could not stay in your apartment with two corpses there. Especially when you need especial care. There has been someone with you day and night since then. Your wife, and the lady Julia have both been here for hours – though they have gone with his Excellence, this afternoon, to attend the lying-in-state of Laurentius Manlius.'

Corpses? And collapse? Laurentius's bier? Slowly recollection was beginning to return. I groaned. 'I misjudged you, Fauvus,' I croaked, through throbbing lips. My voice was not my own. 'I should have seen . . .'

He shook his head and held the sponge so I could wet my tongue. 'It was not your fault, master. It was that potion you imbibed. Fortunately you only had a very small amount – but even that can turn the sanest person mad, and make him imagine whole worlds of fantasy. Some people even to talk to chimeras.'

I nodded. 'Josephus . . .' I remembered the imaginary pigs. He gave me a grave smile and took the sponge from me.

'If I had seen him that day at the baths, I might have recognized the drug a little earlier. But, in any case, there is no cure but time – though cooling water is supposed to help. Are you feeling better?'

I muttered that I was. 'Though . . . foolish. Reasoning . . . was false . . .' I was improving. I had managed to produce a sentence, more or less.

'Master, if it had not been for you noticing the signs that Josephus had been killed, none of this would ever have been brought to light. Including what had happened to that ancient slave of his. Properus would have disappeared, dressed in Semprius's clothing – as it is clear that he intended to – and an unknown body would have gone into the pit.'

Unless the authorities assumed that it was Properus himself, which was probably the plan – that's why he moved the head and took the slave-disc off.

'Wanted . . . dress . . . body . . . in his clothes,' I croaked. He'd brought them for the purpose – he actually showed them to me in that sack – and clearly that stained tunic he was wearing at the pond had belonged to Semprius. Perhaps it was even the one he'd given him – though either way they were clearly of a size.

'So the body would have been identified as Properus – unfortunate victim of a Druid raid – while he and Scito disappeared. Two ex-slaves that nobody was looking for – with a fortune in their cart.' Fauvus sounded half-admiring of their audacity.

The gooseboy had already slightly spoiled that plan, of course, by reporting the corpse to the authorities and having it removed. Properus did not know that – as I should have realized – and of course he had not really been called out of town that day. He and Scito with their transport were about to disappear. And then I came along! A wonder that he did not kill me, there and then – he clearly wished he had. Just as he'd murdered Semprius.

Poor Semprius. He knew and trusted Properus, of course, and would cheerfully have confided the message that he was carrying, saying that Laurentius was coming to investigate the fraud. Probably to my patron, which took him through the woods, where Scito followed him. He would not have been difficult to overcome. If that pond was ever dragged with nets, they'd doubtless find his head. I was almost certain it had been hidden there . . .

'Found . . . Scito, then, and he . . . admits?' I asked.

Fauvus grimaced. 'Unfortunately not, though there's a manhunt for him Empire-wide and no doubt they will catch him in the end. An Imperial agent won't go unavenged. But they have traced the cart. Semprius's clothes were on it – and his slave-disc too – and his master's signet ring and seal. What happened to his message, we may never know. It may have been a verbal one, as you surmised.'

I shook my head – which wasn't sensible. I knew what had happened to that writing-block. I had watched the cool young criminal take it from his slave, and pretend it held an urgent message from the guild. Worse, I later saw him erase the words on it over my own brazier and get me – myself – to replace them with the message of receipt I was to sign. No drug, surely, could excuse me that!

But Fauvus hadn't finished. 'They found a blood-stained Grecian robe beneath it all, as well. Clearly Scito's, though he'd washed and changed. Taken the spare clothing from that bodyguard, along with the rest of his possessions. As no doubt you'd guessed. You must have noticed that his baggage wasn't in the flat, although his master's was.'

I hadn't – and I should have! Where was my reputation for deduction now? But all I said was, 'Our money . . . on the cart?'

'Yours, and several other people's too. They have been contacted, and – as you might imagine – they'd been given forgeries instead. Most hadn't noticed it. But they'll all be repaid. The false coins are being packed off – with the silversmith – as evidence, but since there is no citizen involved, it won't be going to Rome. Clodius can deal with plebian punishment himself.'

I closed my eyes. It was patently unfair – the fraud was Properus's and Scito's work alone – the silversmith had merely done what they had paid him to. And would no doubt die a very painful death in consequence. 'The urchin too?' I hardly dared to ask.

It had occurred to me, at last, why our urchin guides had looked so much alike. They were the self-same person – Properus's lookout, and his go-between. He'd been seen to give him money – false, or otherwise! He was a vital link. Which is why they'd sent him to summon Comux and his friends, in Scito's place, since – if the steward had arrived – Brokko might recognize him as the medicus. As indeed he later did.

'The urchin too,' my slave said, soberly. 'Rome makes no allowances for youth. And now, master, if you're feeling well enough, I am to tell you that you have a visitor. He's waiting just outside.'

I was expecting Marcus, but it was Rufus who appeared, clutching a box of honeyed figs for me. 'To tempt your appetite, when you are strong enough.'

In my state of health, it was enough to nod my thanks – which was fortunate perhaps, since I do not care for figs. But I can detect an offering of peace. I gave him a wan smile.

Rufus sat down on the stool that Fauvus had been using earlier, coughed, fingered his toga-folds and fidgeted. After a moment he produced a little speech – which he had obviously rehearsed. 'Libertus, duumvir, I have come today at the suggestion of the curia. They feel – I feel – I should apologize for having been so readily deceived. I confess I never felt that you deserved your rank – by birth, at least, though by ability perhaps – so when that young villain offered me the chance to . . . offered me the chance, I was too slow to question and too ready to accuse.' He stopped and cleared his throat. 'Even now I find it hard to comprehend that he was dissembling, first to last. Properus was so wholesome, and so courteous.'

I bit back the desire to retort that 'the sanctimonious are usually the worst', and simply did my sick-man nod again.

He took that as acceptance of his apology. 'If you were feeling stronger, councillor, I would offer you my arm to shake,' he said, in the tone of one bestowing a signal compliment. 'But as it is, by way of recompense, your patron feels some gesture should be made. Could I – for instance – volunteer to buy that Dacian slave for you? Marcus informs me that he's only yours on loan, and you seem to value him.'

Much as I valued Fauvus – more than ever now – a man should be respected by his slaves, not be reminded by their presence of his foolishness. Yet, there was one thing, perhaps . . .

'Buy his freedom, rather,' I replied, forcing my tongue to answer to my will. 'And if you have a few denarii to spare, equip him with an attendant of his own. There is an ancient maidservant of Josephus's who will require a place. She will be very cheap.' It sounded garbled, but he seemed to understand.

'With pleasure, duumvir,' he murmured, as he left.

I punched my downy pillow into shape. Tomorrow, I thought, I would speak to Marcus about this. Fauvus, I was almost certain, had a trade – and there was an opening in Glevum now for another silversmith, with vacant premises. Marcus could ensure that the Dacian got the lease.

For today, though, I was very tired. I turned over and went straight to sleep.

This time I dreamed of happier things: Gwellia, and the roundhouse and the servant boys – and myself, in a tunic, attending to the fence.